KT-574-348

UNCLAIMED BRIDE

Lauri Robinson

MILLS & BOON

All the characters in this book have no existence outside the imagination of the author, and have no relation whatsoever to anyone bearing the same name or names. They are not even distantly inspired by any individual known or unknown to the author, and all the incidents are pure invention.

All Rights Reserved including the right of reproduction in whole or in part in any form. This edition is published by arrangement with Harlequin Enterprises II BV/S.à.r.l. The text of this publication or any part thereof may not be reproduced or transmitted in any form or by any means, electronic or mechanical, including photocopying, recording, storage in an information retrieval system, or otherwise, without the written permission of the publisher.

This book is sold subject to the condition that it shall not, by way of trade or otherwise, be lent, resold, hired out or otherwise circulated without the prior consent of the publisher in any form of binding or cover other than that in which it is published and without a similar condition including this condition being imposed on the subsequent purchaser.

® and TM are trademarks owned and used by the trademark owner and/or its licensee. Trademarks marked with ® are registered with the United Kingdom Patent Office and/or the Office for Harmonisation in the Internal Market and in other countries.

First published in Great Britain 2012
by Mills & Boon, an imprint of Harlequin (UK) Limited.
Harlequin (UK) Limited, Eton House, 18-24 Paradise Road,
Richmond, Surrey TW9 1SR

© Lauri Robinson 2012

ISBN: 978 0 263 89281 9

Harlequin (UK) policy is to use papers that are natural, renewable and recyclable products and made from wood grown in sustainable forests. The logging and manufacturing process conform to the legal environmental regulations of the country of origin.

Printed and bound in Spain
by Blackprint CPI, Barcelona

Lauri Robinson's chosen genre to write is Western historical. When asked why, she says, 'Because I know I wasn't the only girl who wanted to grow up and marry Little Joe Cartwright.'

With a degree in early childhood education, Lauri has spent decades working in the non-profit field and claims once-upon-a-time and happily-ever-after romance novels have always been a form of stress relief. When her husband suggested she write one she took the challenge, and has loved every minute of the journey.

Lauri lives in rural Minnesota, where she and her husband spend every spare moment with their three grown sons and four grandchildren. She works part-time, volunteers for several organisations, and is a diehard Elvis and NASCAR fan. Her favourite getaway location is the woods of northern Minnesota, on the land homesteaded by her great-grandfather.

A previous title from Lauri Robinson:

HIS CHRISTMAS WISH
  (part of *All a Cowboy Wants for Christmas*)

Also available in Mills & Boon® Historical *Undone!* eBooks:

WEDDING NIGHT WITH THE RANGER
HER MIDNIGHT COWBOY
NIGHTS WITH THE OUTLAW
DISOBEYING THE MARSHAL
TESTING THE LAWMAN'S HONOUR
THE SHERIFF'S LAST GAMBLE

To my mother, Mary Jane Johnson.

It would be impossible for me to list all the things that made her so remarkable, or how deeply she is missed. While I was writing this book, she was still with us, and I consulted her more than once for a recipe. She 'created' many original dishes over the years, and tweaked others that will forever be passed along from generation to generation in our family. The day she passed away, and we were all gathered at her house, my four-year-old granddaughter said, 'Jesus must be happy. He now gets Grandma Mary's coleslaw.'

Love you, Mom.

Miss you.

Chapter One

❦

Wyoming Territory
November, 1877

The bitter wind that whipped the leather curtains covering the stage windows and snuck beneath the buffalo robe now piled on the hard seat could easily have stolen her breath away, but Constance Jennings's first glimpse of her destination already had her lungs locked tight. Pinning her quivering bottom lip between her teeth, she glanced over her shoulder, half hoping the other passenger—an aging pastor who'd conversed pleasantly during the last leg of her journey—would indicate this wasn't their stop after all.

No such luck. Reverend Stillman smiled kindly as he waved a hand for her to climb down the steps.

The trip had been long and cold, and days of

sitting left her legs stiff and her knees popping. As her boots hit the dirt street, tremors seized her toes, and then traveled, snaking all the way up to her scalp until every hair follicle tingled.

Had she completely lost her senses back in New York?

A gust of unrelenting Wyoming wind caught on her headdress. The covering had once been stylish, but was now as tired and worn as the rest of the traveling suit. She grabbed the curled straw brim to keep the wind from stealing the hat, and gulped at the swelling in her throat.

Which one was he? Ashton Kramer—the man who'd ordered a bride.

The men standing along the dusty road were of various shapes and sizes. One so tall he could have flown a flag off his neck and another so squat and round he easily could have been mistaken for a rain barrel except for the black top hat sitting on his round head. The others were in between and every one of them looked as though they'd just been spit-shined. They were an odd assortment, to say the least, and the lump in Constance's throat threatened to suffocate her.

A long-forgotten image of Aunt Theresa's canary, Sweetie, sitting on its tiny swing with Aunt Julia's big orange tomcat, Percival, staring at it through the spindly gold bars entered her mind.

At this moment, Constance could fully relate to the bird.

Every slight movement—one of the men nodding or tipping their hat with a tense greeting—had panic clutching her insides. Now was not the time to give in to regret or alarm. She'd *chosen* Wyoming.

Over jail.

It had sounded better.

Then.

Not one of the men stepped forward, identifying himself as her husband-to-be. Ashton Kramer's letter hadn't held a picture, but had said not to worry, she'd know him straight off.

The weight that fell on her shoulder had her jumping in her boots. The hold increased and a huff sounded as Reverend Stillman took a final step off the springy stage. "Excuse me, Miss Jennings," he offered, leaning a bit harder. "These old bones of mine just can't take a ride like they used to."

Out of habit, and thankful for something to do, Constance wrapped an arm around the man's stooping shoulders while he settled the bottom of his hooked cane on the well-worn dirt beneath their feet.

The reverend gave her a warm smile of thanks before lifting his chin to scan the town. As if that was the signal they'd waited for, the men rushed forward, pushing at each other, vying for the same spot of earth.

Shouts of, "That's her!" "He called her Miss Jennings!" And "Move out of the way!" caught and sifted in the wind.

Constance cowered, wishing she could make herself as small as Sweetie, or better yet, sprout wings.

"Angel!"

The shout rumbled above the rest, and sent Constance's peaked nerve endings shuddering from head to toe. The reverend's bellow could have shaken the sun out of the clouds, but that, too, wasn't to be. The sky remained as thick and gray as her insides.

"Sorry, Miss Jennings," he offered, patting her hand. "I didn't mean to startle you."

A strained grin was the best she could offer. Startled was putting it lightly. Shocked, stunned, close to hysterical, not to mention freezing, were just a few ways to describe why she shook uncontrollably.

To her dismay and relief, the shout had slowed the men. They now shuffled amongst each other, almost as if waiting for a leader. Ashton, perhaps?

Their gazes had shifted, too, then went up the road. Constance couldn't stop hers from following. A tall man standing beside a wagon made something inside her sputter with hope that she'd found her intended. But only for a moment. The steely glare of his eyes not only said he wasn't Ashton, but that he wasn't impressed with the commotion taking place.

It wasn't as if she was, either.

Constance, glad the stone-faced man wasn't Ashton, turned as a young girl wearing a heavy-looking coat arrived at the reverend's side. "Hello, Reverend Stillman." The girl kissed the old man's cheek and wrapped her mitten-covered hands around his other arm. "We didn't expect you this late in the year. It's gettin' colder and colder."

"I know, child," the reverend agreed. "But I promised one last sermon before the weather makes it impossible."

Constance curled her fingers into her palms and struggled to pull her eyes off the girl's thick mittens. They were bright red and looked as thick and warm as fresh-sheared wool.

As if she were a queen and expected her orders followed, the girl gestured toward the men. "Get his bag and help Reverend Stilllman over to Mrs. Wagner's."

The men didn't question the request, matter of fact, two literally sprang forward. "Ma'am," the first one said, landing next to Constance.

"It's *miss*," the second one said, elbowing the first before tipping his hat.

Renewed shivers assaulted her. Constance stumbled backward, giving the men clear access to the reverend as she pulled her shawl tighter around her shoulders.

Moments later, Reverend Stillman was escorted down the road. He waved, but the whistling of the cold, blustery wind swallowed up his departing words. A thick gush of sadness tightened Constance's chest, as if she watched her last known friend disappear. Not that he'd been a longtime friend, but he'd become a short-term one she'd greatly appreciated. His companionship had made the rocky, cold ride more endurable.

"Are you her?"

Constance, releasing the air from her lungs, turned to the girl.

Seriousness covered the young rosy-cheeked face. "Are you Ashton Kramer's mail-order bride?"

Constance's heart jolted. Hearing someone call her Ashton's bride made it too real.

The way the girl surveyed the remaining men for an extended length of time had the hair on the back of Constance's neck standing on end. Under her scrutiny, the men shuffled, as if unsure if they should move forward. The girl shook her head sadly. "They're here for you."

Constance's blood turned cold—in that foreboding kind of way. "Excuse me?"

"They're here for you," the girl repeated.

The men whispered amongst themselves, and

some nodded her way. Constance gulped as her heart made its way into her throat. "Why?"

"I'm Angel Clayton." The girl slipped an arm under Constance's, hooking their elbows. "Someone should have been here to meet you." Abruptly, she spun about.

Constance had no choice but to twirl with the girl and then be led to the back of the stage.

"Buster, just put her things on the boardwalk."

"Will do, Angel," the stage driver said, hoisting himself onto the roof of the stagecoach.

Angel walked away from the stage, tugging Constance along as the men rushed forward, vying to catch the trunks being lowered from the top of the faded red vehicle. Another chill crept over Constance. It wasn't that she'd formed a kinship with the paint-chipped, leather-cracked, rocking box on wheels, but the thought of being separated from the stage gripped her heart.

All too soon her trunks were carried to the wooden sidewalk in front of buildings built of boards as gray as the sky. Everything looked dull, almost lifeless. Other than the men, the settlement could have been a ghost town withering and dying beneath the dreary winter clouds. This isn't what she'd imagined. Then again, she hadn't contemplated what to expect. She'd spent most of the trip convincing herself she could marry a stranger.

Marriage hadn't been a goal of hers, yet Ashton Kramer's letter....

"What do you mean," she asked, "*someone* should have met me? Where's Mr. Kramer?"

The girl let out a long, heavy sigh. Tiny lines of compassion puckered the bit of forehead that stuck out below her red knitted hat. "I'm sorry to be the one to tell you, ma'am, but Ashton's dead."

Constance's knees buckled. Only the girl's tight hold kept her upright. "Don't faint here," Angel whispered. "They'll settle on you like a flock of crows."

Constance forced her leg muscles to work, while a lump of dread as weighty as her trunks swelled inside her stomach. "Dead?"

"Just keep walking, ma'am," Angel coaxed. "We'll sit down over in front of Link's." She waved a mitten-covered hand. "That's the general store. See he has two chairs set outside the front door. You can make it, can't you?"

Her feet grew heavier by the step, but Constance nodded, having barely heard the girl's words with all the buzzing in her head. How could Ashton Kramer possibly be dead? His letter had said he was a young man, and healthy. Even she wasn't so desperate she'd travel across the country to wed a dying man.

That little voice in the back of her head—the one she'd grown to loathe over the past months—

disagreed. She most certainly was. Matter of fact, she'd been so desperate she'd traveled across the ocean after a dead man. A chair magically appeared beneath her and she fell onto it as her thoughts grew as uncontrollable as wild ivy, going in all directions yet tangling amongst itself until it went nowhere.

Since the moment she'd met Byron Carmichael her life had turned upside down, inside out and backward. And it hadn't stopped with his death. It just kept getting worse and worse.

"What's your name?"

The young girl knelt in front of her, looking up with big brown eyes. They were so clear and caring, Constance wondered if the girl was named Angel, or was an angel. She could certainly use one about now. "C-Constance Jennings," she managed to eke out.

"Don't worry," Angel offered, sounding much older than she looked. "I won't let any of them claim you. You're safe with me."

That would be her luck—getting a child angel instead of an adult one who could really help. Not wanting to hurt the girl's feelings, Constance offered a tiny smile. "Thank you." If only her mind would clear long enough for a concentrated thought to take hold, perhaps then she could fully comprehend what was happening.

"Angel!" The deep voice was followed by footsteps sounding off the boardwalk. "It's time to head home."

"Hey, Pa. I'd like you to meet Constance Jennings," the girl answered, standing up.

Constance clenched her jaw to stop her teeth from chattering. The stiffness of the man's features were as bitter as the frosty wind, and the scowl covering his face was even more fierce now than when he'd stood next to the wagon, glaring at the commotion.

"Constance, this is my father, Ellis Clayton," Angel continued.

Tugging the collar of his sheepskin-lined coat up until it almost touched the wide brim of his hat, the man briefly nodded toward Constance—though his eyes never actually landed on her. "Time to go."

"Pa, Miss Jennings needs to come home with us," Angel said as calmly as if she'd just said it was cloudy today.

Constance flinched, and again when the frown on Ellis Clayton's face grew as if a storm built inside him.

"Angel." The warning tone in his voice was colder than the bitter wind.

"Pa." Angel held her ground as firmly as someone twice her age. "Look at them." She pointed toward the men who'd now gathered across the street from where Constance sat. "They're circling in like a pack of wolves on a fresh kill."

Constance shuddered, and the groan thickening her throat could no longer be contained.

Ellis Clayton glanced her way before he took his daughter's arm. "Angel," he said, his patience clearly spent. "She's not one of the injured animals you're always bringing home. You can't save the world."

"Maybe not, but I can save her."

"Excuse me," Constance started, ready to insist she didn't need to be saved, but the man's sideways glare made her lips clamp shut.

"What if it was me, Pa?" Angel continued. "What if I was in a strange town without a familiar face in sight? Wouldn't you hope some kind stranger would take me in?"

Constance held her breath, both at the thought of such a young girl being on her own and at the bone-chilling wind gusts penetrating her layers of clothing.

"That's not likely to happen. You're my daughter and—"

"But what if? We don't know what the future will bring. It could happen." Beneath her heavy coat, the girl shrugged. "Somewhere, sometime, it could happen."

The man rubbed his forehead, then glanced at the group of men and stared for an extended length of time. Constance's heart throbbed in her stomach. She should say something. Offer some type of solution, but try as she might, she didn't have one. Angel was very close to the truth. Constance did need a kind stranger. Her final fifty cents had paid for last night's meal.

A shrill whistle split the air, followed by the crack of a whip. Groaning and creaking, the stage pulled away from the boardwalk. Moments later, dust swirled as the horses picked up speed. The animals appeared excited to leave the tiny town of Cottonwood, Wyoming Territory. For a moment, Constance pictured herself bundled beneath the buffalo robe on the bouncing stage seat. The vision faded along with the wagon, leaving her chest extremely heavy.

"Widow Wagner only has one spare room, Pa, and Reverend Stillman just settled in it. He came to perform the ceremony."

Constance assumed the girl referenced the wedding between her and Ashton Kramer, which also explained how the reverend had known she was a mail-order bride even though she hadn't provided the information when he'd climbed into the stage in Fort Laramie.

Time ticked by as Ellis Clayton's gaze went from the men to the house the reverend had entered, and then landed on her. Though she was frozen stiff from the wind, heat penetrated Constance's cheeks.

"You're Ashton's bride?" he finally asked.

Biting her lip, Constance managed a nod.

He didn't respond, but Angel did. "She'll need a decent coat, Pa. What she has on won't get her halfway to the ranch."

Constance tugged the gray shawl that had once been Aunt Theresa's tighter around her shoulders. Bits of snow clung to the knitted yarn. The wind had picked up. It now carried swirling and growing flakes through the air with a stinging force. Once again, the girl was right. Constance had on her warmest dress, a beige wool two-piece, but had been close to freezing during the last leg of her journey, even with the buffalo robe.

Qualms piled inside her faster than she could comprehend. This had not been a good plan. Not only was she out of her element, her wardrobe was as out of place in Wyoming as the ocean would be. What she wouldn't give for the red velvet cape lined with rabbit fur she'd left England with. She'd sold it, along with a few other of her more elegant pieces, hoping to find a way to financially support herself. The amount she'd gained had paid her room and board for the week, but hadn't been enough to replace the overcoat, let alone anything else. That had contributed to her ultimate decision: become a mail-order bride.

The way Ellis Clayton glared down his nose at her made Constance doubly wish she'd never seen Ashton's first letter.

Something she could only assume was disgust flickered in the man's eyes as he scanned her shawl. When his gaze met hers, he asked, "Are you interested in coming home with Angel?"

Constance forced herself to breathe. The men across the road still leered, but other than the wind, it was deathly quiet. About ten buildings, built along both sides of the street, made up the town. Paint was nonexistent on most of the weathered boards, and only the two-story home, separated from the other buildings by a small yard, held the image of curtains on the inside. Since that was where Reverend Stillman had been escorted to, she assumed it was Mrs. Wagner's. Besides herself, Angel was the only trace of a female she'd seen.

Knowing the man waited for an answer, Constance prayed the thickness in her throat would allow words to come out. "Perhaps, I…" Her mind couldn't fathom a single suggestion. Fighting to hold an iota of dignity, she voiced her options, "I apologize, but at this moment, your generosity appears to be my only hope."

The man's expression softened and the sight did something to Constance's insides. She couldn't figure out exactly what, but then again she'd been greatly out of sorts since stepping off the stage.

His gaze went to his daughter, who smiled brightly. After shaking his head, he gestured to one of the men. "Put her stuff in my wagon, would you, Jeb?" When a young man moved toward her trunks, Ellis spun on one heel. "Come on, then."

Angel grabbed Constance's hand, and tugged her in the man's wake. "He's not as grumpy as he makes out to be."

The girl's assurance didn't do much for the quaking in Constance's limbs, nor the churning in her stomach. She willed her feet not to stumble as she matched Angel's quick pace into the building. Shelves and tables held an array of goods and foodstuffs, making the tiny space cluttered and claustrophobic. Nonetheless, Constance sighed at the relief of being out of the wind.

A large man, in height and breadth, emerged from behind a curtained doorway. "What you forget, Ellis?"

"We need a coat, Link." Ellis closed the door he'd held wide and moved toward the waist-high counter.

The man, Link it appeared, wrinkled his wide forehead as he stared at Constance with an all-consuming look. "So you're Ashton's bride. Poor sap. He's probably kicking like a mule trying to get out of the pearly gates. He'd sworn you'd be a looker. We buried him yesterday. Had to do it before the ground froze, you know."

Constance swallowed around the glob that had never left her throat, but now doubled in size.

"Just get us a coat, Link," Ellis demanded roughly.

"You claiming her?" Link asked, lifting his spiky brows high on his glistening forehead.

Even covered with his thick coat, Constance noticed Ellis's back stiffen, yet he didn't answer. Probably because his daughter did. "I am," Angel piped proudly.

Link guffawed. "You? You can't claim a mail-order bride, Angel."

"I'm not claiming her as my bride. I'm claiming her as my friend." Angel pointed over her shoulder with a thumb. "You can tell the passel of men out there that anyone who wants to claim Miss Jennings will have to come through me."

"Angel." Ellis sounded extremely frustrated.

Once again, the girl ignored her father. Not in a rude way, but with confidence she was right. "I'll send word for you to post a sign when we're ready to start interviews."

"Interviews?" Link's frown was back.

So was Constance's.

Angel folded her arms across her chest. "Yes, interviews. If anyone wants to court Miss Jennings, they'll be interviewed first. By me."

"Link, get us a coat," Ellis snapped and then turned to glare his daughter.

Angel grinned.

For the millionth time in the past months, Constance wished she'd never left England.

As if he couldn't remain angry at the girl, a tiny grin flashed on Ellis's face. Constance's insides fluttered again. This time the man's face had been transformed into a remarkable image that sparked a memory in her troubled mind.

Link shook his head, as if in disbelief, and then moved back to the curtain. "I'll see what I got, but I doubt it'll fit her. She's not much bigger than Angel there."

As quick as he'd disappeared, Link reappeared. With a flip of his thick wrists, he shook the folds from a garment. The coat looked similar to the one Angel wore. Light brown twill with what appeared to be a buffalo-hide lining. Not fashionable by any sense, but, oh, did it look warm. Constance balled her fists, trying to hold in a new wave of shivers as her body begged to have the garment cloaking it.

Ellis turned, looked at her expectantly. Her trembles increased, but she managed an agreeable nod. "It'll do," he said, taking the coat from Link and holding it up for Constance to slide her arms into the sleeves.

The weight was great, but the warmth heavenly. Angel rolled up the cuffs, and Constance quickly hooked the leather and wood frogs down the front. She should thank both the girl and her father, but something inside Constance—not the irritating little voice, but her own common sense—said Ellis Clayton wouldn't appreciate that right now.

She held her silence even when he insisted Link retrieve a scarf and pair of mittens.

"How much?" Ellis asked Link.

The amount the store keeper said made Constance gasp. The glance Ellis shot her way had her lowering her eyes to the floor. It was almost as much money as Ashton Kramer had sent her, which had paid for the train from New York to Cheyenne, the stage ride to Cottonwood and all her meals along the way.

"That seems kind of steep considering the coat doesn't even fit her," Ellis replied.

The coat was several sizes too large, but Constance could deal with that. She'd dealt with a whole lot worse than ill-fitting clothes. Keeping her gaze off the men, she flipped the scarf over her straw hat and tied it beneath her chin before pulling on the thick, cozy mittens.

"It's called supply and demand, Ellis. You know that," Link answered proudly.

"Yeah, well, someday you're going to demand yourself out of business. People are moving into the Territory every day. A new merchant, one not set on robbing his customers, will have you rethinking your prices." Ellis counted out bills as he spoke.

Link laughed, taking the money. "Yeah, well it ain't gonna happen today, is it?"

They left the small store then, but before Ellis pulled the door shut, after he'd held it open for Constance and Angel, Link shouted, "Be sure to send me word to post, Angel."

"I will!" Angel's words were cut off by the solid thud of the door.

The men now stood next to a long wagon parked beside the boardwalk. One man, the bean pole guy, asked, "You claiming her, Ellis?"

"Get in," Ellis directed Angel before he turned to the crowd. "You men better head home." Pointing to the weather-filled sky, he added, "There's a storm moving in."

Angel had climbed onto the seat of the wagon, and held a hand out, helping Constance up beside her. The back of the buckboard was loaded high, including her luggage. Ellis walked around the back, and Constance swiveled to stare straight ahead. When he planted himself beside Angel, the three of them were packed tighter than her trunks.

"But what about the bride?" another man asked.

"Don't worry about her right now. Worry about your own hides." Ellis threaded the reins between his gloved fingers and snapped the leather over the backs of the matching buckskins harnessed to the wagon.

Constance grabbed the little fluted edge near her hip as the wagon jerked forward.

Other questions filled the air from the men,

some running beside the wagon as the horses picked up speed. Angel started to speak but Ellis insisted, "Be quiet, Angel."

The girl listened this time, but the smile she gave Constance said she wasn't miffed. Actually, Angel seemed quite satisfied.

Constance couldn't return the grin. Though she was thankful to the girl and her father, the day had quickly escalated into a predicament that left her deeply indebted to the Claytons—with no imaginable way to repay them.

Ellis flexed his chin. His jaw was set so tight, his teeth ached. Angel, at times the daughter every man could only hope to have, made him question her parentage today. Hauling home injured animals was one thing, but a woman—a mail-order bride, no less—was out of the ordinary even for her. He also had to agree with Link. Ashton Kramer was probably screaming from his grave. Constance Jennings was about the best-looking woman the Wyoming Territory had ever seen. The contrast between her coal-black hair and summer-sky-blue eyes could make a man stop dead in his tracks. He, himself, who'd never been overly affected by a woman's looks, had been half afraid to take a second gander at her. She'd barely uttered a word, but her stance, and the way she walked, gave the impression she was no ordinary gal. Nope. Miss

Constance Jennings had been born and bred as a lady. How she'd ended up Ashton Kramer's mail-order bride should be investigated. Not by him—he wasn't that curious. Yet, if whoever did take her on didn't do a bit of researching they might find themselves in a whole mess of trouble.

He'd always had a sixth sense about such things, and knew when to listen to his gut. Right now, the milk he'd had at breakfast was churning itself into butter. The only thing that had ever overridden his instincts was his daughter. And she knew it. The little scamp. Asking him how he'd feel if that had been her in a strange place, with nowhere to turn for help. That had hit home, so had her words about not knowing if it would ever happen. He'd known it for a long time, but today Angel once again proved she was much too smart for her thirteen-year-old hide.

Angel was also more like her mother than she knew. She'd been too young when Christine had died to imitate her behaviors, but she'd inherited them just as she had her mother's looks, and used them to rule him on a regular basis. Christine would have hauled the mail-order bride home, and she'd have made him buy her a coat before doing so. Which he'd gladly done. The tiny shawl Miss Jennings wore wouldn't warm a flea.

The snow now fell in huge flakes, the kind that would cover the brown ground within no time, and more than likely, stay until next spring. Ellis tugged his coat collar up to cover his ears and then reached down to pull out the woven blanket from beneath the wagon seat. He flicked it open with one hand, splaying the edges over his passengers' knees. Miss Jennings caught the other end and quickly tucked it under her thigh after straightening it to cover them all evenly. He switched driving hands, and stuck his end of the blanket beneath his outer leg.

While the snow fell, collecting in tiny drifts along the sides of the road, they traveled onward, straight west into the foothills of the Big Horns. His ranch, Heaven on Earth, was nestled there, right where the earth rose majestically into the sky. It was good land. Rich soil, an unending water supply and more acres of sweet grazing pastures than anywhere else in the nation. Come June, it would be fifteen years since he and Christine had topped the little ridge of the valley still a few miles ahead for the first time. She'd shouted for him to stop the oxen. He'd done so of course, wondering what had caught her attention. She'd jumped from the seat, and with her blond hair twisting and turning in the wind, she'd declared, "This is it, Ellis! This is our heaven on earth."

She'd been right of course, as always, and they'd set to building their new lives together. A right fine life they'd had, too, until the birth of their second child eight years later had taken her and the babe from him forevermore.

He'd mourned the great loss, still did, but in the same right, he held thankfulness for what their years had given him. Happiness, joy, one of the largest ranches this side of the Mississippi and more precious than all else, his Angel.

As if she understood his thoughts, his daughter leaned her head against his shoulder and settled those big brown eyes on him. Warmed, he winked. She grinned, and as the snow continued to pile up on the trail, the horses clomped onward.

By the time they topped the little ridge an hour later, the sun, which hadn't quite given up trying to brighten the gray winter sky, broke through for a moment to grace the homestead below with a welcoming glow. Even the wind stilled when the horses stopped, as was their normal routine, giving Ellis the opportunity to appreciate home from his favorite overlook.

Swirls of smoke spiraled out of the house and bunkhouse chimneys. The other buildings, the barns, sheds and lean-tos, sat quietly as snowflakes landed on their shingled roofs. Steam rose around the cattle near the barns, and men mingled between the buildings and pens, making the ranch look like a miniature city. It practically was. There were few things the ranch didn't provide. The only reason he and Angel had gone to town today was to pick up the fixings for the holiday gathering they'd host next month.

"That's it, Miss Jennings," Angel said, staring at the site below. "That's Heaven on Earth."

The woman turned slowly, as if trying to keep one eye on the homestead. "What?"

"Heaven on Earth," Angel repeated. "That's the name of our ranch." Angel looked at him before she turned back to the woman. "Welcome home."

Ellis sucked in air as if he'd just been stomach punched. He actually braced a hand to his abdomen, wondering where the sudden lurching had come from. Swallowing, he realized it was from the way Miss Jennings's blue eyes stared at him.

He tucked the brim of his hat down, and flicked the reins over Jack and Jim, encouraging the animals to begin the final mile—all downhill—of their journey. He kicked the edge of the blanket away from his left foot, making a clear path to the brake if needed. He had no reason to be nervous, he'd traipsed the trail a million times over, but for some reason his nerve endings were dancing a jig beneath his skin.

The decline went as usual, swift and uncomplicated, and the unloading of the wagon happened just as smoothly. The ranch hands were used to unloading Angel's purchases, and since ninety percent of what they hauled went into the house, it didn't take long before one of the hands led Jack and Jim off to the barn.

Ellis entered through the open front door, carrying the last of the bundles. The foyer, though piled with boxes, crates and bundles, was empty. A faint voice, Angel's, filtered down from above—no doubt she was showing Miss Jennings to a room. He set the last package on top of the others, silently admitting he was clueless as to what Angel had purchased, even though she had given him a full accounting of what she needed.

Miss Jennings's trunks were not amongst the other stuff, which meant Angel must have directed they be carried upstairs. His daughter was like her mother in that sense, too, good at giving orders and expecting them to be followed.

Shrugging out of his sheepskin coat, Ellis walked across the foyer and down the hall that led to his office. He'd purchased a few things himself and had some accounting to do—now was as good of a time to do it as ever.

Settled into his high-backed steerhide chair, he flipped open the ledger sitting on top of his desk and reached for the inkwell. A loud thud shook the ceiling. The scream accompanying it sent him flying out the door. Taking the stairs three at a time had him at the top of the steps and shooting down the hallway before his ears picked up the sounds now filling the house. He skidded to a stop in front of the first open bedroom door.

Angel and Miss Jennings were on the floor, covered in an assortment of women's underthings. The lid of one of the round-top trunks rocked back and forth on the floor. It had been years since giggles had echoed off the walls of the big house, and the way these two were going at it, the men in the bunkhouse had to hear it. An unusual fluttering happened in Ellis's insides.

Angel plucked a few frilly garments off her head. Seeing him, she giggled harder. "Oh, Pa." She covered her snickering mouth. When she caught air again, she continued. "You should have seen it. As soon as we released the latch, the top flew off like a blasting cap."

Miss Jennings had one hand covering her lips, and her tiny shoulders shook with mirth. Lace hung over her head. He couldn't tell if it was a petticoat or a pair of pantaloons, but the sparkling gaze of those unique eyes and the flush of her dainty cheeks sent a shiver racing up his spine like a mini bolt of lightning.

Chapter Two

Constance had put it off long enough. She'd been scrounging up courage all evening. Squaring her shoulders, she walked down the dark hall to Ellis Clayton's office and, before she lost her nerve, rapped on the door. He hadn't joined them for dinner, nor had he been back from the barn when Angel showed her where she could take a bath—which had been heavenly. But an hour ago, while staring out her bedroom window, she'd seen him cross the yard, once again hoisting his coat collar up against the snow. After checking her image in the mirror and making a few minor adjustments to her hair, she'd left her room. The past half hour, she'd paced the upstairs hall, listening to his downstairs movements. She may have found an ounce of courage, but a solution to her current situation remained as far away as England.

The opening of the door made her flinch. She'd knocked, so the action shouldn't have startled her, but it did.

Ellis lifted a brow. "Miss Jennings? Is there something you need?"

Tugging the shawl about her shoulders and twisting her fingers deep in the yarn, she nodded. "I'd like to speak with you, if you have a minute."

His lag increased her anxiety. She curled her toes to keep them from twisting her about for a fast exit. After what seemed like an eternity, he stepped back, holding the door wide, and waved an arm for her to enter.

Thick carpet softened her footsteps. The office was as elaborate as the rest of the home. Totally unexpected in the wilds of Wyoming Territory, but in some ways, so similar to her childhood home in Richmond, she wanted to sigh with memories. Shelves stacked with books from the floor to the ceiling covered two walls, and a large fireplace not only warmed the room, but provided a friendly glow. A massive desk sat in the center of the room, positioned so one could gaze out the large windows framed with olive-colored drapes that were tied back to sway along the glass panes from ceiling to floor. The familiar scent of leather-bound books filled the air and had Constance taking a deep breath.

"Have a seat," he offered, pointing to the set of

matching armchairs in front of the desk while he walked behind it.

Memories snuck forward, of her father stationing himself just as Ellis was. She'd often sat on the corner of Papa's desk, thudding her heels against the wood. Now wasn't the time for childhood recollections. She had to quell her nerves, and offer her proposition, which would include sharing some of her past. Ellis deserved an explanation in exchange for his kindness if nothing else, but there were some things she'd never be able to tell anyone.

The mantel clock ticked away, mindless to the noise its steady movement created. Constance took another deep breath before she began, "I'd like to start by saying thank you. I know Angel put you in a predicament by offering me lodging, and I appreciate how you handled the situation."

Ellis leaned back in his chair, eyeing her in an interesting way. Almost as if he was cautious or surprised. Even without his thick coat and big brimmed hat, he was a large man. As he folded his arms, the dark brown shirt stretched over the bulk of chest, straining the buttons holding it together.

He didn't offer an acknowledgment. Her mouth had gone dry, she wet her lips before continuing, "I would like to explain my situation, and hopefully work out an agreeable arrangement."

One dark brow, the same rich shade as his hair, arched, but he quickly relaxed it. Ellis was good at hiding his emotions, and reactions, but she'd already seen that. "I—" she started again.

"Excuse me, Miss Jennings," he interrupted, "where exactly are you from?"

She wasn't surprised. He'd want facts not justifications. "I was born and raised in Richmond, Virginia. My family owned a tobacco plantation. Prior to the war, that is."

"And afterward?"

"There was nothing left afterward." She'd never been back to Virginia, but had heard everything was gone and believed her source.

"Your family?"

"Nothing left, Mr. Clayton. They all—my father, mother and three brothers—perished in the war. My brothers died on the battlefields and my parents during the raid that left our home nothing more than ashes."

"I'm sorry," he said respectfully.

She nodded. Years had eased the pain, but the loss would forever live in her heart. Memories of a happy childhood helped. As did her belief someday she'd find a place she could call home again.

He leaned forward and rested both elbows on the edge of his desk. "How did you survive? If you don't mind my asking?"

"I survived because I wasn't there. When the war broke out, my parents sent me to England. I had two great aunts in residence there and I lived with them."

"When did you return to the United States?"

So this is how it would be, him asking questions, her answering. It wasn't as she had planned, but it might be better. Once in a while she tended to ramble and could accidentally say more than she meant to. She'd already done that once today. "A few months ago."

"Really? The war ended a dozen years ago."

"I know. After my family perished, there was no reason for me to return. Besides, my aunts were elderly and depended on me to care for them. One died in December of last year. The other in January of this year." Constance hoped that was enough to satisfy his curiosity, but not so much that he'd want to know more.

"I see," he said. "It's my understanding you lived in New York?"

A quiver rippled her spine. Ashton must have shared that bit of information. Keeping her chin up, she nodded. "Yes, that's where I saw Mr. Kramer's request and responded to his call for a wife."

His expression said he wasn't satisfied with her answer, but once again, he didn't ask specifics. Instead he offered, "I'm sorry about Ashton's untimely accident."

"Thank you. I am, too. Though I had never met him, I mourn his loss." It was the truth. Without

Ashton, her future looked pretty bleak. "Could you share with me how he—it happened?"

"Angel didn't tell you?"

Fighting the urge to fidget, Constance refolded her hands in her lap. "No, but then I didn't ask her to. I apologize, Mr. Clayton, Angel is a wonderful girl. Very bright and compassionate and understanding, but I do not feel it would be appropriate for me to ask her about such things."

A faint grin curled the corners of his lips and a shine appeared in his eyes. "Don't apologize, Miss Jennings. Angel can appear more mature than she is. I appreciate you recognizing she is still a child."

This man loved his daughter above and beyond all. Constance remembered a time when she was such a daughter. History made her warn, "She won't be a child for much longer though." She often wondered if she'd "grown up" the instant she'd arrived in England.

His smile increased, but was accompanied by a somber nod. "Unfortunately, I'm aware of that."

Her heart pitter-patted, acknowledging the brief connection she and Ellis Clayton shared. There would come a time when this man would have to say goodbye to his daughter, and it would affect both him and the girl—deeply. The only time Constance had seen tears in her father's eyes was the day he'd set her on the ship to sail for England. Though she had many other memories—happy and good ones—that was the one that stuck in her mind like a splattered drop of paint. No matter how hard she tried, it wouldn't dissolve. It had barely faded over the years.

With one hand, Ellis wiped his face, as if erasing the smile. It worked, because when his hand went back to rest on the desk his face was serious. "I guess I should tell you, since you'll no doubt hear it from half the territory."

She frowned, utterly confused for a moment.

"About Ashton's death," he said, eying her critically.

"Oh." Her cheeks stung. She wiped her palms, which all of a sudden had grown clammy, on her skirt. "Yes, Mr. Kramer's death. How did it come about?"

"He took a fall off a horse." Ellis's gaze settled over her shoulder for a moment. When it returned to her, he added, "Doc said a broken rib punctured his lung."

She pressed a hand to the thud behind her breastbone. "Oh, my."

"He was bedridden for three days before he died. Some may tell you he hung on because he knew you were on your way."

She gulped. Ellis Clayton certainly didn't mince words. Sorrow that she'd never meet Ashton Kramer, nor get to know a man who'd awaited her arrival made her sigh heavily. "The poor man."

Ellis didn't linger nor stay on one subject for an extended length. "So, are you going back to New York? Or Virginia perhaps?"

His question caught her slightly off guard. Her mind was still processing Ashton Kramer's untimely death. "No." She shook her head. "No, I left New York for good. And I haven't been back to Virginia since I was eleven."

"Eleven?"

"Yes, that's when I went to live with my great aunts."

His frown was back, tugging his brows deeply together. "So you're twent—"

"Six. I'm twenty-six." There were days when she felt a hundred and six. Hoping to avoid any further questions about herself, she asked, "Have you always lived in the Wyoming Territory?"

"No, my wife, Christine, Angel's mother, and I came out here shortly after we married. Before the war broke out. She died when Angel was six."

"How?" She bit her lip at how fast the question shot out.

"Childbirth." He pushed away from his desk and walked to the fireplace where he removed the grate, stirred the flames with a gold-handled poker and then added a couple split logs. He replaced the poker and the grate before he turned back around. "What are your plans, Miss Jennings?"

He still mourned the loss of his wife. Constance

easily saw it—for it was the same thing she'd seen in the mirror for years. She'd already witnessed enough to understand Ellis's depth and character. He must have treasured his wife. Once, not so long ago, Constance had thought she might have that— a husband who'd cherish her, and had married the man. But Byron hadn't treasured her, nor had he bothered to tell her he was already married. The truth, and the way she'd discovered it, had been demoralizing and humiliating.

The memories, painful and degrading, made a heavy sigh escape before she could stop it. "To be perfectly honest, Mr. Clayton, right now I have no idea what I'm going to do." For the past nine months she hadn't had a concentrated plan that propelled her forward. She'd thought she had, more than once, but fate had stepped in and left her reeling in another direction over and over again.

Ellis opened his mouth. Unwilling to let anything else slip, she quickly changed the subject. "But I would like to offer, or suggest, an arrangement."

He contemplated her statement, silently and thoroughly it seemed, before he walked back to his chair. "And that would be?"

"I mentioned that I took care of my aunts. They had a country estate outside of London. I managed the household for them, and would like to offer you my services in exchange for room and board until

I can decide what I should do." His silence forced her to add, "I've also had experience tutoring children. I know Angel is a very smart young woman, but it's my understanding she hasn't had any formal education. I could offer those services as well."

His chair squeaked as he repositioned. He wasn't quick to respond, which had her nerves ticking beneath her skin in tune with the mantel clock.

"How long do you plan on staying, Miss Jennings?"

"I guess that depends."

"On?"

"Several things." Including if the lies surrounding Byron's death found their way to Wyoming. If so, her chances of starting over would be greatly diminished. She had no proof she hadn't killed Byron, just as she had no proof he'd caused her injuries and left wounds that changed her life forever.

Ellis watched the emotions playing across Miss Jennings's features. Her expressions told him more than her words, in some instances. In others, he'd been downright surprised by what she'd said. Snap decision-making wasn't his way; he'd left that up to Christine and more recently Angel—hence the mail-order bride sitting in his office. Yet he knew firsthand how quickly life could leave a person vulnerable and hopeless.

Unable to stay seated, he pushed out of his chair

again and walked to the window. The snowstorm continued to blanket the earth, and hinted that it would hang around for the next day or so. It was early for such a dumping, but stranger things had happened. Ellis turned and met the apprehensive eyes watching and waiting for his response to her offer.

"I have a cook, Miss Jennings."

The straight, fine wisps of black hair that had escaped her loosely pinned bun fluttered against the elegantly curved line of her neck as she primly shook her head. "I know, sir, and I don't wish to undermine the job Mr. Beans is doing."

"Beans," he corrected. "Just Beans, there's no mister." Beans had a great aversion to being called mister. Just as Ellis had an aversion to being called sir. He worked for a living and didn't appreciate a title he felt was held for those who were born of honor or suggested one man was of higher rank than another. It reminded him of the slave days—something else he had greatly disliked.

She gave a graceful nod. "I apologize. Beans does a fine job. The stew I had for supper was quite delicious."

"Yes, he does," Ellis agreed, but then had to admit, "For the ranch hands. It would be good for Angel to learn more about the kitchen. She tries, and does a good job, but…" An invisible draw made him turn back to the window. High above the earth, beyond the hovering snow clouds, a tiny star twinkled and then shot across the sky. Blinking, he searched for more, but the clouds once again obscured the view. His daughter needed a woman's touch. He'd known it for some time. "Angel could use some formal education as well. She's a sound reader and has a head for numbers, but there are other things she should be studying. Things she should be learning about."

He hadn't turned around, and wasn't ready to do so yet, either. His daughter was the reason he woke up every morning. For the past few years he'd wondered about sending her to a school out east, but the thought of being separated from her made him ignore the considerations as quickly as they formed. Miss Jennings's arrival seemed like a good solution, but… He sighed. There was more to it than that.

Turning about, he leaned back, resting his backside on the windowsill. The wood was cold and penetrated his wool pants, but it wasn't overly bothersome. "You can't see it right now, but out the window behind me, on the far side of the backyard is a small barn. It says Angel's Barn across the front doors. Angel painted the letters several years ago."

Constance nodded again. It had been years since he'd seen someone as elegant and refined as her. He wanted to close his eyes, block the view and the memories of when he'd lived in Charleston and come across stylish women every day. Not that he'd been attracted to them. Simply put, the memories reminded him of how long Christine had been gone.

"I haven't been out to her barn for a week or so, so I don't know for sure," he said, pulling his mind out of the past, "but the last time I was there she had a one-legged rooster, a blind porcupine, a skunk…" Nothing about the animal came to mind. "I don't really know what's wrong with the skunk other than it wants to live here. There were also a couple of birds, a squirrel that ate too much butter and a litter of motherless rabbits."

Constance had a serene smile on her petal-pink lips, as if the array of Angel's pets didn't surprise her.

He gestured toward the other side of the window. "Although I'm sure he's hibernating right now, sometimes there's a bear out in the north pasture. Teddy was a half-dead orphaned cub when Angel found him." He had to huff out the chuckle pressing on his lungs. "He never fails to startle a cowhand or two when he decides to wander through."

"Have you ever considered just getting her a dog?" Constance asked.

That made him crack a smile, but he forced it to leave as quickly as it had appeared. "There are several of those around here, too. As well as cats and kittens." He pushed away from the window, moving toward his desk. "For Angel it's not about the companionship. It's the nurturing. The act of healing, of saving something no one else cares about." It was hard to describe to someone who didn't know Angel. "There have been so many critters over the years I couldn't name them all if I had to. Some have died, some have stayed around, others have healed up and left, never been seen again. Then there are those, like the bear, who wander past every once in a while."

"I have a feeling I'm being compared to one of Angel's animals." A grin lifted the corners of her mouth, but her eyes held a touch of conviction.

"With all due respect, Miss Jennings, I don't mean to offend you, nor do I wish to be rude, but yes, you are like one of her animals. And when Angel sets on healing a critter, no one changes her mind." He half sat on the corner of his desk.

"Because she couldn't save her mother."

The whispered words echoed around the room, making Ellis shiver. The softness of Constance's expression made his throat swell. The thickness was raw and gritty. "She's not looking for a mother."

"That's not what I mean, Mr. Clayton," Constance said, shaking her head. "Forgive me. I spoke out of turn. It's just that I can relate. Losing people we love can leave us wanting to protect others from experiencing the pain."

The authenticity in her eyes and voice was too sincere for him to acknowledge. It made a part of him feel vulnerable—something he refused to let into his life. Shifting his weight, he mulled the decision he'd already made around for a moment before saying, "I'll accept your offer of an arrangement—household management, including cooking and tutoring Angel, in exchange for wages that include room and board until spring. That should give her time to do what she feels she needs to do."

Constance gave a slight nod, not as confident as it had been earlier, which was just as well. He had more to say before he completely agreed to her suggestion. "I appreciate you coming to me and sharing part of your story. I know there's a lot you haven't told me, but I respect your privacy. I do, however, want you to know I'm going to deal with this situation just like I do when Angel hauls home an animal. I'll stand back, not interfere unless she asks..." He paused so his next statement would be more effective. Holding Miss Jennings's gaze, he added, "Or if I feel she's in danger. If that occurs, I will put an end to the arrangement—immediately."

The color had drained from her face, but she held her stiff posture. "I understand, Mr. Clayton, I wouldn't expect any less. I assure you, the last thing I'd want is to see Angel injured."

He held her stare. "There are many types of injuries, Miss Jennings. The ones we can't see are often worse than the ones we can."

She blinked, and respectfully bowed her head. "I agree, sir."

The word grated his nerves too deep this time. "I'd appreciate if you called me Mr. Clayton, or simply Ellis."

"Very well, Mr. Clayton."

"I'll run some figures by you tomorrow as far as pay is concerned. I ask that you complete a list of duties you feel should fall to your position."

"I'll have it ready first thing in the morning. I'd also like to document the funds I already owe you." She clarified, "The coat, scarf and mittens."

He stood and extended a hand. "Very well, Miss Jennings. I wish you a good night, then."

She rose and gave his hand a surprisingly firm shake. "Thank you, Mr. Clayton. I appreciate the opportunity." Pulling her hand from his, she nodded. "Good night."

Straight-backed and head held high, she left the room. It wasn't until the door quietly snapped shut that he repeated, "Good night."

A log rolled in the fire, shooting sparks against the wire mesh grate. Ellis walked over and rather than remove the grate, slid the poker between the grate and the stones. Breaking apart the glowing log until it was little more than small-sized coals that would soon die out, he wondered about the arrangement he'd just agreed to. Constance Jennings hid a very large secret. It was written on her face as bold as the headlines of the *Territory Gazette*.

His brother Eli still ran the family plantation back in the Carolinas. He'd write Eli, ask a bit about pre-war plantations near Richmond. Protecting Angel came before all else, which meant learning more about Constance Jennings. After replacing the poker, he went to his desk and penned a short letter before he blew out the lamps and made his way up the stairs.

The lamp in his room had been lit, as well as the fire set. Tugging his shirt off, he paused near the dresser where the picture of Christine, taken shortly before her death, sat. He picked up the silver filigree frame. "I saw you tonight," he whispered, "shooting across the sky. I hope you know what you're doing."

She didn't answer of course, but his mind did. Christine always knew what she was doing, and had rarely, if ever, been wrong.

He set the picture down. "There's always a first."

Day comes early on a ranch, and a morning that carried a blizzard meant the first set of chores would take twice as long as usual. Ellis donned layers, knowing how the wind could steal away the body's heat, and made his way down the front set of stairs. A scent caused him to pause on the bottom step. Coffee? Beans never entered the house in the morning. He and Angel dealt with that meal themselves.

He made his way to the swinging door off the foyer.

"Good morning, Mr. Clayton." She didn't turn from the stove.

The fine hairs on his neck stood. How had she known he was here? He'd barely pushed the door open, and it didn't squeak. "Miss Jennings," he greeted, stepping into the room.

"Coffee's on the table. The biscuits will be done in a few minutes as well as the gravy." Her trim hips swayed as she stirred a spoon about in the pan.

"I usually wait until after chores and breakfast with Angel." He hadn't meant to sound as rude as it came out, but his nerves were ticking again.

"Oh, I'm sorry. I assumed with the storm you'd need to be out early this morning. I'm sure it'll keep if you want to wait." She pulled the pan off the heat and set it near the back of the stove before she spun about. Dressed in the same dark blue outfit she'd worn last night while they'd talked in his office, he wondered if she'd slept.

There were no bags under her eyes. Actually, she looked quite rested and healthy. Her black hair was neatly pinned in a bun, and she'd tied a flour sack around her waist for an apron, which enhanced the feminine curves he had to drag his eyes off.

He gripped the back of the closest chair, but needing something more to do, snatched the steaming cup off the table. The wondrous smells filling the kitchen had his stomach growling. "As long as it's ready, I might as well eat. It may be a while before I make it back in."

"Wonderful." She spun back to the stove.

Did she mean it was wonderful that he wanted to eat, or wonderful that he'd be gone for a while? He sat, scratching his head at the conflicting thoughts. It was almost as if he was in the wrong skin, the way his nerves twitched and itched. Mere seconds later, a plate of biscuits smothered with glossy gravy was set down in front of him. "Thank you," he mumbled.

She hovered near the table. "Angel gave me a tour of the house last night. I assumed our arrangement would start this morning." Tugging her fingers apart, she pointed to a sheet of paper on the table.

Written in slanted, perfect penmanship, was a long list of duties. He didn't take the time to read them all. "Yes, that's fine." He picked up his fork. "I'll meet with you later today, to go over your wage and such."

"Very well," she replied, walking across the

room. "Enjoy your breakfast. There's more on the stove."

There were times she acted like a scared little girl, others where she appeared to be a wise old woman and still others—especially when a slight hint of an English accent filtered her words— where he was convinced she should be sitting in a tea parlor surrounded by ladies-in-waiting. All in all, she made him feel as confused as a cat with two tails.

"Aren't you going to eat?" he asked.

"I'll wait for Angel." She transferred the pan of biscuits into a basket and covered them with a cloth, and then stirred down the bubbling gravy.

He pulled his eyes back to the breakfast before him, and lifted his fork. Beans had never made something taste this delicious. The gravy had big chunks of sausage and had soaked deep into the golden-brown biscuits. He ate two helpings before he excused himself to gather his outerwear from his office.

A scraping noise said someone was in the front parlor when he reentered the foyer. Walking to the doorway, Ellis paused. Crouched down, Miss Jennings swept the cold ashes from the fireplace in the large front room and deposited them in the ash bucket. Frowning at the sight, he said, "Thomas Ketchum is my wood man."

She flipped loose strands of hair aside with the back of her hand as she turned. "Excuse me?"

The action teased his mind, made him think of her attractiveness. "Thomas," Ellis repeated, reminding himself of what he'd been saying. "I pay him to cut wood during the summer and tend to the fires in winter. He does other things as well. Part of his job is to clean out the fireplaces and keep them burning all day. He should be in any minute."

She finished the job, replaced the ash brush to its holder and then stood. "I thought that was just because you were gone yesterday. He comes in even when you're home?"

"Yes. That's his job." He gestured toward the front door. "A ranch this size requires a lot of wood. It takes one person dedicated to it."

Wiping her hands on the flour sack, she said, "I do apologize. I'll remember that in the future."

He nodded, but a feeling as if he'd just chastised her for no reason settled in his chest. Shrugging against the sensation, he went to the door and stepped out into what might prove to be one of the biggest blizzards of all time.

Chapter Three

The wood man, Thomas Ketchum, turned out to be a bulk of a man with a cheerful disposition. Upon his arrival, he'd not only cleaned out and set fires in the fireplaces but had refilled all of the wood boxes—which totaled over a dozen—shortly after Ellis had left the house. During the morning hours, Constance had explored the home thoroughly, making notes of things that needed immediate attention, such as cobwebs in hidden corners a child or man wouldn't notice. She'd noted other things that could use slight adjustments in the future—rugs showing wear and curtains that had become sun-faded—but overall the home was in excellent condition and was well run.

During that quiet, early morning time, the expanse and elegance surrounding her had childhood memories dancing in her head like a figurine on a music box. Matter of fact, part of her had wanted to skip along the halls and slide down the wide banister. The house, the surroundings, produced a contentment she'd never found in England, one she already cherished.

Curiosity had led her to ask Angel why the home was so large, for just her and her father. "Pa said he promised my mother the exact home she'd left behind in the Carolinas—only bigger," Angel had said.

Now, several hours later, Constance listened with one ear as Angel explained the upcoming holiday party. The other ear was tuned into the doors of the ranch house, both the front and back. Ellis had yet to return. Noon would soon be upon them, the roast a ranch hand had delivered to the back door which she'd seasoned and set to bake was nearly done. She'd gone to the door several times, wondering if she heard something, but the blizzard created a whiteout that made seeing the edge of the front porch impossible.

She and Angel were settled in the large yet cozy front parlor, where the fire roared with warmth and the wide windows, despite the blizzard, filled the room with light.

"Last year, I made divinity. I found the recipe in a cookbook, but it didn't turn out very well." The girl scrunched up her face. "Not even the animals would eat it."

Constance focused her waning attention on Angel and smiled. "We'll make it again. It'll help with two people. Whipping the egg whites becomes tiring for one."

"It certainly did," Angel admitted. "And turned out as hard as rocks. Good thing Pa didn't break a tooth. He was the only one brave enough to try it."

"That sounds like something my father would have done," Constance admitted.

"Oh? Where does he live?"

"He used to live in Virginia, but he passed away many—" A thud outside the front door had Constance jumping to her feet. Regardless of Angel's earlier assurance that Ellis was fine, was used to working in such extreme conditions, Constance couldn't help but fret for his well-being.

The noise came again, and Angel ran from the parlor, pulling the front door open as Constance turned the corner.

The bitterly cold wind swirled into the house, stinging Constance's face and eyes, but it was her heart that froze. The blizzard had made her compliant. Let her believe travel would be hampered. The man lying on the front porch wasn't Ellis. It was a complete stranger. Could he be the authorities? All the way from New York? Who else would travel through a blizzard? Though fretful, concern for his lifeless state flared inside her. "Help me get him inside."

Between the two of them, Angel tugging and Constance pushing, they managed to roll the man over the threshold. His face was beet-red and ice hung on his eyelashes.

"Mr. Homer?" Angel patted the man's ruddy cheeks. "What are you doing here?"

The man groaned, and Constance sighed with relief he was indeed alive. "Mr. Homer?" she asked, brushing aside the snow covering his clothing.

"One of the men from town. He works at the bank," Angel explained as she pushed the door shut.

Constance now recognized the man as the one she'd compared to a rain barrel yesterday. "What's he doing out here?"

Angel, with her long blond curls bouncing about, shook her head ruefully. "My guess would be to claim you."

Constance pressed a hand to the alarm thudding in her chest, recalling the men outside the stage. "In a storm like this? He must be crazy."

The man groaned again.

For a few hours the reason for her being at the Clayton home had escaped her. The panic in her chest turned into annoyance. It was a dismal situation she found herself in, but in all circumstances there was a solution, and she'd find one now, too. As soon as she saw to the tasks at hand. Constance huffed out a puff of frustrated air. "Help me drag him into the parlor so he can thaw out. The poor man's lucky he didn't freeze to death."

Along with much tugging and pulling, she and Angel managed to get Mr. Homer in front of the fireplace in the parlor. Pressing her hands against her muscle-strained thighs, Constance took a moment to catch her breath from the laborious job before she began removing the man's coat by rolling him from side to side while Angel went upstairs for a blanket.

After a few minutes, the man regained consciousness. "Oh, thank you, thank you," he mumbled several times as he flopped closer to the fireplace. "Heat. Heat."

"Not too close, Mr. Homer," Constance warned, glad the grate kept the man from climbing into the flames.

A rap sounded on the front door. She and Angel stared at one another for a brief moment before they rose and went to the door again. This time the man was upright on the porch, but he leaned heavily on the door frame, shaking and shivering from head to toe. "G-g-g-goo-d-d-d d-d-d-ay."

Constance ran a hand over her aching forehead. This was too absurd to be happening. Surely these men didn't believe she was so destitute she'd— A lump formed in her throat. She was destitute. Lord knew where she'd be right now if not for Angel and Ellis.

Angel grabbed the man's arm. "Good day to you, too, Mr. Aimes. Get in here before you freeze to death."

Constance took his other arm as the man stumbled in, mumbling and leaving a trail of snow on the rug.

After that, there was barely time to get one man settled when another would be knocking, or in some cases, falling against the door. The final count was five. Mr. Homer, Mr. Aimes, Mr. McDonaldson, Mr. Westmaster and Jeb. Angel said she didn't know Jeb's last name, and the way his teeth chattered, Constance couldn't understand what he'd said.

Constance had just removed Jeb's frozen coat when the front door slammed shut. "Oh, no, not another one," she groaned, much louder than intended, but she was quite exasperated. Was every man in the Wyoming Territory without a lick of sense?

"Not another whaaat the hell?" Ellis stared into the front parlor from the doorway, his gaze making a full circle of the room.

Constance held her breath. It was quite a scene. Men wrapped in blankets, some holding hot water bottles on their frozen heads, others soaking their feet in tubs of warm water. Some had water dripping from the ice chunks still clinging to their hair, and most were groaning with shivers or their teeth were chattering loud and uncontrollably.

"They came," Angel said, squeezing around her father to enter the room, "to claim the bride." She walked over and flipped the blanket in her arms around Jeb. "I knew they wouldn't wait. I should've made a post with the date we'd start the interviews and left it with Link."

Constance's heart sank, and then jolted. Quickly, she stepped around and between the men. Though his face held an astonished look, Ellis must be furious. Rightfully so. This was all because of her. Stalling until she could come up with an appropriate explanation, she asked, "Mr. Clayton, can I get you some hot coffee?"

He glanced at the steaming cups set beside some of the men. "Is there any left?"

"Yes, I just put on a fresh pot." Constance froze midstep. His broad frame filled the doorway and she didn't dare squeeze around him as Angel had. "It should be about done," she offered, glancing toward the kitchen door on the other side of the arched opening.

He stepped aside, providing the space she needed to slip through the doorway. His attention remained on the parlor. "This explains the horses that showed up at the barn door."

Constance scrambled across the foyer to the swinging kitchen door. Once beyond it, she took a breath and slowed her pace, wishing she could slow her pulse as easily. The pot was perking loudly on the stove, and she grabbed a cup from the cupboard along the way. The last thing she'd expected was a horde of men traveling through a blizzard to claim her hand in marriage. A heavy foreboding once again pressed on her chest. Besides being overly disconcerting, it gravely added to the long list of debt she owed Ellis. He'd probably send her back to town with the men—tired of the problems she caused in such a short span of time. Heat stung her palm and she pulled her hand away from the hot pot.

"Did you burn yourself?"

Shy of jumping out of her skin, Constance shook her head. How had he come to stand right beside her and she not hear him? Ignoring the smart in her palm, she grabbed a towel before attempting to lift the pot this time.

"Thanks." He took the cup and moved a few steps away to drink the coffee.

Constance sought solace in the space separating them.

His silence lasted several minutes. "How many are there?"

Her relief was short-lived, if it had existed at all. "Five." She set the pot on the back burner, wishing she could make the unexpected visitors disappear as fast as they had arrived. An apology seemed trivial, and the justification she hadn't expected the men sounded like a flimsy excuse.

His gaze was on the door. "At least all their horses are accounted for." He spun around. "Unless there are more?"

Despondent, she shrugged. The action made the weight on her shoulders grow heavier. "I have no idea"

He held out his empty cup. She filled it. Flimsy excuse or not, it was all she had. "Mr. Clayton, I…" Another sigh left her chest. "I apologize. Please understand I had no idea—"

"I know you had nothing to do with this."

Shocked by the gentle undertone of his voice, she glanced up.

His gaze was on the coffee in his cup. "You didn't invite them. I was there yesterday. You have nothing to explain." He set the cup down and shrugged out of his coat. "It appears there'll be a few more than just the three of us for lunch, and supper."

Constance pressed a hand to the fluttering in her stomach. She could have sworn there had been humor in his voice, and from his profile, it appeared a smile sat on his lips.

The most remarkable thing happened then. He laughed. A sincere, deep baritone. "Can't say I've ever seen anything quite like it," he said, still staring at the closed door.

The image of the packed parlor flashed before her eyes. It could appear rather comical to some, Constance had to admit, through trying not to. An unexpected giggle slid up her throat. She pressed a hand to her lips, but it was too late. He'd already heard it.

The fine lines around his eyes deepened as his smile grew. "Don't upset yourself, Miss Jennings. It's truly not your fault." Shaking his head, he laughed harder. "They are a sorry looking bunch, aren't they?"

The giggle in her throat escaped, and along with it went some of the tension eating at her insides. His reassurance felt good. Really, really, good.

As their laughter died down, she chided herself, "Oh, goodness. It's not funny. I shouldn't be laughing. Those men could have perished."

"Yes, they could have," Ellis agreed. "But they didn't." He picked up his cup, emptied it in one swallow, and then set it back down on the counter.

Constance grasped he was an understanding man, his relationship with his daughter was proof of that, but she couldn't help but admit, "I was afraid you'd be upset."

"I could be, and I hope no one else is out there in this storm." He folded his arms and leaned back against the table. "But my wife was a very wise woman. She taught me years ago not to get angry over the little things. To save it for the things that matter. Angel is a lot like her." He glanced to the door again, as if he could see beyond the wood and into the parlor filled with men. "Besides, I expected it. I didn't think they'd arrive in the middle of a snow storm, but I knew they'd come."

It dawned on Constance that Ellis used his dead wife as a shield. The past affected him as much as it did her. Maybe there was no hope she could get beyond it. If he couldn't, how could she?

She pushed the coffeepot to the very back of the stove. "How did you know they would come?"

"Miss Jennings, surely you've noticed the lack of women in Wyoming. Or heard of it. Out here a woman is worth more than her weight in gold. The ad you saw from Ashton, that's just one of hundreds that have been posted places. Very few are responded to, and if they are, not many women actually show up after the man sends her money."

The thought of keeping Ashton Kramer's money and not upholding her end of the bargain had never crossed her mind.

His gaze was apprehensive. "You didn't know that?"

She shook her head.

"Where did you see Ashton's post?" There was a touch of skepticism in his voice.

She bit her lip, wondering just how much would be revealed by her answer. Several explanations rolled in her head, she chose one. "Someone in New York gave it to me."

His brows furrowed. "Gave it to you?"

"Mmm hmm," she murmured, trying to sound indifferent. His silence waited for more, so she added, "I traded some used clothes for it."

"Traded used clothes?" The doubt in his voice increased her apprehension.

She folded her trembling fingers together, squeezing them tight. Though she wasn't lying, the bubbling in her stomach made it feel like she was. "Yes, I had several things I no longer needed, and a woman offered to sell them for me. She gave me Mr. Kramer's letter for a dress she wanted to keep for herself."

"Was she wanted by the law?"

His question knocked the air right out of her lungs. She couldn't breathe, let alone respond.

As her ears buzzed, he said, "More than one woman's become a mail-order bride instead of going to jail."

She had to breathe or she'd faint. Sucking in enough air to get by, she managed to answer, "Stella wasn't wanted by the law."

Just then the kitchen door opened and Angel strode into the room. Constance had never been happier to see someone. "They'll all live," Angel said offhandedly. "I do wonder about Jeb's toes though, they're already turning black."

Ellis pushed away from the table. "I'll go take a look." He chucked Angel under the chin. "We even fed your animals, so don't consider going out there today."

"I won't, Pa. I figured you'd remember them."

Before he went out the swinging door, his gaze settled on Constance again. The silence grew thick and heavy. She stared back as long as she could, but shame made her lower her eyes before he looked away. He must know there was more to her story, just as he'd known there were more details to her past than she'd shared last night. An ugly glob of regret settled in her stomach. Stella hadn't been wanted by the law, that much was true. The girl couldn't be more than a few years older than Angel. She'd stolen Ashton's letter from a stack of others that had been delivered to Rosalie's—the large home down the street from the New Street Boarding House where Constance had first purchased lodging. Later, when her funds had become depleted, she'd washed laundry for room and board.

Stella had said Rosalie had dozens of letters from men who'd paid her to post notices for them. Rosalie never posted the advertisements. Instead she sold the letters to girls who thought becoming a mail-order bride would be better than working in one of Rosalie's second floor rooms. Constance had no doubt as to what went on in those upstairs bedrooms even before meeting Stella. The young girl had stolen the letter, thinking she might like to travel west, but upon reading Ashton's description of Wyoming, changed her mind. Stella said she didn't dare replace the opened letter, but wasn't going to part with it free of charge, either.

Constance had read the description, and though it didn't sound rosy, it did seem like a brighter future than washing sheets until her hands bled the rest of her life. She'd responded to the letter the morning after seeing Byron's headstone. A gravesite didn't completely convinced her he was dead, but it did make her believe the inheritance from her aunts was gone, and when she was told the authorities would soon be after her, she'd known she had to leave New York.

"Constance? Are you all right?"

The concern in Angel's voice had Constance twirling around, and searching for an answer. "Yes, yes, I'm fine. I'm just wondering what we should fix all those men for lunch." Could it be true? That a woman could choose being a mail-order bride over jail? Maybe, but what if the crime was murder? Not that she'd murdered anyone. But if Byron really was dead, they'd have to blame someone.

"Well, you could turn the roast you have in the oven into stew. Stew goes a lot further and will warm them up at the same time." Angel walked toward the pantry off the side of the kitchen. "I'll peel potatoes."

The girl's common sense was astounding, and the way she flashed those big brown eyes had the ability to catch Constance's heart off guard. "How did you get to be so wise?" She followed Angel into the pantry. Shelves went from the floor to the ceiling and held more provisions than Link's store had back in Cottonwood—not to mention it was better organized.

Angel handed Constance a big pot. "I don't know. Living out here maybe. But I think it's just one of those things you either have or you don't. Like good horse sense. Some folks know a good horse when they see it, others get swindled every time." Angel gathered items as she talked, plopping potatoes, carrots and onions into the pot. "There are times when I see an injured animal, and I just keep riding. I know no matter how hard I try, I won't be able to help it. Not because of its kind or the size of their injury, but because of their will to let me help."

There was truth in Angel's unabashed philosophy. Sometimes a person just had to keep riding. Ignore what they'd seen, where they'd been. Focus on the here and now—like a house full of hungry people.

Constance set the kettle on the table. Angel was a lot like her father. That explained why they got along so well, and how they'd occasionally butt heads. Ellis not only loved his daughter, he respected her, and because of that others did, too. It was evident in how the men responded to Angel, both yesterday in town and today at the ranch.

"I saw it in you," Angel said as they transferred the vegetables onto the table. "I knew you'd let me help."

Constance caught the authenticity in Angel's admission, and a tender wave of warmth, similar to how a morning fire warms a room, spiraled inside her chest. Moved by the genuine fondness blossoming inside her, Constance wrapped her arms around Angel's shoulders. "Thank you. I appreciate your willingness to help me. And I treasure your friendship."

Angel snuggled in for an extended hug. "I knew we'd be friends right off. We'll forever be friends."

Constance rested her chin atop Angel's head. Though their age difference was great, she felt a kinship to the girl like no other she'd ever known. Something else wafted over her, a sense of protection. Of keeping Angel safe. Perhaps if she wrote a letter to the authorities in New York, not necessarily telling them where she was, but explaining everything to them—again. When she'd gone to them before, they'd said without a body there wasn't a crime. This time she could tell them where Byron's headstone was. Surely the undertaker could identify who was buried there. Her heart balled itself inside her throat. Maybe that wasn't a good idea. That might be the proof they needed.

In the crowded front parlor across the hall, Ellis lowered Jeb's darkening toes back into the tepid water. "They'll be fine, Jeb. Sore for a while, but they didn't freeze all the way through."

"Thanks, Ellis. They sure do sting." Jeb spoke through clenched teeth.

"I'm sure they do. It was foolish to leave town in the middle of a blizzard." Ellis sat back on his haunches, and included all of the men in his gaze. His frustration at the disaster that could have been laced his voice as he spoke, "Why would any of you do such a thing? You all know better."

Every man started talking at once, pointing fingers at each other and creating excuses. Ellis crossed his arms and waited for the commotion to die down. When it did, he pointed to Buford Homer, the one man he'd been shocked to see huddled beneath a quilt. The banker had more sense than the rest of the room put together—or should, leastwise. The man lowered his head, clearly unwilling to speak. Ellis turned instead to Fred Westmaster, the blacksmith, and maybe the second smartest man in the bunch.

"Well, Jeb there said the storm was lifting and that he was gonna ride out to talk to Ashton's bride." Fred glanced around. "Word got out. We all want a chance at asking for her considerations."

"Are there any others?" Ellis hated the thought, but if there were, he'd have to see about finding them.

Fred shook his head. His cheeks, burned from the elements, were now redder than the man's hair and beard. "No, not that I know of."

The rest of the men shook their heads. "Well, gentlemen," Ellis used the term lightly, "I'm afraid your trip was useless. Miss Jennings hasn't decided if she'll stay in the Territory."

"Not stay?"

"Why not?"

"Says who?"

Ellis held up his hand, stopping the onslaught of questions. He'd dealt with men for years. They were by far easier to deal with than women. Not that he'd had much experience with women—but that's what he'd always heard. Christine had been the only woman he'd ever dealt with, and her tender and kind heart had never been a challenge. Matter of fact, there were times he wished she'd have been less amicable; it would have better prepared him for raising Angel. His daughter definitely had a mind of her own. So did Constance, traveling all the way from New York City on little more than the promise of marriage. There was more to it than that, and his mind tumbled with what he should do about it.

"Whatcha mean, Ellis? Not staying?" Jeb asked. His young eyes looked as sad as his frostbit toes.

"She's had a shock, fellas, in learning about Ashton's death." He seized all of their attention. "Miss Jennings needs time to catch her breath and then decide what to do. Running her down like a rabbit won't speed up her decision-making."

The room filled with low grumbles as his statement hit home.

"Sorry, Ellis," Mr. Homer offered. "We should've thought before we acted. Now, it appears we're indebted to you to let us stay until the weather breaks. I have no desire to venture back out in that storm, as I'm sure is the case with the rest of the men."

The men nodded, gladly agreeing with what the banker said.

"You're welcome to stay, but don't expect Miss Jennings or Angel to wait on or entertain you." Ellis wanted the ground rules laid out, and followed. Every man on his ranch knew their position when it came to his family. His mind tried to dart in another direction, telling him Constance wasn't family, but he brought the thought to a halt, and glared around the room. "Understand?"

"Yes, sir, we understand," Fred Westmaster assured. The man was the size and shape of a grizzly, and the gaze he shot around the room said he'd be enforcing the ground rules. "Don't we?"

Agreeable nods and comments guaranteed everyone understood.

Ellis gave a single head bob, accepting their responses. "Good enough, then. I'm sure lunch will be ready shortly." He rose, prepared to seek some thinking time in his office.

"Mr. Clayton," Sam McDonaldson said. "Are you interested in claiming Miss Jennings?"

The man owned a farm between Heaven on Earth and Cottonwood. Ellis didn't know him well, but had no reason to dislike him. Prior to this moment, that is. Ellis didn't answer right away, not because he didn't have one, but because he didn't think anyone needed to know his business.

McDonaldson must have made his own conclusion from Ellis's silence. "It seems a bit unfair to the rest of us, if you are, with her living here and all."

Ellis met the man's stare. McDonaldson had to be well over forty, and it appeared the man had less sense than he had hair. "Do you have a daughter, Sam?"

"No, you know I don't," Sam answered. "I ain't never been married."

Ellis turned, making a wide sweep of the room with a steady stare. "What about anyone else? Does anyone have a daughter or a female that could befriend Miss Jennings?" The room was full of negative gestures. "Then wouldn't you agree the most appropriate place for Miss Jennings is here at the ranch—with Angel?" Some of the men nodded, while others simply stared at him. His throat wanted to swell up, as if it, too, wondered about his explanation. "Besides," he added, "I've hired Miss Jennings to be a tutor to Angel for the time being. You all know the girl needs some formal education."

No one dared argue that point. His daughter—as much as he loved her—could be considered a little rough around the edges at times, not to mention a bit domineering.

Ellis spun on his heels and left the room, not willing to answer the array of questions his last statement might conjure up.

The fire in his office needed to be stoked. Understandably, he'd told Thomas not to worry about the house fires after his morning visit, and Angel and Miss Jennings had their hands full with unexpected guests. Ellis crossed the room, threw in a couple of good-sized logs, and then strolled to the window. The blizzard raged on. The hands had been prepared for it. Most of the cattle had been brought close to the ranch and a good supply of hay had been laid out. The brunt of the morning chores had been for the homestead animals, including Angel's flock. He'd stayed outside as long as he could—contemplating his house guest all the while.

Ellis made his way to his desk. Every time he encountered her, Constance said or did something that had his mind and guts rolling with questions. A smile played on his lips. She certainly had a sweet laugh. It hadn't been funny—those men could have died—but once it was known everyone was fine, there probably wasn't a person around who wouldn't have broke out laughing upon seeing his front parlor. It resembled a Civil War infantry, a comical looking one.

He'd told her the truth: he *had* known they'd come. Once word got out that there was an available female in Cottonwood, men from as far away as Montana would descend on the town. He'd have to prepare for it, but hadn't thought it would start today, in the middle of a blizzard.

There was also the consideration of how to prepare her for the onslaught of suitors. He'd expected to someday have this chore ahead of him, but assumed it would happen in a few years, when Angel became of age.

That thought lurched his stomach to his heels. When melancholy hit like this, he grew more thankful he'd only been blessed with one child. He'd have loved them all as much as he did Angel, of that he had no doubt, but the older she grew, the more he understood why his mother had cried when he and Christine had left the Carolinas.

He could only hope the man Angel would eventually fall in love with would be interested in living in Wyoming. Maybe not right on Heaven on Earth, but close by would be the next best thing.

Someone tapped on his door. He glanced at the mantel clock and was surprised by the length of time he'd been wallowing in thought. "Come in," he instructed.

Angel stuck her nose in. "Lunch is ready."

"Enough for everyone?"

She grinned, entering the room. "Yes. Constance could out-cook Beans."

"Oh?" He slapped shut the notation book he hadn't made a mark in. "She could, could she?"

The door closed behind her. "Yup," Angel said confidently. "You already tasted her breakfast. She knows how to make fancy holiday candies and cookies, too, beside lots of other stuff."

"How do you know that?" He rose and pushed his chair in, but didn't move to the door.

"She told me." Angel skipped across the room and jumped up to sit on the edge of his desk. "We were planning the holiday party when Mr. Homer arrived." She rolled her dark eyes to the ceiling. "Followed by the rest."

"You like Miss Jennings, don't you?" He held in his other thought, that of asking his daughter if she was looking for a mother. The thought clung to the back of his mind like a pesky cobweb.

"Yes. And you will, too, once you get to know

her. She's lived in England and has lots of recipes from there. And she promised to teach me all about the kings and queens over there."

"Kings and queens?" He ruffled her hair. "You're interested in that kind of stuff?"

"I suspect." She gave a nonchalant shrug. "I promised to teach her all about Wyoming, and in exchange she said she'd teach me about England. It would have been rude to not accept her offer."

"I suspect it would have been." He'd already spent too much time mulling thoughts, so took a hold of Angel's hand. "Come on, scamp, let's go get some lunch before our guests eat it all."

"Why do you think she goes by Miss Jennings instead of Mrs. Jennings?" Angel asked as they walked to the door.

The question brought Ellis to a skidding halt. He planted a hand on the wood, keeping Angel from pulling the door open. "Because she's not married?" It was a question, but he hoped it sounded like a statement.

"Not now, but she was."

"No, Ashton died before she arrived," he argued.

"Not Mr. Kramer."

"Who then?"

"I don't know. But when I helped her unpack there was a ring in one of her trunks. She said it was a wedding ring." Angel stared up at him with open, honest eyes.

"Maybe it was her mother's or grandmother's. Women often pass their wedding rings down in the family." The bubbling in his stomach said no matter how plausible that sounded, he didn't believe it.

Angel shook her head. "Nope. She said it was hers, but that her husband died."

His hand slipped from the door.

"I don't think she meant to tell me though, since she clammed up right afterward." Angel had pulled the door open and was crossing the threshold when she spun about to whisper, "Oh, and if any of the men ask, I cooked lunch. Constance doesn't want to encourage them. Something about the way to a man's heart being through his stomach."

Ellis rubbed at the invisible hammers pounding against his temples, drumming up a headache like he'd never known. Constance Jennings was becoming more than he'd bargained for. Much more. What kind of woman keeps a dead husband a secret?

Chapter Four

Feeding the men without letting them know she was the cook was not an easy thing when a blizzard held everyone indoors. It wasn't as if Constance thought herself an excellent cook, but years of preparing meals for Aunt Julia and Aunt Theresa had provided her with the ability to create very palatable dishes. She didn't want the men to think she would make an acceptable wife just because she knew how to cook. Actually, the more she encountered the men roaming the house, the more she questioned her ability to marry anyone ever again.

She snuck a peek to the group sitting at the table. There was no doubt Ellis had said something. The guests were practically tripping over themselves attempting to help with any and all household chores. Two of them had washed the lunch dishes, and had managed to not break a single plate, which was a relief considering how awkwardly they'd gone about the duty.

Constance put aside the dust rag and walked across the room. "Angel," she whispered near the girl's ear. "It's time to check the ham."

The girl scooted her chair away from the table. "It's time you boys cleared out. I gotta check the ham and show Miss Jennings how to peel potatoes." There were times, especially in how Angel framed her words, that made it crystal clear she'd been raised in a man's world.

"We can help," Jeb offered. The man had hobbled into the kitchen earlier, and knowing how badly his feet must hurt, Constance hadn't had the heart to shoo him out. His attendance had encouraged others to gain entrance, and before she knew it, all the men sat around the kitchen table. Angel had taken control of the situation by pairing them up and dealing out a game of whist. Constance had feigned interest in removing dust from the far corners of the room, while wondering where Ellis had gone.

"Nope." Angel handed the deck of cards to Constance. The girl also knew when to play a trump card. "Pa wouldn't want you in here underfoot. Skedaddle now."

The men listened, pushing in their chairs before they left. When the door clattered shut behind the last one, Constance turned to Angel. "You know, sometimes a lady makes a subtle suggestion rather than giving orders."

Angel cocked her head, as if deeply contemplating the suggestion. "Does it work?"

"Most of the time." Constance picked up the potholders and opened the oven door. "For instance, you could have said, 'Excuse us, gentlemen, but Miss Jennings and I have things we need to complete. Perhaps you'd be more comfortable in the parlor.'"

Angel laughed. Not just a little giggle, but an outright hee-haw.

Constance lifted a brow, attempting to chide Angel with a stern look.

"Do you honestly think those fellers would have listened to that? They'd still be sitting here telling us how comfortable they are," Angel said, shaking her head and huffing out extra giggles.

Hiding her smile, Constance basted the ham before pushing the large roasting pan back into the oven. "You may be right. It's just food for thought."

"I'll chew on it for a while," Angel responded.

This time Constance couldn't help but giggle. She playfully tossed a pot holder across the room. "You are going to be a challenge, aren't you?"

Angel plucked the knitted pad out of the air with one hand. "Yup." Eyes sparkling, she tossed the potholder back. "Life's full of challenges. They make us stronger."

Constance tossed the pot holder onto the counter and leaped forward. "You are full of it," she teased, tickling the girl's sides.

Twisting and giggling, Angel spun about and dug her fingers into Constance's side. It had been years since she'd joked around. Her brothers had been masters at tickling. Joyful prickles shot up and down her sides and in and out of her heart as she and Angel playfully attacked one another.

The tickling match continued as they twirled from one end of the kitchen to the other. While both of them were whooping with glee the back door opened.

Ellis shed his coat and stomped the snow off his boots by the door. "Every time I find you two together, you're giggling up a storm."

His entrance had stalled their fingers, but while smoothing the wrinkles from the flour sack tied around her waist, Constance bit her lips at the fading bits of laughter now mingling with the flutter flipping her insides.

Angel, still openly giggling, wrapped an arm around Constance's waist and laid her head on her shoulder. "I know. I haven't had this much fun in years."

Touched deeply, Constance hugged the girl back. It was quite profound, this tenderness she felt for Angel.

When Constance glanced up, the scowl on Ellis's face shattered her joy like someone throwing a rock through a window. She pulled her eyes off him as the not-so-old scar on her abdomen stung with renewed pain, telling her she'd never know the love of a child. Swallowing against the thick glob forming in her throat, she patted Angel's arm, and moved to the pantry. The ache in her heart wasn't new, yet it had never been quite this strong.

Months ago she'd dealt with the scar, how it had come about, and how it had changed her life forever. There was no sense in reliving it. Her focus was best used on the present and the situation at hand.

Her mind shift wasn't any better. She barely knew Ellis Clayton, yet the man had an overwhelming effect on her. Probably because he held her ability to survive in his hands. One word and she was out in the world—alone. She'd been there before, but this time around, she knew what to expect and didn't want it back again. The path she walked was a rickety one, and she'd best tread carefully. If she had any hope of staying long enough to figure out her next steps, she'd best remember that.

"Can't you find something?"

Constance spun about, grabbing a shelf to keep from falling.

Ellis reached out a hand, but pulled it back shy of touching her. His eyes latched on to hers though, and his gaze was penetrating, as if he searched for something. Constance was on the brink of suffocation by the time he finally said, "Angel's been without a mother for a long time."

Fearful no matter what she said would be taken wrong, she nodded. "I-I assure you, I'm not trying to replace her mother."

"No one could ever replace her."

"I know that."

"You do?"

Believing honesty was her only friend in this instance, she explained, "I lost my mother as a child. No one could ever have replaced her, either."

He nodded, slowly, silently, and then his hand touched her shoulder. The way he gently squeezed it sent a tidal wave of emotions rippling her system. "You haven't had an easy time of it, have you?"

There was so much compassion in his words a part of her wanted to blurt out her entire life story, beg him for help.

"What I said last night was true," he said. "If I believe Angel's in danger, I'll step in."

His hand was still on her shoulder, and she feared he felt the way she trembled.

"But," he continued, "I'll also step in if I believe I can help. I have a lot of resources, Miss Jennings, and I'm not opposed to sharing them when needed."

She had to respond, knew that's what he expected. "Thank you, Mr. Clayton," she said as evenly as possible. "Your generosity, what you've already provided, is more than I could have hoped for."

His penetrating gaze was back, and it lingered until her heart pounded against her rib cage.

After another soft squeeze, he lifted his hand off her shoulder. "My daughter, Miss Jennings, is the most important thing in the world. I'll do anything to see she's happy."

"I believe you will," she whispered.

He didn't move, yet the air in the pantry that moments ago had felt charged and heavy, grew light. Her heart still hammered, yet dread no longer shrouded her. Confused, Constance glanced around. The only thing that had changed was his expression, a soft smile now pulled on the corners of his mouth.

As he took a step back, out of the pantry, he pointed to a barrel of apples. "Angel loves applesauce."

Something inside her flipped and stirred up a soft, gentle sensation that cascaded all the way to her toes. No one had believed her in a very long time, yet he did. He believed she only wanted what was best for Angel. "Then we'll have applesauce for supper."

Cooking, Angel's never-ending chatter and the house full of men kept Constance busy the rest of the evening. The meal passed without an event, other than the men showering Angel with compliments on her cooking and applauding Ellis for having such an amazing child. Constance gave Angel a secretive wink, happy the girl was gaining acknowledgment outside of how well she could ride, shoot or rope.

After the meal, Constance insisted she'd do the dishes—alone, wanting the time to determine exactly how much she'd tell Ellis, and when. Of course, sooner would be better, but with a house full of men, she couldn't very well insist they closet themselves in his office; yet it was her duty to tell him the truth—as much as possible, as soon as possible.

When the dishes were done, after a few interruptions from men offering to help, she made her way to the parlor, still not prepared with her next action step.

Faint music had made its way into the kitchen. She'd assumed it came from one of the men, but for some reason, seeing Ellis strumming on the guitar surprised her. Pausing in the doorway, she rested the side of her face against the arched framework and let the gentle tune fill her soul. She cherished guitar music, and hadn't heard it in years. Her older brother, Edwin, had played guitar and often serenaded her to sleep.

The gentle, soothing music continued. It was as

if the war and all the awful things that had happened disappeared and she was once again in Virginia, snuggled in her bed with Edwin sitting on the foot of it. Eyes closed, she welcomed a sense of security she hadn't known in a very, very long time.

The music left her soft and mellow. Exhaling a relaxed breath from her lungs Constance lifted her eyelids, half wondering why the strumming had ended. Every eye in the room was on her, she felt them, but the only ones she saw were Ellis's. They were a rich brown, and extremely expressive. Another sigh left her chest. They were remarkable eyes.

He squinted then, and it was as if his gaze had the ability to enter her mind and read her thoughts as someone reads a periodical. She bowed her head, breaking the connection, and gasped for air to refill her empty lungs at the thought of him learning her darkest secrets.

"Play another one, Pa," Angel pleaded.

"No, our guests are tired," he said. "It's time for all of us to turn in."

Constance stepped into the hallway, out of the way as men mingled toward the stairway. Upstairs, there were seven bedrooms, three of them occupied by the family and her, and the additional four would house the men, leaving Jeb on the couch in the back parlor. Ellis had arranged the sleeping arrangements this afternoon. Angel had popped in the kitchen more than once to update Constance on the guests' activities.

Following some of the men out of the parlor, Angel hooked her elbow with Constance's. Together they walked across the foyer. "I love listening to Pa play. It was nice, wasn't it?"

"Yes," Constance admitted, glancing over her shoulder to where Ellis extinguished the parlor lamps. "It was very nice." Tonight wouldn't do to talk with him, not with all the men here, but tomorrow she'd make sure it happened.

At the girl's bedroom door, Constance gave Angel a hard squeeze. "Good night, Angel. Thanks for your help today."

"Good night, Constance. Sleep tight." Angel disappeared into her room, and Constance slipped into hers directly across the hall.

She walked to the bed and sat, but didn't attempt to remove her clothing. Not yet, she had to go back downstairs once she was sure the household was asleep. Second guessing herself, she reached down to unhook her boots. Stocking feet would be quieter on the stairs. Wiggling her freed toes, another realization came to mind. No one else would be up, so she pulled the pins from her hair. After giving it a thorough brushing, she climbed onto the bed and propped the pillows behind her head and shoulders.

Reading from a book she'd brought with her

on her voyage across the ocean, Constance waited for the house to grow still with slumber. After re-reading the same paragraph four times, she set the book aside. No wonder she hadn't read the story on the long trip. The tale about two families torn apart by a war was compelling, but extremely boring. Or maybe it was the fact she didn't want to know what happened. She'd already lived through such an event, why indeed would she care to read about it?

Once again she reminded herself some things were best forgotten and climbed off the bed to lay a log on the dying flames. Someone, most likely one of the guests, must have stoked all of the fireplaces earlier in the evening. She'd been responsible for the fires back in England, but that had only been one fireplace, a parlor stove and the kitchen range. It seemed like eons ago, whereas it hadn't even been a year since her aunts' deaths and her marriage to Byron.

She spent another hour or so fidgeting and contemplating circumstances before she guessed the guests would be sleeping and moved to her door. The back stairs that led directly to the kitchen would cause her to pass too many doors, namely Ellis's room, so she chose the front set.

Ellis, two rooms down and across the hall, heard a door open. The click was loud enough to have been his own door. He trusted the men, his house-guests as they were, yet when he'd entered his room a while ago, a sixth sense had told him not to get undressed, that he'd soon be leaving again.

He bolted to his feet and eased open his door. Constance glided out of her room, and with her skirt hitched well above her ankles, tiptoed down the hall to the stairway. After counting to ten, he followed, frowning to the point his forehead ached. At the bottom of the stairs, she made a beeline for the kitchen, but when he entered the room a moment later, the space appeared empty. Willing his eyes to focus in the darkness, a soft thud drew him toward the pantry.

Ellis grabbed a match from the holder near the stove as he made his way across the room. The pantry door was open, and he propped a foot against the wood as he struck the match against his pant leg.

The flare had her spinning around. Round-eyed, not unlike a fox that had just swallowed an egg, she clutched a package to her chest.

"Looking for something, Miss Jennings?" The match fizzled out.

She let out an enormous sigh, and then sharply whispered, "Mr. Clayton, you startled me."

This woman had him twisted inside out. Her secrets were driving him crazy. "I wouldn't have if you hadn't been sneaking around my house in the middle of the night." He wished he had another match so he could see her face.

"I wasn't sneaking." She lowered her voice, whispering again, "Well, I was, but with good reason."

"Oh? And what's the reason?"

"I need to mix up a batch of bread or there won't be any for breakfast."

"Why didn't you do that earlier?"

"Shhh. I don't want any of the guests to hear."

"Why not?" He whispered this time.

"Because they believe Angel did all the cooking. I don't want to encourage them."

His fingers easily found her elbow in the darkness, and leading her from the small room, he assured, "Whether you can cook or not won't hold a lot of bearing on their pursuit."

"It won't?"

Her disappointment was so heartfelt he had to smile. "No, it won't." He retrieved another match and used it to light the lamp on the table. After the wick caught, he replaced the globe. His breath tried to catch in his lungs as her face, twisted in a frown, came into view. "Those men have been cooking their own meals for years. That's not the reason they're looking for a wife."

She set a tin of flour on the table and then tucked her long hair behind her ears. "Well, nonetheless, we need bread for morning."

"You stayed up until everyone else was sleeping just so you could make bread?" He'd heard it, but had to repeat it to make sure he had it right.

She nodded. "Angel already helped so much today, I didn't have the heart to ask more of her. It won't take me long to mix it up and set it in the pantry so it won't rise too high before morning."

Her soft whispers were messing with his insides. Though their actions were completely innocent, whispering in the dim-lit kitchen felt clandestine and somewhat exciting. It was crazy for him—a man just shy of the ripe old age of forty—to become excited over such things, but there was a youthfulness swirling in his insides he hadn't felt in years.

"I'm sorry I woke you," she continued.

"I wasn't sleeping," he admitted. Then, quite remarkably and unusually, he made a snap decision. "Tell me what you need. I'll help."

"Oh, that's not necessary." She turned about and glided back to the pantry.

He followed, whispering, "You need someone to guard the door. We don't want them learning the truth now, do we?"

Even in the shadowy corner of the room, sparks danced in her blue eyes.

"Do we?" he repeated.

Nibbling on her bottom lip, she cocked her head. "Mr. Clayton, I have a feeling you're enjoying this."

"So are you, Constance." Her name slipped out before he had a chance to stop it, and he was amazed at how easily it rolled off his tongue.

"I don't believe I've ever considered making bread fun."

Feeling twenty years younger, he moved past her, slipping into the pantry. "Tell me what you need, and I'll show you how fun it can be." The space was tight, and twisting sideways as she reached around his bulk had tiny jolts zipping beneath his skin.

When his arms were full, she picked up a large bowl and led the way to the table. "Have you ever made bread before?"

"No," he admitted as she unloaded his arms. "Have you ever made bread at midnight before?"

"Midnight? Is it really that late?"

"Yes."

"Then no, I've never made bread at midnight before." She tugged her hair aside so it fell evenly down her back and then reached over and lifted the lid off the flour tin.

He grabbed the cup nestled in the powder. "Then it's a first for both of us." Meeting her eyes, he offered an olive branch. If he was ever going to learn more about her, he was going to have to give her reason to trust him. He held the cup up. "How many?"

She stared at it, as if contemplating a great decision. Her long, thick lashes lowered for a moment, fluttering against her cheeks. When they lifted, she smiled. "Twelve."

"Twelve?" he repeated, wondering what she referred to.

"Yes, twelve cups. We need to make a double batch." She padded across the room in her stockinged feet to retrieve the flour sack she'd had around her waist earlier in the day. "We don't need the flour, yet, though. I have to get warm water from the reservoir for the yeast and heat the milk first."

She was slender, almost too slender. Then again, the amount of traveling she'd done to get from New York to Wyoming was taxing; anyone could lose a few pounds along the way. It would do her good to eat a couple of loaves of bread herself.

He'd told the truth. Never, not once in thirty-six years had he made bread. And, he decided, he looked forward to the experience. "What else do we need?"

"It's all right there," she said. "Oh, and we'll need a touch of sugar and salt."

He helped as he could, but mainly watched her flutter around the kitchen with the ease of a spring butterfly, stilling for such brief moments he couldn't quite keep up with her. Cautious, not wanting to disrupt the harmony growing between them, he asked simple questions about her aunts in England, the things she'd cooked for them and such, and he told her about his grandmother back in the Carolinas and all the tasty pies, cakes and cookies she used to make. Funny thing, he hadn't realized he missed the sweets as much as he did.

"You act as if you've made a lot of bread," he said, standing at the stove.

"I guess I have." She sprinkled a handful of flour on the table. "How's the milk?"

"Butter's still not melted." He had to grin at himself. Unbelievable—that's what it was—him stirring a pot of milk and butter in the middle of the night. "Constance, will you promise me something?"

"Well, I guess that depends on what it is."

He grinned at her honesty. "Just that you won't tell anyone about this. If word got out that the owner of Heaven on Earth makes bread in the middle of the night...well, it might damage my reputation."

She giggled. "Your secret is safe with me, Mr. Clayton. Don't worry."

When the milk was ready, he poured it in the bowl.

"Now we start adding the flour," she said.

He set the pan aside and scooped up a cup of flour. "Twelve, right?"

"Yes, but not all at once." She continued to stir the mixture with a long spoon.

"How much then?"

"Dump in six or seven."

"Six or seven?" he asked, simply because he liked hearing her talk. The twinge of southern dialect mixed with her English accent was rather addictive to his big ears.

"Six or seven, here they come." She stirred while he dumped, slowly dragging the spoon around the circumference of the bowl. Keeping track of the number of cups he poured grew difficult. "Was that five or six?" he asked.

"You don't know?" Her amusement tickled the air.

He chuckled, and honestly admitted, "No, do you?"

"No."

Holding a cup of flour over the contents, he confessed, "I can't start over."

She giggled while setting the spoon aside and gently shoved his hovering hand away from the bowl. "Don't worry, it doesn't matter." In a quick, fluid movement, she dumped the bowl out on the floured table. Her fingers dove into the mixture. "Sprinkle another cup on, and keep dumping cupfuls until I say stop."

With skill and precision, she worked the flour into the dough, turning the lump and folding the edges in with quick yet smooth movements. Every once in a while she'd nod his way, and he'd sprinkle another cup over the mixture. His mind was tumbling again—for whatever reason it imagined how those hands would feel massaging his skin, smoothing the kinks and knots out of his back and shoulders as finely as they worked the flour into the dough.

Almost magically the mass on the table went from sticky and stringy to smooth and pliable. "I'll be damned," he muttered.

"What?"

He dropped the cup back in the flour tin. "I've eaten enough bread to fill a boat, but I've never made it. Never even paid attention while someone else did."

"Who makes your bread now?"

"You," he said a bit too quickly.

A flush covered her cheeks as she brushed her hair aside with the back of one hand. "Before me."

A smudge of flour sat right below her eye. He wiped it away with the pad of his thumb. Her skin was soft and smooth, and unable to stop his fingers, he tucked her hair more firmly behind her tiny ear. "Beans," he said, before he forgot to answer. He pulled his hand away and not sure what to do next, he resettled the cup in the flour tin. "Beans bakes all the bread around here."

She plunked the dough back into the bowl. "There, that's it. I'll just put it in the pantry."

His heart hitched, not ready for their encounter to end. "I thought you had to put it in bread pans."

"I will in the morning." She wiped her hands on the flour sack again. "And let it rise again before baking."

"Oh," he said, disappointed the event was almost over. "Are you sure you don't want to bake it right now?"

"We can't. It has to rise once over night, and then again in the morning before it'll be ready to bake." She'd already gathered an armload of the supplies as well as the bread bowl and was heading back to the pantry.

He snatched up the other items and followed. "How often will you have to make bread?"

"It depends on how much gets eaten on a daily basis. Why?" She took his items and placed them back on the shelves.

"Oh, just wondering," he croaked as heat snuck up his neck. "We eat a lot of bread around here." It was crazy, a grown man wound up about making bread of all things, but there was something about doing it with her that made him want to do it again.

She was back at the table, wiping the flour residue off the surface. Walking across the room, he wondered about the way his body tingled from head to toe. It had been a long time since a woman had graced his house. Actually, a woman had never graced this house—not as it stood today.

The thought caused him to pause for a moment in reflection, or maybe it was perception.

"Constance, can I ask you something?"

"Sure," she answered.

"What happened to your first husband?"

Her face turned ashen, and he reacted, caught her elbow as she wobbled. Regret gripped his throat. "I'm sorry."

Chapter Five

Constant couldn't move. The wood beneath her fingers throbbed in tune with her pulse. *Ka-thump, ka-thump, ka-thump.*

"Constance?" Ellis's grasp on her elbow tightened.

This was her chance to tell him. She'd planned on doing it, but all of a sudden fear paralyzed her. "He died."

His fingers moved up her arm, tenderly, soothingly. "How?"

"He was shot," she answered, unable to look up. Not because Byron's death was too painful to relive, but because if Ellis knew the truth, he might send her away. No one else had believed she hadn't shot Byron, and there was no reason for him to, either.

"I heard noises. Is something wrong?"

Constance closed her eyes at the sound of Jeb's voice across the room. She hadn't heard the door open. Fear raced around in her stomach. How much had the young man heard? It wouldn't do for the entire territory to hear about Byron. Though it wasn't something she could keep hidden forever.

"No, nothing's wrong. Miss Jennings just needed some help in the kitchen."

She didn't turn about, but opened her eyes at Ellis's answer. He hadn't moved, still stood in front of her, and his fingers continued to softly rub her upper arm. Pressing her toes harder against the floor, she willed her legs not to give out.

"Is there something I can help with?" Jeb asked.

"No." Ellis shook his head. His gaze lowered and captured hers. "Everything's done now. You can go back to bed, Jeb. Thanks for checking."

"Good night," Jeb offered, somewhat reluctantly.

"Good night," Ellis repeated.

The ability to drag her gaze from his couldn't be found. It was back—that glimmer in his eyes that said he could see directly into her head, knew all there was to know. Yet there was that softness in his eyes she'd seen earlier today, while in the pantry discussing Angel, that once again made her want to press her head against his chest.

Constance drew in a deep breath. He would never understand about Byron, or how or why she'd married the man. Half the time she didn't understand it herself. Looking back at how quickly it all had came about, things grew blurry and convoluted. Which is precisely why she didn't look back—no good could come of it. This escape to Wyoming, becoming Ashton's bride, proved one thing: she couldn't run from the past. Sooner or later, she'd have to face it.

A frown had formed on Ellis's brow. "Constance?"

She had nowhere to go if he sent her away. All she needed was a little more time. To what? She couldn't gather proof against Byron from Wyoming. Couldn't gather proof against a dead man no matter where she was. The desire to ask Ellis for help was back. He'd know what to do. But she couldn't. Things were too unsettled. Maybe in a few weeks, when they knew each other better, she could ask him for help.

"Constance?" he repeated.

"Well," she attempted a lighthearted tone as she walked to the sink with stiff knees. "It's late and morning will come quickly." After rinsing the rag, she smoothed it to hang evenly over the edge of the built-in sink, waiting for him to leave. He didn't. She could feel him. Hear him breathing.

This was getting to be too much. Everything catching up to her at once. Her shoulders attempted to droop, but she tightened her neck muscles, refusing to be overwhelmed by the plague of history trying to overtake her like a storm of grasshoppers. Memories had the ability to take her down, and she wasn't about to let that happen now. There was too much at stake.

"Thank you, Mr. Clayton, for your assistance with the bread." Taking a fortifying breath, she thrust her chin out and her shoulders back, and strolled across the room. Her footfalls were as unsure as a toddler's just learning to walk, but she pushed on, not breathing until she set a foot on the bottom step of the staircase that went from the kitchen to the upstairs hall.

He hadn't moved, and the way her back stung said his gaze followed her. Pressing a hand to the wall, she used it to assist her climb up the steps. When she reached the top, where moonlight filtered through the window at the end of the hall, the space at the bottom of the steps went dark. She leaned heavier against the wall.

A soft thud echoed up the stairwell. The kitchen door, no doubt. She could almost hear him climbing the front steps. A rush of unease had her flying down the hall. Once inside her room, she let out a burning gust of air and leaned against the closed door. There wasn't time for relief before a quiver raced her spine. Ellis was on the other side of the door. Would he knock? Would she answer?

No sound entered her room, but her shoulders drooped to her elbows. He was gone. She trudged across the room, removing the makeshift apron and unbuttoning her dress.

It was a terrible ending to what had been a re-markable experience. She'd known companionship in the kitchen before. There was a time where Aunt Theresa had been a pest when it came to sticking her fingers in the bowl for a lick when she thought Constance wasn't looking. That of course had been before Aunt Julia had become ill. Aunt Theresa had grown frail as well, but she, being younger, hadn't succumbed as quickly as Julia had.

Poor dears. It was still hard to believe they were both gone, and making bread beside Ellis had brought back just how lonely life had been since they'd died. No matter how menial the task, it was always more fun to have someone at your side. She'd felt that all day, but Ellis's kitchen help had touched her deeper. In a spot she hadn't known existed.

Constance pressed a hand to the tenderness swirling around her heart. It was apparent Ellis never spent much time in a kitchen. His big hands made the teacups look like doll dishes. Hopefully the bread wouldn't be tough from her zealous kneading. He'd seemed to be in awe of the pro-cess, and therefore, she'd been reluctant to stop.

The chill of the night seeped through her thin underclothes, making her finish undressing and pull on a heavy flannel nightgown. The spacious room held fine, darkly stained furniture including a large bed with pinecones carved into the head and foot posts, as well as bedside tables and a short dressing table, which she moved to and peered into the mirror. What did Ellis see when he looked at her with those all-consuming eyes?

Abruptly she spun around, forcing her thoughts to stop wandering. After she banked the glowing logs in the stone fireplace, she climbed into the big bed, all the while begging her mind to remain in the present.

The crisp, clean sheets crinkled beneath her weight, and she shivered against their iciness. Twisting, she turned down the wick on the lamp beside the bed, watching until the flame extinguished, and wishing it was as easy to douse foreboding memories. Curled on her side, rubbing her feet together to warm the sheets beneath her toes, she recalled the warmth that had emitted from Ellis's body. Downstairs it had flowed around her like a summer breeze. Snuggled beneath the covers, her lids grew heavy, and she gave into the cozy glow she'd felt back in the kitchen.

An inner clock had her crawling from bed a few hours later. With the fire now nonexistent, the cold air encouraged her to dress and attend to morning necessities swiftly. In record time she slipped from her room and hurried down the back stairs.

Kindling leaped to life in the cook stove with

the touch of a match, and while it started to warm the thick cast iron, she gathered the bread dough and several pans. Her mind attempted to fill with visions from the previous night, but she squelched them before they could form. When the bread was set to rise, she prepared the coffeepot and, refusing to allow her mind to waver off the morning tasks, retrieved a large slab of bacon and started slicing thick strips.

Pancakes, bacon and bread would fill the guests' stomachs. The window over the sink said light had yet to break. Hoping the storm had calmed enough for the men to take their leave, she crossed the room to gather a pan and paused to peer over the large crescent of frost clinging to the glass on the back door. Beyond the porch, whiteness covered the ground, but the faint light of dawn revealed flakes no longer fell. The curtain slipped from her fingers, and she moved back to the bacon, cutting until the entire slab was reduced to a pile of slices. She would owe Ellis an enormous amount of money by the time this was over. It was her fault the house was full of men, and she couldn't expect him to absorb even the food costs the episode caused.

Ellis would protest. The warmth stealing its way into her heart said he was too honorable not to. Perhaps that's why she experienced a deep draw to him. His honor. It had been years since she'd encountered that quality in a man. Living with two elderly spinsters who were keenly set in their ways hadn't provided opportunities to encounter men very often. There had been kind men on the ship, and others along the road from New York to Wyoming had been benevolent, but Ellis projected respect toward others with a unique way that demonstrated he expected it in return. Only admirable, commendable men had the ability to do that.

"Good morning."

The knife slipped from her fingers, clattering upon the floor. That's all it had taken. One minute of allowing her thoughts to focus on him and he appeared.

She willed indifference. It wouldn't do anyone an ounce of good for him to know he'd been the center of her thoughts. Though a smile sat in her heart, she kept it concealed. Turning, she took the knife he'd retrieved. "Good morning."

"Sleep well?" he asked with eyes that sparkled brightly.

"Uh-huh." She nodded affirmatively. While pretending she had complete control of her insides, she carried the knife to the sink. "You?"

"Very well, thanks." He'd followed and pulled open a cupboard door. "Coffee?" he asked, holding up a thick ceramic cup.

The image of the fine bone china cup he'd used the night before to dump the flour into the bread dough flashed before her eyes. The heavy stoneware he now held fit his fingers and matched his personality much better.

"Coffee?" he repeated.

"It's not quite ready. I didn't expect any one up yet."

"I heard you leave your room."

She had no choice but to accept the flood of tenderness swirling inside her. He'd probably lain awake all night, listening. The house was full of men, and Ellis was not a man who'd sleep if there was even the possibility one of the men might wander about. "I had to set the bread to rise." Almost breathless, her words came out hushed.

"I know. Do you need any help?"

His whisper tickled her ears. Constance locked her knees. It wouldn't do to encourage a repeat of last night—when his companionship had allowed her to forget where she was and how she'd come to be here. Her resolve returned, but the smile on her lips couldn't be contained. "No, I don't need any help. Thank you." She reached for the two cups he held by their handles in one hand. "Sit down. I'll get your coffee."

The roots of his hair were damp, as if he'd combed it back after splashing his face with a fast morning cleanse, and the skin on his cheeks and chin shone from being freshly shaven. Heat flushed her cheeks, thinking of such personal tasks.

"I can get the coffee. You sit down. No one else is up yet." He tugged on the cups.

She didn't let loose, as if this was a tug-of-war she had to win. "Which is precisely why I'm cooking. The men will be hungry when they wake up. I want everything ready." With a nod toward the table, she added, "Sit down. I'll get the coffee."

His grin increased. "All right. You get the coffee."

She waited for him to move, walk to the table, but he didn't. Jittery, with jerky movements, she filled his cup and absently handed it to him while pretending the need to reposition the frying pan on the stove. It was a ruse. She couldn't start frying bacon yet. The bread still had to go in the oven. Besides, the smell of bacon cooking would probably wake every man in the house.

"Constance?"

"Hmm?"

The sensation of his hands loosely gripping her upper arms had her drawing in air and curling her toes. She'd wanted it, deep down she'd wanted him to touch her again. It affected her like no other ever had.

He twisted her around. The urge to step forward, to stand nose to chin, had her pressing her heels onto the hard floor and balling her fingers deep into her palms.

"Come sit down," he urged. "So we can talk."

It was clear where Angel got it. The girl had inherited Ellis's charm, an allure that had Constance unable to deny anything he asked. She dipped her head, indicating she'd follow him to the table.

"Good morning. Is that coffee I smell or am I dreaming?" Mr. Homer, the banker, rolled his round frame into the kitchen like a barrel with two short legs.

Ellis's fingers slid down to her elbows, where after a slight squeeze, they left her. He picked up his cup from the edge of the stove and turned to the other man. "Morning, Buford, have a seat." Ellis met the man at the table and handed him the cup of coffee. He then returned to the stove and accepted the other cup Constance had filled with an apology in his eyes that had her heart thudding.

From then on, one by one, men filed into the kitchen. Constance kept the coffee cups filled, and the pot perking, while poking the bread pans in the oven and filling the frying pan with the thick strips of bacon. It wasn't until Angel appeared, rubbing the sleep from her eyes as she padded down the back stairs, that Constance remembered she wasn't supposed to be the one cooking.

Men sat around the table like chickens to a feed bowl. She couldn't very well shoo them out. Ellis caught her gaze. One of his brows arched, and a knowing grin sat on his lips. His teasing made her wrinkle her nose and shoot him a mock glare.

He chuckled as he rose from his chair. A moment later he stood beside her and Angel. "Good morning." He dropped a kiss on his daughter's forehead. His hand then landed on Constance's shoulder. "Miss Jennings has been waiting for you to wake up. She's not much of a cook, you know."

Constance willed the heat in her cheeks to dissolve. It didn't, but a bright smile formed on Angel's face. "I'm up now, and ready to help." Angel walked around her father and then spun on one heel. "Pa, aren't there chores that need to be done? Too many cooks in the kitchen spoils the pot."

Chair legs scraped the floor. "Of course we'll help with morning chores," Fred Westmaster assured. "Come on, fellas, get your coats."

In a matter of seconds the room was clear. A groan and a giggle danced with each other in Constance's throat. It was the giggle that won out, but only after Ellis emitted a deep chuckle.

His eyes twinkled with merriment and when he winked one eye, Constance had to bite the tip of her tongue to keep from giggling again. More than that, she had to once again lock her knees to keep from swooning.

"I'd best go help them," Ellis said when the last man made his way out of the kitchen.

"Yes, you'd best," Angel supplied. "Give us an hour and we'll have breakfast on the table."

"Oh, you will, will you?" he asked.

"Yes, we will." Angel nodded and then twisted around. "What are we making?"

Constance rushed to the stove. Luckily, the bacon hadn't had time to scorch. "Bacon, pancakes and bread." Of their own accord her eyes sought out Ellis.

He moved to the doorway, but paused to glance over his shoulder. "I'll have Jeb start the house fires. He shouldn't be out in the cold with those feet yet."

"All right, Pa." Angel said, moving toward the pantry. At the doorway, she turned to Constance. "What do we all need for pancakes?"

It was a moment before Constance could respond. She was too busy watching the door swing shut behind Ellis. Drawing in air, she turned to Angel. "You get the big bowl, and I'll get the ingredients."

Ellis examined Jeb's toes before he handed the man a pair of socks. "You can't go around without socks, Jeb. What were you thinking? No wonder your toes got frostbit."

"I know. I bought a bath in town the day Miss Jennings arrived, and with everyone else taking one and buying new clothes, Link ran out of socks. I didn't have time to go out to Ashton's place to get another pair." Jeb's cheeks were blazing red as he pulled the socks on his feet.

Up until now, Ellis hadn't noticed most of the men sported new clothes. Link had to be smiling like the cat who caught the canary. The man probably hadn't sold that many pairs of britches on the same day since opening his store fifteen years ago.

"Thanks for the socks, Ellis. I'll buy you a new pair." Jeb planted his feet on the floor to stand.

Ellis placed a hand on the man's shoulder. "Don't bother. For the price Link charges I can order a dozen from the store in Cheyenne."

Jeb nodded. "I suspect so."

After hitching his pant legs, Ellis sat down in the armchair across from where Jeb sat on the sofa. "I guess I haven't given much thought to Ashton's farm. How's it going out there? Did he have any family to come take over for him?"

"Nope. Just me and Miles." Jeb shrugged his shoulders. "I went to town to tell Miss Jennings about Ashton's accident. Miles and I figured she'd still want to move into the place. We figured wed or not, she was Ashton's bride." Rubbing his chin, Jeb continued, "I never expected half the town to be lined up waiting to ask her to marry 'em. Did you?"

Ellis drummed his fingers on his knee. "I can't say what I thought. I never really took any of it into consideration." Ashton's ordered bride had been the talk of the town, as well as the bunkhouse. Everyone was itching to see if she'd actually show up. Bets had been laid she wouldn't.

"The farm should be hers, shouldn't it? Ashton wanted that. She's all he talked about since getting her first letter. Miles and I figured we'd offer to go on working for her." Jeb lowered his voice to whisper. "Neither of us—Miles or me—are interested in marrying her, but once I got to town, I figured I best line up, too, so I could tell her about Ashton's place."

"Ashton's place is a long ways from town, Jeb. I don't know if Miss Jennings would like living way out there."

"It ain't no further than your place. Just in the opposite direction." Jeb's cheeks grew red again. "No offense, Ellis."

What Jeb said was true, yet from what Ellis recalled the place wasn't fit for a woman. "The last time I was out at Ashton's—" Ellis paused, not wanting to offend a dead man "—the place needed to be cleaned up. Fixed up."

"We've been working on that. Put a new brace bar on the door, and plastered all the cracks between the logs. Ashton even ordered a new cook stove and curtains for the window. We built some cupboards, too." Jeb glanced around. "Sure it ain't nothing like Heaven on Earth, but no place in Wyoming is." His gaze went to the floor. "Miss Jennings most likely wouldn't want to live out there after being here, would she?"

"Well, that's not our choice to make. It's Miss

Jennings's. If she wants to move out to his place, then that's what she will do." The words left a rotten taste in his mouth.

"You think so? You think she might want to move out there?" The hope in the young man's voice was impossible to miss.

Ellis shrugged. "I don't know." His mind churned almost as hard as his stomach.

"What about you?"

He snapped his head up to glare at Jeb. "What about me?"

"Well, you said you hired her to teach Angel manners and such. She can't go back on that, can she?"

Ellis stood. He'd wasted enough time talking with Jeb. There were chores to be done. "It's impossible for men to even pretend to guess what a woman will do, Jeb. Trust me, if I know nothing else, I know that." His eyes were locked on the door across the hall, the one that led into the kitchen, where Constance was frying bacon and baking bread. Would she back out of their deal and move out to Ashton's?

"Well, I'll get the house fires going," Jeb offered.

"Thanks," Ellis mumbled as he made his way out of the parlor. The idea of her living anywhere except here, in his house, was a startling notion, one that would gravely upset Angel.

With all the extra help, the barnyard chores had barely started before they were done, including feeding Angel's critters. Still, Ellis found a few odd jobs for the men to do, giving Constance and Angel time to cook breakfast. The snow had stopped, but the gray skies and crisp air said it would merely be a short reprieve before the flakes started filling the air again. If they hurried, his guests might make it home before the second round hit.

At that thought, he sent the men into the house and made his way over to where Hank, his foreman, oversaw the cowboys replenishing the hay for the herd in the back pasture.

"You feel up to making a trip to town?" Ellis asked. The man was getting on in years, but never appreciated others pointing it out.

"Sure," Hank agreed. "You want me to make sure they all make it home safe?" The grin on his face, as well as the way he shook his head, said the man couldn't fathom why anyone would chase down a woman in the dead of a snowstorm.

"Actually, I want you to pay a visit to John Hempel."

"The lawyer? What for?"

"It appears Ashton didn't have any other family. I want to know if Miss Jennings could legally claim his property."

The man let out a whistle. "That would be

enough to start a range war. A woman owning that amount of land."

"I know. It wouldn't be safe for her to claim it, but if it's rightfully hers…" Ellis let out a gust of air as his gaze wondered across the snow covered land. A woman was a highly sought after commodity, but one that owned five hundred acres would be even more sought—be in more danger.

"I'll be ready to ride as soon as your guests are."

"Thanks. I'll go write a note to send with you. And if the weather worsens, stay in town."

"You don't have to tell me that." Hank gave Ellis's shoulder a good-natured whack. "I was born in this country, and though I plan to die here, I don't plan on it being this year."

"Let me know as soon as you get back."

"Will do."

Ellis turned to make his way toward the house. He tucked his chin into the collar of his coat. For some reason the air seemed colder and chilled him to the bone. There was no way in hell he'd let Constance move out to Ashton's place. Jeb was just a kid, and Miles was as old as the hills. Those two couldn't offer protection against the hordes of men who'd come calling if the ranch was legally hers.

A gust of wind tugged at his hat. As he pulled it down, he grumbled, "Damn you, Ashton Kramer. Why'd you have to go and get yourself killed? Better yet, why'd you go and order a sweet little thing like Constance for a mail-order bride?"

When he opened the front door, the wondrous smells of breakfast greeted him, but so did laughter. His temperament soured even more. Maybe he should let her move out to Ashton's place. After all, he wasn't responsible for her. She wasn't *his* mail-order bride.

His spine stiffened, like when someone says your name, and you know they are about to lecture you for something you did but thought no one knew about. He spun around, half expecting to see Angel behind him.

The foyer was empty. He glanced into the parlor, but it, too, was empty. No one spoke, but nonetheless, his mind heard the words. He was responsible for her. If for no other reason than he wasn't the type of man to leave someone vulnerable to the elements.

"I'll help her," he muttered. "But only because I know you'll haunt me until I do." In the years since her death, Christine had filled his mind, but this was the first time she irritated the pants off him.

He could almost hear Christine's soft laugh, and then a new message landed between his ears. *Angel needs her.* Ignoring the message, he shrugged out of his coat and walked toward his office to write the note for Hank to take to Hempel.

"Pa?" Angel pushed the swinging door to the kitchen open. "Aren't you going to eat?"

"I'll be there in a minute," he said, but kept moving. It was getting to the point he had more women telling him what to do than a man could take.

"Well, hurry up. The pancakes are going faster than beer on Saturday night."

He stopped and spun about. Steam hissed inside his head. "What did you say?"

Constance appeared then. She tugged Angel into the kitchen by the girl's shoulders and took her spot holding the door open. "She said breakfast is done. But don't worry, there's plenty."

The little voice singing, *I told you so*, in his head was enough to make him stomp the rest of the way down the hall and throw his office door open with sufficient force it banged against the wall.

Chapter Six

The thud of the door down the hall made Constance shudder clean to her core and caused a wave of doubt to wash over her. Maybe she wasn't cut out for this job. Not only did she not have much experience with children, the amount she had with men was next to nil.

Letting the door slip shut, she hurried to the stove. "Where did you hear something like that?"

Angel shrugged her shoulders, flipping pancakes. "From one of the cowboys I suspect."

Constance picked up a platter for the pancakes and held it out. "I suggest you not say it again."

Angel snickered as she transferred the cakes onto the platter.

"It's not funny," Constance insisted. She moved the platter to catch a pancake falling from the spatula, but wasn't quick enough. It landed on the floor near her feet.

Angel glanced to the men, bent down, grabbed the cake and set it on the plate. "No one saw."

Constance gave the girl a stern look. "I saw. Furthermore, *you* saw." She tossed the pancake on the counter and carried the platter to the table. When she arrived back at the stove the pancake was gone. Angel was chewing.

"You didn't eat that, did you?"

Angel nodded as she swallowed. "The floor's clean."

Appalled, Constance glared at the girl.

"You scrubbed it twice yesterday," Angel replied, losing a bit of her defiance as a blush rose on her cheeks. "I didn't want it to go to waste."

Thankful patience was a virtue she'd been blessed with in abundance, or had found living with her aunts, Constance poured out six pancakes and waited for the sizzle to ease before she whispered, "No you didn't."

The girl bowed her head, telling Constance all she needed to know, except why Angel had purposefully tried to irritate her and Ellis. "As soon as the men are gone, you and I are going to have a talk." She set the bowl down and emphasized, "A long talk."

Angel grinned, but there was no sparkle in her eyes. "About kings and queens?"

"No, about manners."

The chatter at the table quelled a bit as Ellis walked into the room. The frown on his face said he wasn't out to make friends.

Whatever reason Angel had to annoy him, Constance had more reason to right the situation, for all their sakes. She prepared a plate and handed it to Angel. "Here take this to your father and apologize for what you said."

Angel lingered, as if the thought distressed her.

"You can just whisper it in his ear," Constance insisted, allowing a hint of compromise, "and kiss his cheek."

Angel rarely had to answer for her behaviors, and the struggle inside her was evident. Constance turned her about, unwilling to back down. The girl let out a weary sigh and walked across the room. Constance wished she could hear, but then knew she didn't need to. The surprised expression on Ellis's face, and the way his eyes shot across the room told her Angel had followed her instructions.

His gaze then went to his daughter, and Constance could almost feel his anger easing as he grinned at the girl. Relief eased out of her chest, but only until Ellis's gaze returned to her. It was a serious look, as if he was deeply contemplating what had just happened.

Constance kept her chin up. Discipline was a part of education, and if he questioned that, her job in reforming Angel would be impossible. Doubt seeped in. He probably shouldn't entrust his daughter to her. She really didn't know anything about raising children.

He cocked his head slightly, and then the edges of his lips curled as he gave her a slight nod before he lowered his eyes to his plate. His approval had a shattering effect on her body. Pride as she had never felt, along with delight, swirled around her heart.

Angel had six more cakes sizzling on the grill. Constance grasped the spatula. "Go fix your plate and eat with your father."

"No," Angel said, tugging the spatula from her fingers. "I'll wait for you. So we can talk." Shifting so her shoulder touched Constance's, she added, "I owe you an apology, too."

If all of life's lessons were as easily combated as this one, the world would be a remarkable place. "Accepted," Constance said, wrapping an arm around Angel. The twinkle in the girl's eyes had her adding, "You are an imp."

Angel leaned against her. "I know. But you love me."

Emotions flooded Constance's system, locking her lungs and making her knees tremble. Angel's statement was laced with hope, something Constance knew a lot about. It had been a long time, but one never forgets what it feels like to want to be loved, or to love. Constance increased her hold. "Yes, you little imp. I love you."

Angel emitted a happy little squeal. "I knew it. I love you, too."

Ellis couldn't hear what Angel and Constance whispered about, but he didn't need to. Ashton's unclaimed bride had been claimed—by his daughter. He should have known this would happen. Angel never did anything halfway. It was all or nothing. Just like her mother.

Trouble was, Constance was good for Angel. It had been years since Angel had apologized for something. Then again, it had been some time since he'd made her apologize. Instead he'd sloughed off the occasional smart mouth or action, blaming himself for her rough edges.

He pushed away from the table. "The storm's let up. If we leave now, there should be enough time to get to town before the next wave moves in."

"We?" Fred Westmaster leaned against the door frame. "You got business in town, Ellis?"

"Yes, I do." Ellis couldn't say when, but the decision had been made. He'd go to town and speak to John Hempel himself. The sooner he had a plan for Constance Jennings, the sooner his life would get back in order. "And the sooner we head out, the better off we'll be," he added aloud. More for himself than anyone else.

The others finished their meals, swiping up the

thick syrup left on their plates with hearty chunks of bread and gulping down the last bits of coffee in their cups. His gaze went to the plate of thick-cut bread slices in the center of the table and a tenderness wedged its way into his heart. Frowning, he left the room.

His mind was in worse shape now than it had been earlier. Notions and thoughts swam amongst each other like minnows in a shallow creek. He tried to snatch on to ones that made sense. Ashton's place probably wasn't that bad. Jeb said they'd fixed it up. The two of them, Jeb and Miles, had lived out there for several years, so they knew how to weather a storm, and would provide for Constance. If she was to leave, it would be best now, before Angel got any more attached.

He pulled his coat from the hook, but while working the buttons through their holes, his fingers stalled and his gaze roamed the office. Constance had eyed his bookshelves as if there was a hunger in her for the stories between the pages. They were all here—the long-ago written classics, as well as the newer novels of life, love and journeys to find the meanings behind conscious thoughts. He could loan her a few to take to Ashton's. They'd give her something to do while the winter winds kept her indoors.

The chatter of the men donning their winter gear floated down the hall. Who was he trying to fool?

Miles and Jeb wouldn't be able to hold off the horde of men who'd descend upon her. Leaving the note for Hempel on his desk, he grabbed his gloves and, slapping their stiffness against his thigh, left the room as if it were on fire.

"Let's go," he directed toward the men, walking straight to the door.

"Mr. Clayton?"

His feet stuck in such a manner he wondered if they'd all of a sudden glued themselves to the floor. Holding his breath, he turned. Constance held the door to the kitchen open. "We have to go while the weather—" he started.

"Why do you have to go, Pa?" Angel interrupted, poking her head out beside Constance's shoulder. "We got everything we needed the other day."

"There's someone I want to talk to. I'll be home before nightfall." He turned and pulled open the front door.

"You will be careful?" The apprehension in Constance's voice was highlighted by the grimace on her face. There were already enough thoughts rolling around in his head, adding where her concerns came from would be useless. With a brief nod, he exited the house.

Cold air greeted him like a scorned woman, and he paused to fasten the top button of his coat and pull on his gloves. Snow had been cleared away to make a wide path from the house to the barn, and the heels of his boots crunched against the hard crust as he trudged forward. The choice was suddenly made, and he wasn't one to go back on a decision. The thought of a freezing ride to town was about as thrilling as walking all the way to Mexico, but Constance wasn't moving out to Ashton's, whether she could claim it or not. Angel needed her right here.

The barn could have doubled for a train depot with the amount of men moseying about. Ellis gathered his tack and went to saddle a roan.

Hank appeared next to him. "What you doing, Ellis?"

"I decided to go to town myself."

"Mind if I ride with you?"

Ellis shook his head. The good thing about men who'd worked for you for years was they knew you, and didn't question decisions. Hank wasn't a flap-jaw, either. Good thing, 'cause Ellis didn't feel like talking.

"I'll go tell Thomas to check in on the woman folk a couple times today and meet you out front." Hank disappeared as quickly as he'd appeared.

That was the other good thing about Hank; he knew what needed to be done and saw to it. A finer foreman would be hard to come by. Ellis mounted and led the group of travelers out of the barn. On the way, he nodded to the cowboy holding the big door against the gusts of wind that had picked up. He had a lot to be thankful for—good men working for him was part of what made Heaven on Earth what it was today. And he was grateful. Tried to remember to thank the Good Lord every night.

So why in tarnation was he so out of sorts? He kneed his horse, leading the way through the homestead and up the winding trail where the winds were sure to be stronger and colder. Hank caught up at the bottom of the draw, giving a nod in greeting as he hunkered down deeper in his coat.

The wind was bitter, but Ellis didn't bow to it. Rarely did he stoop to anything. That wasn't his way. Then why the hell was he bending over backward to make sure a little snip of a woman didn't have to go live in some crude cabin? Was it just because of Angel, or was that an excuse he was trying hard to believe?

Topping the hill, he turned, taking a quick glance at the view below. The wind raced by, whistling a wintry tune. What he saw—the homestead surrounded by thousands of acres of plentiful land—was all he ever wanted. Ever needed. So where had the hollow feeling in his chest come from?

He turned and flicked the ends of the reins aside the roan, jolting the horse into a canter. It would be cold the entire way to Cottonwood. He'd want a warm fire and hot coffee badly by the time he arrived, but arrive he would. If Constance Jennings had inherited Ashton's place, she had a right to know about it, and he'd be the one to tell her. Then she could decide if she wanted to stay in his warm and comfortable house this winter—fulfilling their agreement—or go live in a cracked and drafty cabin.

Surely she'd understand the risks of living with Jeb, a greenhorn with frozen toes, and Miles, an old coot who didn't take a bath but twice a year.

Planting his feet firmer in the stirrups, Ellis urged his mount into a steady but quick pace. "Let's ride, boys. The quicker we get off this hill, the better."

Constance's fingers tightened on the curtain as the tiny dots disappeared over the top of the snow-covered hill. Who did Ellis need to talk to? She'd intended to speak with him as soon as breakfast was over. If he learned her tale from someone else, she was worried the details would be skewed.

A thud caused her to let the curtain loose. There wasn't anything she could do about it right now. "I said book. Not books," she explained, picking up three books in Angel's trail.

"I know, but I didn't know which one we should start with." Angel arranged her load into a pile on the table in front of the sofa and plopped onto the cushion with a sigh.

Constance flipped one of the books around, reading the spine. *An Etiquette Guide for Young Ladies.* She spun the next one about. *True Politeness.* The third one was titled *The Church Society Handbook.*

"Oh, goodness."

"What?" Angel flopped one leg up to rest an ankle on her opposite knee.

Constance set the books on the table and then, one by one, read the covers of the rest of the stack. All six of them were similar to the first ones, having to do with manners and young ladies. Momentarily at a loss, she tapped Angel's foot. "A young lady sits with both feet on the floor."

Angel lowered her foot, rearranged her skirt and gave a look that asked, *Is that better?*

Gesturing to the books, Constance said, "These look brand-new."

"They are. Pa bought them last year. I started to read that one." Angel pointed at the one titled *The Peacemaker.* "I thought it was about the gun." She leaned back and rolled her eyes to gaze at the ceiling. "But it was about how to behave so you don't ruffle anyone's feathers. I only got through the first few pages." She shivered and groaned dramatically.

The sight sparked a memory for Constance. "Wait here." Entering Ellis's office, a smile twitched her lips. The entire house was wonderful, but this room was already her favorite. The rich, wonderful aroma of books and the lingering scent of leather and rawhide mixed together created the one fragrance she'd never been able to find in England. It reminded her of her home in Richmond. Somehow the smell instilled an assurance of well-being and happiness.

Remembering exactly where she'd seen the novel, she plucked it from a shelf of many and darted around the desk. Her flaying skirt caused something to flutter to the floor. She picked up an envelope with the name John Hempel penned across the front and laid it in the middle of the desk.

Back in the parlor, she held out the book she'd collected. "Here. We'll start with this one."

"*Little Women?*" Angel's tone sounded as if her life was in jeopardy.

"You'll like it. Trust me."

"Little Women?" Angel repeated. "Are they leprechauns?" The sound of hope in her voice made Constance smile.

"No, they aren't leprechauns." Constance sat down on the sofa. "It's a wonderful story about four sisters. I've read it a couple of times."

"Is it from England?"

"No, it was published here in the States. In Massachusetts a few years ago." She ran a hand over the top of the book identical to the copy she'd once owned. Her aunts had given her the book for her birthday. "It's written by Louisa May Alcott. It's been said the one character, Jo March, is a reflection of who the author was growing up."

Angel rested her head on Constance's shoulder. "What's it about? Are they short?"

"They're young women. Girls really. Just like you. It's the story of them growing up and how they discover who they are." She touched the tip of Angel's nose. "They also must overcome some natural imperfections. For Jo, it's her temperament. For Meg—she's the oldest sister—it's vanity. Beth is younger than Jo, and is very shy. And the youngest is Amy. She's a tad selfish."

Angel's eyes proved her interest was piqued. She opened the front cover. "You promise it's not boring?"

"I promise." Constance snuggled deeper into the sofa and tugged Angel with her. "Turn to chapter one and read it to me."

"Out loud?"

"Uh-huh," she mumbled. "I love having stories read to me."

"Why? Don't you know how to read?"

Constance opened one eye, peering down at Angel. "Hasn't anyone ever read to you?"

"My mother did, before she died. I can kinda remember it. And Pa did, but not since I learned how to read myself."

The trials and errors of Ellis raising his spirited daughter by himself tugged at Constance's heartstrings. With her free hand, she thread through the first few pages until she found their starting point. "You read chapter one to me, and I'll read chapter two to you."

"You will?"

"Yes, I will." She rested her cheek against Angel's head. "Go on, start reading."

That's how it went for the next few hours, each of them reading, pausing to discuss a character or the twisting and turning plot. They were on chapter four, with Constance reading and feeling each and every word, when the front door opened.

Before they climbed off the sofa, Thomas Ketchum, with his red-bearded face, poked his head around the door frame.

"It's just me, ma'am. I thought I better check the fires."

Constance handed the book to Angel and smoothed her skirt as she rose. "Thank you, Mr. Ketchum. I'm afraid the time has gotten away from us."

"It'll only take me a few minutes, and then I'll refill the wood boxes." He tipped the front brim of his hat before he moved down the hall.

Constance turned to Angel. "Run into your father's office and find a scrap of paper to mark our page."

"Can't we read some more? It's really good."

"I know it's really good." Constance flicked

a finger over Angel's nose. "And waiting to read more will make us get the household chores done even faster."

Angel giggled and then skipped to the doorway. She flipped around before exiting the room. "Constance?"

Pausing to lift her head as she gathered the stack of books off the table, Constance replied, "Yes?"

"Thank you. I like reading to you. And I like you reading to me." Angel was gone then, racing down the hall.

"You're welcome," Constance whispered. The enjoyment she'd experienced the past two days was quickly becoming a highlight of her life. Times she'd remember when she was old and gray, and long for when they were no more. Her fingers shook as she picked up the books. Her time here was temporary—Angel wouldn't need her for long. Self-imposed insight continued to flood her mind. She wasn't a young girl like Angel, or the March sisters. And she had discovered what her flaw was. History. Her past. It not only haunted her, it repeated itself. Two dead husbands—well, one husband and one soon-to-be husband had he not died. How could a person outgrow a flaw like that?

Thomas Ketchum entered the parlor, causing her to gather the books and leave the room. Her mind wasn't done, and as she walked down the hall, her family came to mind. It wasn't just husbands. Everyone in her life died—tragic, unexpected deaths that left her reeling.

A gasp had her glancing up when she entered the office. Angel's cheeks were flushed and alarm filled her eyes. Something fluttered out of the girl's fingers. The envelope Constance had knocked on the floor earlier sat opened on the top of the thickly varnished desk.

"Angel!" Constance crossed the room quickly, replacing the books in the empty space on one of the many shelves. "I know you know better than to read someone else's mail."

"It's not mail, it's a note Pa wrote to—"

"That constitutes mail," she interrupted. Aware of Mr. Ketchum across the hall, Constance moved to the desk. "Mail is a very personal and private thing. I'm ashamed of you. And you should be, too."

"But—"

The glare she sent stifled Angel. Shamefully, the girl bowed her head.

Constance pointed at the letter lying open-faced on the desk. "Now put that back. It's time for lunch." Without waiting to see if the girl complied, she left the room.

Angel was little more than a step behind her. "Constance, are you mad at me?"

It appeared today's life lessons were hard ones—for both her and Angel. Constance pushed the kitchen door open, and held it for Angel to enter the room. "No, I'm not mad at you. But I am disappointed in you. Stealing someone's privacy is easy, and it's one of the most painful thefts a person can experience." Draping an arm around Angel, Constance gently consoled, "Sometimes our curiosity gets the best of us, but when it comes to other people's belongings, we need to let our inner conscience lead our actions. Your stomach told you not to read your father's mail didn't it?"

Angel nodded.

Constance ran her hand down the back of Angel's golden curls. "Next time, remember how sad you feel right now, and your conscience will be even stronger."

"I will," Angel vowed. "I promise."

"Good." Constance placed a quick kiss on the top of the mass of curls and let the girl loose. "Now, what do you want for lunch?"

Angel, still glum, shrugged. Constance took her hand and led her toward the pantry. "Let's see what looks good."

"Constance, if you had somewhere else to live, would you?" Angel asked, stopping as Constance opened the pantry door.

An odd vibration raced up Constance's spine. Frowning, she turned to gaze into Angel's face, deeply concerned by what the girl wasn't saying. Or maybe it was disquiet deep within herself she picked up on. There wasn't any place else she'd rather live. In the short time she'd been at Heaven on Earth, she'd grown attached. Both to the home and the occupants. The knowledge wasn't something she was prepared to accept. Yet, a deep sense of homecoming had planted itself within her soul the moment Ellis had stopped the wagon on top of the far hill to gaze down on the homestead, and had expanded until it was deeper and wider than the ocean she'd crossed from England.

She turned back to the pantry. It seemed a lifetime had passed since she'd packed most of her belongings in trunks and closed the door on her aunts' home for the last time. Had she been excited that day? Byron had been waiting for her in the rented coach. It had been their wedding day.

"Would you?" Angel asked again, this time urgency laced her tone.

Constance released the foggy memories and stepped into the pantry. "Well, since I don't have any other place to live, it really doesn't matter, does it? Now, what looks good? I could make some more applesauce. Or I could make candied apple rings. Have you ever had those?" She knew she was rambling, but she had to. Leaving here— leaving Angel—was not something she wanted to talk about. "They're delicious. Aunt Theresa taught me how to make them." After handing Angel several apples, she took a large wheel of cheese from the shelf. "We can have a cheese sandwich with them. How does that sound?"

Angel looked at her speculatively, and then, as if she concluded it was the only answer she'd get to her question, nodded and moved toward the table.

Constance pressed a hand to the churning in her stomach that had nothing to do with food and swallowed against the bile bubbling into the back of her throat. The wave of understanding washing over made breathing difficult. That letter on Ellis's desk was the reason Angel had asked the question. She'd read something. Had he found out about Byron's death? Was he writing to ask someone for more details?

The envelope had been addressed to John Hempel. She couldn't recall ever hearing the name. A flood erupted inside her mind. Angel had asked if she had somewhere else to live, would she. Was Ellis writing to people, hoping to find another place for her to live?

Dread, thick and heavy, settled around her. History was repeating itself again—she was being sent away.

Chapter Seven

His toes were stiffer than cowpies in January. Ellis rubbed his arms and stomped his feet to get the blood flowing and then led the roan into the stables behind Link's place. The snow held, and hopefully would continue to wait until after he'd met with Hempel and made it back home.

Several times during the past few hours, he'd questioned this trip to town. Not his ability to survive it, but his reasoning. His mind paraded Constance Jennings around in his head like a campaigning politician, shouting promises that could never be kept. Yet the memory of baking bread with her that kept bounding in had kept him warm enough to survive the long, cold ride.

He stepped onto the boardwalk and, after a quick rap, opened the door to John Hempel's office. In no time, the lawyer, a young man who'd moved to the territory last spring, confirmed Constance had every right to move out to Ashton's place. Upon his deathbed, Ashton had had Hempel draw up a will, leaving most everything to his soon-to-arrive mail-order bride.

The visit was short. Hempel was fighting a cold, and clearly needed to go home and get some rest. He did ask Ellis to tell Constance as soon as he felt up to the ride he'd be out to tell her about Ashton's will.

Ellis wasn't ignorant of the law, but telling Constance she had someplace else to live didn't settle well. Angel would be heart broken, not to mention the horde of men pursing Constance would probably double once they heard she was a landowner. The ride home would be longer with all this on his mind.

Hank was just where Ellis thought he'd be—at Link's, sided up next to the tiny stove in the corner. Besides the usual smells of coffee beans and leather, a sweet scent floated on the air. It wasn't a sickly odor, just different, somewhat tantalizing, and coming from the two good-sized canvas bags sitting on the countertop.

Link emerged from the back room, where he and his wife, Lula Mae, resided in quarters more cramped and cluttered than the store. "Aw, Ellis," he greeted. "Just the man I wanted to see." Untying the rope securing one of the bags, Link added, "I got something here you're gonna like."

Ellis wasn't in the mood for one of Link's sales pitches, but when Link pulled out an odd tube-shaped thing—about the ugliest looking object he'd seen yet—curiosity had him taking a closer look. "What is it?"

"A banana," Link said. "It's a fruit. Folks over in Europe love them."

Ellis handed it back. "It looks like it's half rotten if you ask me."

Link replaced the object in the bag. "That's only 'cause they froze. A cargo wagon was taking them up to Fort Laramie. The government bought a boatload of them for the soldiers. The wagon master said an army general ate one at a fair out in Pennsylvania last year, and ever since then has been on a mission to buy up all he can. Said they're sweeter than candy."

"They are." Hank moseyed away from the stove, toward the counter. "I ate one," he explained. "It was good, but kinda mushy."

"That's 'cause they froze," Link insisted. "The wagon master said they got to get used up 'afore they go bad. That's why I bought the lot. Figured you'd be interested in them."

"I don't have any use for them," Ellis told Link, shaking his head.

"You might not have any use for them, but I bet Miss Jennings does."

A shiver spiraled Ellis's spine.

"The driver said people from England love bananas. I bet Miss Jennings hasn't had one since she left the old shore. I bet she'll be happy as a clam to have one." Link was taking his time tying the bag closed. "Yes, sir, I bet that little gal would love to have a banana or two."

Ellis breathed through his nose, questioning the way his insides took to flipping at the thought of Constance's face shimmering with delight.

"And I bet Angel would jump for joy at the thought of being the only one around with bananas. That girl loves being the first to try something," Link continued. "Yes, sir, those two gals back at your place will think you are something, bringing them home these here bananas."

He'd go on and on. Link wasn't the best salesman, but he could talk a customer to death if you didn't give in or leave. Ellis chose to give in, already anticipating Angel's smile. And Constance's. "All right, I'll take a few home."

Link patted the sack. "Got 'em all bagged up for you."

"I said a few. I don't need the whole bag. Con— Miss Jennings and Angel can't eat that many."

"It's an all or nothing deal, Ellis."

The man could try, but he wouldn't get the best

of him. Smile or no smile, he wasn't hauling home the whole bag. "Then it's nothing."

Link hung his head, shaking it like a forlorn dog. "That's a shame. No one else is gonna know what to do with them. I bought them just for Miss Jennings, knowing she'd lived in England and all."

"How'd you know that?"

"Ashton told me. 'Afore he died of course. I bet he'd have bought them—the whole kit and caboodle—for Miss Jennings. She'd have been his wife by now of course, and he'd want to do anything to make her feel more at home out here in the wilds, knowing she was used to the finer and gentler things in life. Yes, siree, Ashton would have bought every last banana to make her happy."

The balling of his insides made Ellis groan. "All right, I'll take the lot." The words were out before he knew what he'd said.

"I'll just put them on your account."

Never one to carry a balance, Ellis moved back to the counter. "No, I'll pay you now." He pulled out a few coins.

Link patted a bag. "It'll be ten dollars."

Ellis stopped his jaw before it dropped open. "Ten dollars?"

"Yup."

"For rotting bananas?"

"Frozen. They froze. They aren't rotten."

"Either way, they aren't prime," he insisted.

There wasn't much use in arguing—not while the anticipation of surprising Constance with the fruit danced inside him like spring calves frolicking in the pasture. Besides, Link might just take it upon himself to deliver the lot to Constance himself. Ellis pulled money out of his hip pocket. The ranch had already experienced more than enough unexpected visitors.

"As prime as you're gonna get out here. And the prime price is ten cents a piece." Link took the money, counting out the bills one at a time.

"They aren't going to be able to eat a hundred bananas no matter how good they are," Ellis grumbled, moving to the door where the cold air might slap some sense into him. Wasting money was as unusual for him as bananas were to Wyoming. But here he was, spending ten dollars on mushy fruit the rest of the state hadn't even heard of.

Constance added another log to the fire. The same wind rapping on the windows sucked the smoke, along with a goodly amount of the heat, up the chimney. Darkness had descended some time ago, cloaking the earth with a blanket so black a person would believe it was midnight instead of seven in the evening.

Supper was over, and Angel was on the couch, reading aloud from *Little Women*. Constance had no idea what chapter they were on now. Her ears had been tuned in to the door, her mind conjuring up reasons why Ellis hadn't returned yet.

"Constance, do you want me to read it again?"

She pushed off the mantel and walked toward the sofa. "Read what again?"

"That last part. It was very exciting. Jo just read her writing to her sisters."

The March sisters sharing Jo's publishing joy had always been one of her favorite scenes. "Hmm, yes, that was exciting."

"But you didn't hear when I read it. You were staring off like you were dreaming of finding gold under the rocks in the creek."

Constance sat down next to Angel. "I was picturing the story. Go on, keep reading."

Angel looked at her curiously for a few seconds before she bent her head over the book and started reading again.

The story held Constance's attention for a few sentences, but then she drifted off again, hoping something hadn't happened to Ellis along the route. Angel wasn't concerned. Several times the girl had explained how well her father knew the land and the weather. Most likely she was right. Ellis had lived in the territory for years.

The wind rattled the windows again. Last time she'd checked—a few minutes ago—snow was coming down at a steady pace. If the sun had been shining, perhaps she wouldn't be so apprehensive.

Sunshine always lifted her spirit. No matter where a person was, whether England or America, November was a gloomy month, full of gray skies and cold breezes.

Then again, maybe if she wasn't so concerned over that letter, she wouldn't be sitting here fretting up her own storm. The envelope still sat on his desk. She couldn't read it. Wouldn't read it. Yet she wanted to know what Ellis had written on that piece of paper as badly as Angel wanted to read the next chapter of *Little Women*.

Was he offering her to John Hempel? It wouldn't do. Not only was she not willing to become engaged to another man, Ellis had offered her six months of employment. They had a deal, and she wouldn't allow him to back out of it. This time the past wasn't going to repeat itself. Furthermore, Angel needed her. Without the influence of another woman, the girl would grow into the spitting image of the cowboys filling the bunkhouse. Today was proof of that.

She was needed here, and no matter what Ellis decided, she'd stand her ground and remain at Heaven on Earth for the next six months. Come Hell or high water. She flinched as the expression floated over her mind. Angel had said those exact words not long ago, when talking about her father's safe arrival. When Ellis did arrive home, she'd tell him everything. About Byron. About the authorities. And she'd ask for his help. He was an influential man. Perhaps he even knew the governor.

Even though she'd been a child, she remembered her father meeting with the Governor of Virginia. If she told her story to Ellis, and he told it to the governor, maybe that would clear her name once and for all.

Footfalls stomping up the front steps had Angel dropping the book. "I told you he'd be home soon."

"I never said he wouldn't." Constance stood, smoothing her skirt with both hands while fighting the urge to run to the door—or for her room, she wasn't quite sure which.

"You didn't have to say it. The number of times you stared out the window told me you had your doubts," Angel tossed over her shoulder as she left the parlor. "Hey Pa," echoed back into the room.

"Hi." Ellis's greeting was followed by a loud sneeze.

Concern rippled her shoulders, making Constance hurry from the room. "Mr. Clayton?" His face was bright red, but more so, he shivered from head to toe. She rushed to his side to pull the heavy garment from his shoulders. "Here, give me your coat."

"What took so long, Pa?"

"Hank's horse went down in an icy patch," he offered breathlessly, rubbing his hands up and down his arms.

"Oh, goodness. Is he all right?" Constance asked, duly alarmed.

"Yes, he's fine. We just had to take it slow."

"Was it Jacob?" Angel shook her head. "I warned Hank last week that horse isn't as sure-footed as he used to be. They're both getting up in age you know."

"No, it wasn't Jacob." Ellis patted Angel's head. "And Hank is thawing out in the bunkhouse."

Glad the other man was fine, Constance focused her concerns on Ellis. "Come into the kitchen where there's hot coffee, and I'll warm your supper."

"What's in the sacks, Pa?" Angel asked as Ellis bent to pick up two bundles.

"I'll show you while I have a cup of coffee. I'm frozen to my bones."

Constance held the kitchen door wide, but he nodded for her to enter first. It was silly, the way her insides fluttered whenever he was near. Disregarding the sensations as best she could, Constance gathered a cup and thanked her own good sense for having brewed a pot of coffee just a short time ago. Knowledge of how to run a home wasn't foreign to her, and the ability to do so efficiently coaxed her determination to remain at the ranch. Not only did Angel need her, Ellis needed someone to look after his home, whether he knew it or not.

After setting the steaming cup on the table, she

stoked the fire and transferred the plate of chicken and dumplings from the warming bin to the oven. While it heated she gathered utensils and bread, setting it all in front of Ellis as he told Angel about Hank's horse slipping on the ice.

"Thank you, Miss Jennings," he offered, when she slid the plate with bubbling gravy in front of him.

His smile made her insides do all kinds of things. "You're welcome, but be careful, the plate is hot," Constance warned. She returned to the stove before the gaze of his knowing eyes drove too deep. The letter hadn't been far from her mind all afternoon, but now that he'd arrived home, she could barely refrain from blurting out that she wasn't willing to marry any other man.

Of course they had other things to discuss as well, but in all honesty, neither of her engagements had been well thought-out. With Byron it had happened during the turbulent passing of Aunt Julia and the legal whirlwind that had followed. And with Ashton it had been an impromptu decision while dismal clouds of poverty and homelessness—or possibly prison—had shadowed her vision. Long days and nights of traveling across the nation had given her time to lament both events. She'd have married Ashton, had the poor man not perished before her arrival. A promise was a promise, regardless of how impromptu or regrettable.

Would Ellis understand that? It wasn't that she was thankful Ashton had passed—he hadn't deserved that—but she was happy not to be tied to a stranger for the rest of her life. Maybe she just wasn't cut out for marriage.

"Constance?"

Both father and daughter stared at her in question. They had the same eyes—dark brown and intuitive. "I'm sorry. I'm afraid I didn't hear what you asked," she admitted what they already knew.

"Bananas," Angel said. "Have you ever had one?"

Blessedly thankful the answer didn't require thought, she nodded. "Oh, yes. Several years ago my aunts and I sampled them in London at a fair." Her fingers went to the cameo broach at her neck. Aunt Theresa had purchased it from one of the vendors that day.

"Do you like them?" Angel wanted to know.

"Yes. They're very good. But quite seasonal."

Angel frowned. "Seasonal?"

"Yes, they aren't grown in England. And they ripen quickly, making shipping them a grievous task, which means they're not available year round." Drawn by the expressions on both their faces, she moved to the table. "Why all the questions about bananas?"

"Because Pa's got a whole bunch," Angel answered excitedly.

Perplexed, Constance turned to Ellis. "You brought home bananas?" She bit the tip of her tongue, wondering if he'd catch how easily she used the word *home*.

His smile was genuine and fresh as he nodded.

Now utterly baffled, she asked, "How? Bananas couldn't possibly make the trip all the way to Wyoming."

He reached down to the bag near his chair leg. What he lifted and then held up rather proudly was the ugliest, blackest banana she'd ever seen. The scent was familiar—it said the banana was well past its prime.

"Oh." She flattened her hands on the table top to keep the shivers from rippling her arms. Even the oldest banana off the ships had never looked so…distorted.

The smile on his face faded. "They froze."

His obvious disappointment made her heart sink in a wave of compassion. "Oh," she repeated. As if his explanation was sufficient, she quickly added, "I see." She'd never seen bananas that had frozen, but she had seen ripe ones, and that was one ripe banana.

"Probably ain't good for much." He dropped the fruit on the table. His tone sounded as flat and sad as the banana looked.

"So we can't eat them?" Angel's joy had deflated, too.

Willing to do anything to cheer them both, Constance pasted a positive smile upon her face. "I'm sure we can," she assured, while searching the recesses of her mind. Creating soft foods for her Aunts during their illness had her mind rushing about, but the blackened fruit lying on the table mocked her. She picked it up, flinching at the mushiness beneath the thinning skin. Unwavering, she thought aloud, "Perhaps a pudding. You like pudding don't you?"

Angel shrugged. "Can't say as I've had pudding." She turned to her father. "Have I?"

He shrugged.

Constance took in the way the two of them seemed to shy away from the once-exciting banana. "Well, that settles it. Tomorrow we shall have banana pudding." If the bananas didn't completely rot between now and then.

"How many bananas does it take to make pudding?" Angel asked as Constance was wondering exactly how she'd make a banana pudding.

"I'm not sure." Holding the smile that wanted to slip from her lips—a recipe still wasn't coming to her—she turned to question Ellis, "How many do we have?"

His cheeks were once again bright red as he glanced to the sacks by his feet. Constance stepped around the table. She hadn't really noticed how large the bundles he'd carried in were, but now was rather overwhelmed to see they were half the size of one of her trunks. Swallowing the lump in her throat, she peered back at the black banana in her hand.

"Give or take one or two, I'd say right around a hundred." The self assured, confident tone Ellis usually spoke with had disappeared. He sounded more like a guilt-ridden schoolboy.

"I see." She sounded about as confident as a bird with fins. Her fingers tensed, which caused the bruised and battered banana skin to split. Mush ran between her fingers.

Ellis started chuckling. Shaking his head, he ran one hand through his hat flattened hair, and laughed harder. "I'm sorry, Constance. I don't know why I let Link talk me into the buying those things. I'm sure the pigs will eat them."

Her ears sang at the way he said her name, and his ability to find humor in the situation touched her heart. Afraid the ability to speak might leave at any moment, she assured, "From what I've seen of Link, the man has the gift of gab, and most likely left you little choice but to buy them." Recalling how Aunt Julia had enjoyed eating berries that were past their prime, Constance moved to the cupboard and took down a bowl. This was her chance to prove to Ellis he'd made the right choice—not only in bringing home the bananas but in bringing her home, too. *Please, Aunt Julia, if you're up there and listening, don't fail me now.*

She peeled the banana and plopped the mushy guts into the bowl. Then poured a small amount of cream in the bowl and sprinkled a touch of sugar across the top. After she retrieved a spoon, she set the bowl in front of Angel. With her heart thudding and her fingers crossed, she said, "Try that."

With a pensive look, Angel peered at Ellis.

He glanced up at Constance. Hope had her too stiff to do much more than nod once.

Ellis lifted a brow, but then nodded to Angel.

After sniffing the spoonful, Angel took a bite, and then another before she said, "Mmm, that's good. Try some, Pa."

Constance let out the air locked in her lungs, but it stalled again when Ellis grasped the spoon.

He scooped it full and slid it between his lips. "Mmm," he said. "Not bad. Not bad at all." Smiling, he gave the spoon back to Angel.

"You want some, Constance?" Angel offered her the spoon.

Constance took the spoon, willing her trembling fingers to not drop it. Ellis's approval had her trembling with glee. As the cream-covered fruit rolled across her palate, she wondered if it was what tasted so good, or if there was just a hint of Ellis left on the spoon. Her cheeks flamed at the thought, and she chased the notion away as fast as it entered her mind. "That settles it." She handed the spoon back to Angel. "The pigs will not get the bananas." Meeting Ellis's grin, she added, "But I'm sure they'll enjoy the peelings."

Chapter Eight

By the time Ellis crawled between the sheets of his bed, his head throbbed and his throat was on fire. He'd managed to control the fit of sneezes playing havoc inside his nostrils until he'd closed the bedroom door. What did he expect traveling mile upon mile in the freezing wind? He reached for the handkerchief he'd set on the bedside table and plastered it across his face moments before another attack left him gasping for air.

Pulling the covers over his shoulders and shivering from tip to toe, he closed his eyes, hoping by morning the worst would be over. At least that's what he thought he hoped, whereas actually, his mind had floated downstairs to when he'd been laughing and eating cream-covered bananas with Constance and Angel.

The warm thoughts heated his body and made

a smile form on his chapped lips. He'd forgotten how good it felt to laugh. Not the rough and rowdy joking that happened with other men, but the soul-ripening happiness that occurred when cradled in the shelter of home with loved ones. That type of laughter instilled a peaceful, yet tremulous joy deep in one's heart.

It was also the type he hadn't known he missed until he experienced it again. Angel had missed it, too. She certainly needed Constance, and it was his duty as a father to assure she got what she needed, come Hell or high water.

His lids grew heavy, yet he wondered if he could keep Constance from learning about her inheritance. As his mind had a way of looking at things from all angles, he realized he couldn't keep the information from her. That wasn't the type of man he was, nor wanted to become.

She seemed happy here. He saw it in her eyes and in that enchanting little smile that floated over her lips as soft and gentle as a butterfly floats from flower to flower.

A shudder rippled him as another sneeze tore through his system, and the sneezing fit that followed shook the bed. Afterward, exhausted, he slept, but the chill in the room woke him several times. Shivering uncontrollably, he huddled deeper beneath the covers, sneezing and wiping at his nose that wouldn't stop dripping. When dawn etched against the windows, he crawled from bed, sweating one second, freezing the next, and aching from head to toe. With great effort, he dressed and left the room.

Not even the scent of coffee brewing penetrated his plugged nostrils. Soft noise said Constance was in the kitchen, and that was enough to draw him in.

"Good morning," she greeted as she turned from the stove, cup in hand. Her face grew somber and she rushed across the room. "Goodness, Ellis, you look—" setting the cup on the table she pulled out a chair, gesturing for him to sit "—terrible." She brushed a hand to his forehead.

Her fingers, ice against his sizzling skin, made him sigh at the cooling relief the touch provided. In all honesty, he wanted to lean against her, just absorb her tender kindness, knew it would make him feel better. Chiding himself for the childish thoughts, he picked up the coffee cup.

"Oh, no," she took the cup from his hand. "You're burning up." She hurried across the room, and a second later was back, handing him a glass. "Cold water is what you need."

He opened his mouth to offer a word of appreciation, but the flames in his throat stalled the vibration of his vocal cords. The water helped cool the inside of his mouth, but pain seized his throat muscles when he tried to swallow.

She took the glass from his hand. "That's it. Back to bed for you."

He shook his head, forced out, "Chores."

"You have a bunkhouse full of men who are perfectly capable of doing all the chores." She wrapped a hand around his arm. "Up you go. Back to bed."

The thought of lying down, if just for a few minutes, was so enticing Ellis didn't argue. She helped him up the back stairs, and it took all of his strength not to lean too heavily on her. His bed was like a beacon in a storm. He fell deeply into the mattress, groaning with both pain and relief. A brief moment of clarity entered his mind, telling him she was removing his boots and then his shirt, and that he was too weak to stop her or enjoy her assistance.

Fog, thick and heavy, floated over the thoughts, and something cool and damp covered his forehead. Relaxing into the mattress, Ellis welcomed the oblivion bearing down.

Dreams came, vivid and real. Christine round and plump as Angel grew to full-term in her belly, and the two of them greeting their tiny daughter for the first time. Other firsts came, too, Angel's first tooth, her first steps and her first pony. The visions grew dark then, turning into those he never wanted to recall. Christine in agony as the doctor worked to turn the baby. His wife and infant, cold and still in the pine box.

He fought, but the nightmares were uncontrollable, coming at him from all directions. Only an outside force—a steady, soft voice whispering in his ear—slowed their onslaught. When the voice left, the nightmares returned. And so it went until he begged the voice to stay. To never leave.

It assured him it wouldn't.

Dreamland overtook him again, and this time they were exciting, dazzling visions of two people sharing their lives, their love. They chased each other through the spring fields dotted with daisies, kissed each other and teased and kissed some more until they were rolling across a downy-soft bed with great abandonment, flesh on flesh, lips on lips. Her kisses and caresses were wild, taking as well as giving, leaving him gasping for air as an all-encompassing and burning desire built between them. He buried his hands in her long, black hair and his heart soared seeing the love glimmering in her blue eyes.

Panic-stricken, Ellis wrenched himself out of the dream so quickly it was a moment before he knew where he was. Who he was. The dream, so real he was swollen and hard, screaming for release, hadn't been him and Christine, but him and Constance.

Staring at the ceiling, watching the tiny shadows made by the flames in the fireplace, he sought betrayal, wanted to feel the painful ache of infidelity. Nothing came. The shadows above were too dim, too gentle. Needing something bold and feral to ignite the bitterness he sought, he turned to the window, wishing for the raging blizzard that had attacked with bitter winds earlier in the week.

The curtains were drawn, giving no solace to his body begging for the fulfillment the dream promised. He turned to where a picture sat atop the dresser. Light wasn't needed for him to see the image preserved forever in the photograph. Christine had been reluctant to have it taken, saying it was a foolish waste of money, though she'd been adamant about having several of Angel taken.

A cherished love spread across his chest. There were so many memories he treasured, would never forget no matter how many years separated them from the present.

Ellis begged the need throbbing in his veins to dissolve. The dream, the desires it left behind were interfering, overriding the void he'd come to trust in. As he lay there, with the intimate cravings storming, an indulgent perspective overtook him. It was as if someone had laid a patch over the hole inside him—the one left by Christine's death—like they would mend a tear in a canvas tent.

His throat swelled. "No," he whispered, never taking his eyes from the photograph. "I'm not through loving you."

The flames in the fireplace sputtered, as if caught by a gentle wind, and the shadows on the ceiling danced with renewed brilliance. He closed his eyes, knowing it was Christine and that she'd heard him.

The door opened, and he feigned sleep, not wanting anything to disturb the solace of Christine's intervention. When a hand, soft and gentle, touched his forehead, he damned his heart as it skipped every other beat.

"Thank heavens." Constance's whisper was so soft he barely heard it, but that didn't stop his body from reacting. It was a battle to keep his breathing low and slow with the way his blood, still heated from the dream, pulsed against his skin and the intensity in other areas increased to mammoth proportions.

The tinkle of water sounded and then a damp cloth floated over his forehead, barely touching, yet leaving the skin refreshed. "You had me scared," she whispered, and he strained to hear more. "I've lost too many loved ones, couldn't bear another."

The cloth brushed his cheeks next and his chin and neck. "But, I knew you'd survive," she continued. "You're so big and strong. Too powerful for something as mundane as a cold to get the best of you."

Her words and caress had his heart pounding, and her sweet, heady scent filling his nostrils heightened the already raging desires sweeping his body. He dug his hands into the bottom sheet when the cool cloth went lower, swiped across his chest and dipped toward his abdomen.

"You had me scared though. Very, very, scared." She ran the wet cloth from one side of his rib cage to the other.

He was about to snap, about to grab her hand, when the cloth stilled, sat on his stomach as she whispered, "What would we do without you?"

Fighting the urge to pull her down and kiss her was like battling the weather—useless in so many ways.

"There, now." She pulled the top sheet up to cover his chest and tucked it beneath his chin. "Sleep and heal."

Ellis, still trying to keep his breathing even, highly doubted sleep was in his near future, but remained prone. He did, however, lift one lid, watched as she stirred and banked the fire, but snapped the eye shut when she turned. Moments later, unprepared, his breath caught as her lips pressed tenderly upon his brow. "Tomorrow," she whispered, "you'll be as good as new. I promise."

He held his breath until his lungs burned, but still her lips lingered on his forehead. It happened then, just as he'd feared, his resolve snapped. The air in his chest left with a gush, and his hands, as uncontrollable as his breathing, caught her face. Like magnets, drawn to each other by natural pulls, their lips met, momentarily, sweetly, softly, then separated.

For a split second it was as if he was in limbo, wondering if the kiss had happened or not. Then a charge shot through him and their lips met again with an urgency he'd never experienced. His fingers dug into her hair, held her face against his as the kiss bestowed even more excitement than the dream had promised.

He couldn't get enough, and when he shifted, just wanting to slide his hands down her back, she escaped his hold.

Ellis shot up, stared at the door closing and searched for an ounce of sanity, but that too must have left him.

Constance tucked a clump of hair behind her ear and dumped another cup of flour into the bowl. Her eyes glanced first to the dwindling pile of black-skinned bananas and then to the back stairs. It had been an hour since she'd checked on Ellis. Several since his fever had broken.

She wrenched the spoon through the batter, forcing her hand to stop trembling and her mind to focus on what she was doing, not on what she'd done. It was only supposed to have been a soft peck on his forehead, and for the life of her she couldn't figure out how it had turned into a kiss that she'd never forget. It had to have been the fever. People did strange things while feverish. Ten minutes after the kiss, when she'd sent Angel in to check on him, he'd been sound asleep.

She stirred faster. At least he had an excuse. She didn't. She was as healthy as a horse—as the saying goes. His illness had come on fast, and his body had responded, spiking a fever that forced the sickness to run its course quickly, and she'd taken advantage of his feverish state.

He'd recover now that it had broken, and her only hope was that he'd have no recollection of the kiss, or how she'd sat by his side, whispering for him to relax, and wiping his brow with a damp cloth for a good portion of the day—long after he'd asked her not to leave and she'd promised she wouldn't.

Still stirring the batter, she plopped onto a chair. Here she was again, worrying about herself when it was him she should be concerned about. A fever was a good thing. If it hadn't come upon him, then she'd have had the right to be concerned. Neither Aunt Julia nor Aunt Theresa had had fevers prior to passing, which had been disconcerting. Running a temperature was the body's natural way of fighting.

"It smells wonderful in here. What are you making now?" The door swung on its hinges as Angel sauntered into the room.

"How's your father?" Constance asked.

"Still sleeping, just like he was when you sent me up there fifteen minutes ago." Angel stuck a finger in the bowl and twirled it deep in the batter. "Mmm." She licked her lips thoroughly before asking again, "What are you making this time?"

The kitchen smelled of bananas. For good reason. She was working as fast as she could, but still hadn't found a good use for all of the fruit. A platter of cookies sat on the open shelf of the pie cabinet beside a layered cake covered with boiled frosting, and a pan of what she considered to be banana cobbler baked in the oven. "I'm creating what I'm naming banana bread right now."

"Banana bread?" Angel asked from where she plucked a cookie off the platter.

"Yes." Constance used the spoon to point at the pile of bananas on the table. "These bananas will rot right there on the table if I don't figure out what to do with them." She was not about to let that happen. If she lived to be a hundred she'd remember the pride in Ellis's eyes when he pulled out that first banana. She wanted to see that pride again—when he told Link about the delicious things she'd made out of those "frozen" bananas.

Angel swallowed and held up the other half of the cookie. "These are good."

"Thank you, but they are a bit too soft and crumbling for cookies. Besides, we could never eat enough cookies, or cake, to use up all these bananas." The pantry had plenty of spare jars, but for the life of her she couldn't figure out how she'd go about canning bananas.

"Want me to try the cake? See how it tastes?"

"You can try the cake after supper." Using her spoon again, Constance waved it at the stove.

Angel bent down to sniff at the pie sitting there. "Pie? We're having pie for supper? Is it banana, too?"

"No, it's beef." Constance poured the batter from the bowl into two bread pans. There was also a small pan of broth, just in case Ellis did wake enough to eat something.

"Beef?" Angel asked.

"Yes." Her answer was automatic, while her mind was upstairs. Once the bread was in the oven, she'd check on Ellis herself. And this time, she promised, she wouldn't kiss him. Would not. No matter how hard her lips begged to touch his again.

"You don't make pies out of beef. You make pies out of berries or apples or pumpkin. I like pumpkin pie."

"In England we make pies out of lots of things besides fruits." Constance carried the bowl to the sink. Perhaps she should send Angel up to check on him again. That would be safer.

Angel peered closer at the pie. "Beef, uh?"

Constance walked over and kissed the top of Angel's head. Not only did she love the girl, she was very grateful for the distraction. Otherwise, Constance would already be in Ellis's room. "Yes, with carrots, potatoes and onions."

"Hmm, like stew between the crusts?"

"I suppose so. It needs to set for a few more minutes." Constance walked back to the table. "You can help me clean up."

Angel gathered things from the table, carrying an armload to the pantry. "Constance, how do you know how to make all these things? Did your aunts teach you?"

"Some. Some I learned from experimenting," she answered off-handedly. Her aunts had taught her many things, but nothing she could use right now. They'd known less about men than she did. Which totaled nil.

Angel picked up one of the bananas. "So what else are you going to make with bananas?"

"Well." Constance let out a sigh. "That has been my dilemma all day. I'm hoping this banana bread recipe works. If it does, I can bake the loaves, then wrap them and set them in a crate outside. It's cold enough that they'll freeze. That way we won't have to eat it all right now." She peered at the looming pile on the table. "If it doesn't work, we are going to be so tired of bananas we'll never want to see another one the rest of our lives."

"Do you think Pa will feel up to joining us for supper?"

"No." Constance drew a breath at the way her heart somersaulted. "I think he'll sleep right through until morning. Which will be best. By tomorrow, I'm sure he'll be fine and dandy."

Angel repeated, "Fine and dandy," with an exaggerated flair. "Oh, Constance, some of the things you say make me want to giggle." She wrapped her arms around Constance's waist.

Constance hugged her back. An eerie bout of fear tingled her spine. Her time was limited. Forgetting that, as she seemed to have done regularly, could cause more problems than kissing Ellis. She released Angel, asking, "How's your book coming?"

"I'm almost done, but..." Angel stepped away, sighing heavily.

"But what?"

"*Little Women* is such a wonderful story. I want to finish it. I want to know how it ends. But at the same time, I don't want to finish it, because then the story will be over." Her eyes grew somber. "Does that make sense?"

It made perfect sense. Actually, that was just how Constance felt about her time at the ranch. She never wanted it to end. "Yes," she agreed, yet didn't want to shadow Angel's joy. "But, don't fret. Your father's office is full of other wonderful books you'll enjoy just as much as this one."

Angel shook her head. "I don't know if there'll ever be another one to compare to this one."

Unable to meet Angel's inquisitive gaze, Constance moved to the sink. No matter where she went, where she lived, nowhere would compare to what she had right now. It was idiotic to become so infatuated with a place—and the people residing there—in such a short time, yet, she had. England had never really been home to her. And New York most certainly hadn't been. But here, it was as if she'd put down roots the minute she'd arrived. Part of her said it was because of the people, which only made it worse. Angel didn't need that much schooling, and once that was completed, the people here wouldn't need her services, for she truly had nothing else to offer them.

Stiffness cracked and popped in his joints as Ellis stretched and flipped around. No water basin sat beside his bed. There was no cloth. Had he dreamt it all?

No, he'd been sick, clearly recalled feeling it come on as he rode home. He brushed the back of his hand to his nose. The constant drip was gone. The tightening and sting in his throat had left as well.

Only a few embers glowed in the hearth, and sunlight, though hazy, penetrated the window and brightened the room.

He tossed aside the covers and went to the window. Due to the fog, it was hard to tell what time it was. Pausing near the bed, he drank from the glass of water sitting on the table, swishing his mouth well before swallowing. At least the illness had left as quickly as it had arrived.

His gaze went to Christine's picture. A light, optimistic sensation washed over him. "It *was* all a dream," he whispered. "Just a dream." A soaking is what he needed, a good washing to refresh his body and mind.

With a full set of clean clothes draped over one arm and his shaving gear in the other hand, he left his room for the back stairway. A wondrous scent filled the air. His stomach reacted, grumbling like a miner seeing gold.

If waking up with no after effects of his illness hadn't been enough, a wave of homecoming—that of cheerful giggles floating up the stairway—had his chest welling with satisfaction.

"Hey, Pa," Angel greeted as he stepped off the final stair. "How you feeling?"

A spoon hit the floor, clattering as it bounced. Constance, with her long hair twirling to catch up, spun from the table. "El— Mr. Clayton, you're up."

For a moment he couldn't pull his gaze from her. She was a remarkably beautiful woman. The gown melded to her curves was the same sky blue as her eyes, and more fashionable than anything

Link sold. Not even the flour sack tied around her waist lessened the stunning picture she made. Her cheeks were bright pink, and the smile she flashed his way before she bent to retrieve the spoon made him think of springtime and a field of daisies.

"Yes, I'm up," he assured. "And I feel fine."

"Sit down," Constance said. "I'll get you something to eat."

His stomach growled, but he ignored it, and hoisting his arm covered with clothes, he explained, "I thought I'd take a bath first. I feel a bit grizzly." Fire burned his ears. Grizzly? Daisies? Maybe he'd been sicker than he thought. Why else would his mind be flapping around like it didn't have the sense God gave a duck.

"I have two pots of water heating for dishes. You can start with those while I heat more," Constance offered, already rushing toward the door under the back staircase that led to the small bathing chamber. "Sit down, and I'll get everything ready."

He stepped into her path. A hint of a memory flashed in his mind, drawing his eyes to her lips as if he knew how they felt, or wanted to. He blinked, clearing his mind of a vision that most certainly had been a dream. "No, I can do it."

She let out a sigh, making him wonder if she'd been holding her breath. "Nonsense, you've been ill. Now go sit down. I'll get the bath ready."

Her practical attitude had surprised him from

the beginning. Though she looked like a lady, with the delicate cameo pinned near her throat and her graceful posture, her sensibility and straightforward approach said she wasn't used to others doting on her. Which was sad. Every woman deserved to be taken care of. He side-stepped at the same time she did and took his clothes back. "I'll do it. You sit down. It looks like you could use a rest."

Her hands flew to her face. She wiped her pink cheeks and then smoothed tendrils of ebony hair behind each ear.

He could have kicked himself. Accepting the urge filling his chest, he trailed a knuckle along one perfectly formed cheekbone. The skin was downy soft, and enticed his touch to linger. "You look fine," he whispered. "I was referring to the kitchen."

A wispy gasp escaped her slightly parted lips, and then she twisted her neck, giving him the view of her stunning profile as she peered over her shoulder at the array of baked goods covering the counters and cupboards.

"Are we having a party?"

Her blush deepened. "No. I—I didn't want the bananas to go bad."

"I'd forgotten about those," he said as his hand slid to her slender shoulder. "I wondered if half the town hadn't showed up again while I slept."

Though the words were meant to tease her, they sent a ball of fire through him.

She trembled beneath his touch, as if she feared more visitors as deeply as he loathed the thought. He squeezed her shoulder. "It smells wonderful. I can't wait to sample the fare."

Slow and thoughtful, she turned back his way. Looking into her eyes was like gazing into a mountain lake, where the clarity allowed one to see deep beneath the surface, yet not all the way down to discover the secret treasures that lay buried below. He couldn't stop himself from staring, wondering what her secrets were, and wishing he had the right to ask.

Too quickly, she dipped her chin, lowering her gaze to the floor. "I'll get the water for you."

The bones beneath his fingers felt as fragile as a sparrow's wing. "I can haul my own water. You go back to your baking."

As if she were a small bird, she flitted away, leaving an empty space where she'd stood and a tiny one inside him. Ellis turned, frowning at the knowledge Constance affected him more than he would like—and had since she'd stepped off the stage. The memory of when she'd come to his office, to offer a solution, appeared then. He hadn't mailed the letter to Eli yet, but would, as soon as he took his bath. Perhaps she still had family; someone who'd survived the war but didn't know how to contact her. That would solve all their problems.

In no time the bath was full of steaming water. He closed the door to the washroom, and stripped down. The commotion brought about since her arrival had left him with little time to focus on anything else. That must be what triggered his insides. Women evoked protectiveness in men, and he was no different. Constance needed someone to look out for her. Comparing her to a little bird was accurate—a tiny blue bird, alone and lost in the vast open range of the Territory.

He cupped his hands and splashed water on his face in an attempt to chase away the image. Next he grabbed the stool holding his shaving utensils and pulled it closer. The tasks consumed him, held his attention as he scraped away the whiskers and then scrubbed from head to toe. But his ears practically heard the charming tweets of an elusive blue bird.

Cleanliness was rejuvenating. Donning fresh clothes, he straightened up the room and exited, ready to face whatever lay before him. He oversaw thousands of cattle and dozens of men. How much trouble could one little bird be?

His stomach grumbled again, so while walking past the cupboard he picked up a cookie. Flavorful and moist, it melted in his mouth. He took another before moving to the table.

"Good, aren't they?" Angel asked as he finished the first one.

"Yes," he agreed before biting into the second one.

"Wait until you taste the bread," she said, grinning from ear to ear.

The word *bread* sparked a tiny little light inside him. Fighting the urge to catch sight of Constance, he kept his gaze on his daughter. Her blond curls were smoothed away from her face and tied on the top of her head with a neat bow. The style was very becoming. She had on a dress he'd seen before, but it looked nicer. A closer inspection attested it had been neatly pressed. A smile tugged at his lips. Little things he hadn't noticed before now corroborated: Angel did need the influence of a woman. He planted a kiss on the top of her head and sat at the table.

A cup of coffee as well as a plate of scrambled eggs was set before him. He brought his tumbling mind to a halt and nodded toward Constance. "Thanks, this looks good."

She slid another plate across the table. It held a few slices of dark bread. "I'm sure you're hungry," she said, fluttering away before he could catch her gaze.

Eyeing the bread, he wondered if she'd been up baking half the night, and wished he'd joined her. He took a piece and popped it in his mouth; a savory burst of sweetness teased his taste buds.

The back door flew open with a clatter. Beans, thrusting his way over the threshold, waving a long spoon with one hand, carried the expression of a badger on his whiskered face. "What the Hell's the meaning of this?" the cook shouted, pointing the spoon at Constance.

"Beans!" Ellis shot to his feet, admonishing the man with a harsh glare. No man, no matter whether he'd worked here for years or not, had the right to approach his family with hostility.

The man bowed his head, accepting the reprimand, but Angel, like a mother hen defending her chicks, flew across the room to stand in front of Constance.

The shock of the startling entrance lessened, and knowing neither was in danger—Beans was all bark and no bite—Ellis watched as Constance gently set Angel aside. She then walked past Beans and calmly closed the door. When she turned about, a tender smile graced her lips.

"What seems to be the matter, M— Beans?" she asked soothingly.

Ellis bit the inside of his lip. If he'd learned one thing about women from his marriage, it was when to step into an argument and when to watch. Right now, he witnessed the gruff old Beans melt like a chunk of ice in the April sunlight.

"I—I—I—" Beans stuttered. He lifted a chin covered in more whiskers than Rip Van Winkle had, and held out his other hand. "This."

"You don't like the banana bread?" Constance asked, reaching for the crumpled piece of bread.

Beans pulled his hand back before she took the food. "I don't mind you cooking for Ellis and Angel, they need good food, but—" the cook turned to Ellis "—sending something this tasty out to the bunkhouse could start an uprising."

Ellis grinned and gave an affable nod as he sat back down at the table. "It's mighty tasty, I'll give you that." He amplified the statement by taking another bite of his banana bread.

"Too tasty if you ask me." Beans ate the piece in his hand. "The men are asking why I can't make something that tastes like this."

Constance pulled a chair away from the table, indicating with a gracious nod for Beans to sit down. As if she expected his company, she handed him a cup of coffee as soon as he settled on the chair.

"I'm sorry, Beans," she started. "I didn't intend to have the men question your fine cooking abilities. I simply made more banana bread than the three of us can eat. I thought the men in the bunkhouse might enjoy some." She set a plate of the bread, with several slices precut, within reaching distance of Beans. "I promise not to do it again."

Beans set his spoon down and took another piece of bread. Something very close to affection sparkled in the man's eyes. "Maybe you could just warn me first," he said, devouring the slice in one bite.

Pondering the gaze, since Beans rarely showed warmth of any kind, Ellis glanced beyond the old man's head. The scrambled eggs setting on his tongue stuck there as he caught the shine in Constance's eyes. Her smile was smug, not conceited nor arrogant, but humble and content in the fact she'd calmed Beans's rant so effectively. It wavered as she found his stare.

His approval was easy to give. Ellis winked one eye and then bowed his head, returning to his meal. A wave rolled inside his chest, not unlike a strong gust of wind. She was no little bird. Constance Jennings had a backbone and knew how to use it perfectly. But then, he'd already seen that in the way she handled the house of men seeking her hand. Ellis forked eggs in his mouth, but discovered his last thought had stolen his hunger.

"You gonna teach me how to make this?" Beans sliced another strip from the loaf since he'd already consumed the other three pieces.

Constance drew in a deep breath. The storm of Beans was nothing compared to the flipping and flopping going on in her chest. When Ellis had first descended the stairs, she'd feared he'd remember their kiss, and then her heart threatened to burst when he'd touched her cheek, but the flurry of activity caused by his wink had her reeling as if she'd just run a good three miles—uphill.

"Well, are you?" Beans repeated.

Snapping her attention back to the cook, she offered, "I most certainly can give you the recipe, but I'm afraid I only have enough bananas for a few more loaves."

"What are bananas anyway? I've never heard of them."

Angel stepped in then—bless her heart—handing Beans one of the deteriorating bananas. The girl set in telling the cook all about Ellis's purchase and how they'd been cooking up experiments ever since he'd brought the bags home. Constance, thankful for a moment to gather her wits, moved to the sink, where she'd been rinsing out the pans for the next batch she planned on making as soon as Ellis finished his meal. She'd baked long after the sun went down yesterday and started again as soon as it rose this morning. When Thomas had entered the house to set the morning fires, she'd recommended he take a few loaves to the bunkhouse, never imagining Beans would be so upset by her actions.

Then again, she'd never anticipated she'd be so affected by Ellis's actions, either. She gripped the edge of the sink. Goodness, it appeared she had a lifetime of learning to do in a very short time.

The rapid beats of her heart had yet to slow, and her fingers trembled so hard she didn't dare pick up a dish for fear of dropping it.

The conversation around the table soon included the timbre of Ellis's voice, and somehow the sound had a calming effect. Her pulse slowed and, drawing on the relief, she set about her chores. When the dishes were done, including Ellis's plate that Angel had carried over, Constance moved to the washroom beneath the back staircase. The space was surprisingly large and not only held the large brass bathing tub, it also hosted two wooden washtubs. A thin rope had been stretched from one wall to the other, creating the ideal setup for winter clothes washing. The amenities of the house had amazed her at first, but as time went on, the thoughtful and careful planning had given her appreciation for those who had constructed it.

Ellis had tidied up after bathing, all she needed to do was hang the towel a bit straighter and reposition the stool along the wall. Still feeling the urge to stay busy while the men talked, she slipped from the room and glided up the back stairs.

She'd stripped his bed and was tucking the edges of clean sheets beneath the down mattress when her nerve endings tapped. Smoothing the sheet, she turned to the open doorway. Once again, Ellis's gaze had her pondering how deeply he could see into her soul. For that's where her thoughts were—remembering the kiss. Their kiss.

Her heart landed in her throat as he moved into the room and picked up the quilt she'd set on the chair before removing the sheets from his bed.

"I thought—" She paused for a moment to get control of her thick tongue. "Your bedding needed to be changed after the fever."

Without answering he flayed the quilt across the bed from the other side. She caught the edge and together they tucked in the bottom and smoothed out the top. It was a thick patchwork covering made of dark browns and deep reds. Her fingers caressed the squares, feeling the cords of the twills and the softness of the flannels as her mind and heart tumbled. She'd jeopardized her chances of staying here with a foolish, impulsive act.

"I hadn't realized I slept almost two days until Beans informed me," Ellis said.

Jarred to attention, she nodded. "You needed it. That's how the body heals." Having already replaced the covers on the pillows, she retrieved them and positioned each one across the top of the bed. Fearful of the silence, she added, "But it wasn't quite two days. It's only a little after noon now."

"I slept all day yesterday and half of today," he disputed.

The mockery in his tone had her glancing up.

A smile sat on his lips. It was a delightful sight—had her heart dancing against her rib cage.

"That's two days," he explained.

The urge to smile had her bowing her head. It was rather remarkable how he made her see the humor in situations. Almost as if he found joy in the simple things in life and wanted others to, too. She gave her head a quick shake. "I suppose you could say it was two days."

"You suppose?"

"I suppose." She gathered the heap of sheets off the floor and escaped to the door.

"Constance."

Her feet stalled near the room's entrance. The wood beneath her boots was smooth, and the thick shimmering varnish kept her eyes busy. "Yes?" she answered without turning around.

"I— Could we talk for a few minutes? I have something to tell you."

Like a nightmare in the depths of sleep, the image of the envelope on his office desk leaped before her eyes. She closed her eyelids, as if that could make it disappear. He not only had a reason to send her away, he had a destination. "Certainly," she agreed. "I just have to put these sheets downstairs."

"In my office then? In five minutes or so?"

She nodded and left the room before the nightmare had her afraid to move. By the time she'd disposed of the bedding and taken a moment to smooth the hair from her face, she was in no better condition. Beads of sweat covered her palms. Wiping her hands on her skirt, she willed all of the reasoning she'd gone over a hundred times to come forth so she'd have the wherewithal to convince Ellis he must fulfill his end of their bargain. Of course she'd come up with all of those reasons before he'd taken ill. She couldn't tell him about Byron, either, not after that kiss.

A sneak peek proved Angel was nose-down in a book in the front parlor. Back straight, namely due to the nerves twisted around her spine, Constance treaded down the hall and tapped on the office door.

It opened immediately. Without a word, Ellis waved a hand, indicating the empty chairs. She'd boarded a ship to sail across the ocean with less trepidation than what ate at her insides right now. A sea squall had been less threatening than leaving—or being sent away.

The first place her eyes went was to the desk top. No envelope decorated the space. It had been there this morning. She'd poked her head in while Thomas was building the fire. Her arrival at the closest chair was timely, for her legs no longer wanted to hold her upright. Sitting down, she was thankful her spine didn't give out. Back stiff against the chair, she folded her hands in her lap, and drew Angel's welfare forward in her mind.

Ellis sat behind his desk, the mantel clock ticking away reminded her of another night when they'd sat as such. She'd grown since then. In the few days since her arrival she'd had the time to contemplate her wants instead of her survival. That hadn't happened since burying her aunts. Perhaps before then even.

"The banana bread is very good." Ellis broke the deafening silence.

"Thank you," she responded, holding her breath at the way her heart skipped a beat.

"Angel said you're going to set it outside to freeze."

Ellis was not one for small talk, he had proven that before, but she was more than agreeable to avoid other topics. "I hope that will preserve it, so we don't have to eat it all at once."

"I have an old ice box in the spring house. I'll bring it up to the porch. That should keep the bread safe from anything that comes sniffing around."

His approval of her plan touched her more than surprised her. "Oh, I hadn't thought of that. Thank you."

"That bread—it was good thinking on your part. A good way to use up those bananas."

There was pride in his voice, just as she'd wanted. Excitement chased away a portion of her anxiety, but increased the other—more intense—sensations swirling in her veins. "Yes, well, I still have a few more batches to make. The bananas are aging quickly."

The sparkle in his eyes was enchanting, making her want to smile in return. "I think they were reasonably aged when I bought them," he said.

She nodded, attempting to hide her grin. "I believe so."

His chair creaked as he leaned back and folded his arms behind his head. "I'm going to enjoy telling Link how tasty they were."

Her heart soared. "You will?"

"Oh, yes." He leaned forward, placing both elbows on his desk. "I'm also grateful for the difference I'm seeing in Angel. I noticed she's in the parlor, reading." His brows lifted.

"Little Women," Constance answered.

He shook his head. "Can't say I've read that one."

"I wouldn't imagine you have." The thought of him reading the tale about the March girls brought her smile out. "But I assure you, I have, and it's quite appropriate for Angel to be reading."

"I'm sure it is. I don't imagine you'd allow her to read something that wasn't appropriate."

She met his stare, wondering if there was more behind his words.

"I mean that truthfully, Constance. I have no

doubt you only have the best intentions for Angel at heart."

Pride, once again instilled by him, wafted over her chest. "Thank you. I appreciate your confidence. Angel is a delightful girl, and a joy to tutor."

"I've also noticed the improvements in her appearance. You've done a remarkable job in a very short time."

"She's an apt student," Constance insisted.

"The manners may take a while. I hope you won't get discouraged."

The smirk on his face said he knew how trying his daughter was, as well as how much he loved Angel's independence. "I won't, but you're right, it may take a while." They shared a laugh, just a small one, but subtle enough to have her heartbeat increasing. "She really is a good person at heart," Constance assured.

"I agree with you." Ellis reached to the edge of his desk and pulled a piece of paper forward. "I'm glad you came along when you did. I may have been a bit hesitant a few days ago, but I've already seen the difference you're making, so I'd like to confirm our agreement."

"You would?" The words were out before she could stop them.

"You sound surprised."

Her insides were snapping like grease on a griddle. Before her was evidence that snooping was ill-fated. Rarely did it turn out to be beneficial. The envelope that had been on his desk must have had nothing to do with her, and yet, she'd anticipated it did, and therefore caused herself nothing but grief. The bout of imprudent imagination now left her feeling foolish. Furthermore, her fears over him recalling her sitting beside his bed had been foolish as well. He clearly had no recollection of the kiss, which should increase her relief. But in an odd way, she was disappointed. She'd thought of little else, even dreamed of it last night. Chasing aside the thought as best she could, she answered, "Not necessarily surprised, but relieved perhaps."

He rubbed a finger over his chin as if pondering deeply. Her insides ticked along with the clock, and she had to bite her lip to keep it from tingling with memories.

"Relieved?" he asked. "How so?"

The truth was out before she could contemplate it. "Because there truly is no place I'd rather spend the next six months than right here."

His features grew soft and mellow, sending her insides into a frenzy, and making her words echo through her head. "Mr. Clayton," she started, searching for a way to clarify her answer. It was the truth, but sounded so forward. So revealing.

"Constance," Ellis interrupted. Her answer had his pulse racing, and the blush on her cheeks had him wanting to move out of his chair and fold his arms around her. She pinched her lips together, which had an unsettling effect on his. Once again they acted as if the kiss hadn't been a dream. "If we're going to be living together for the next six months," he said, thankful his mind still worked, "I'd appreciate if you called me Ellis."

She pressed a hand to her stomach, and bowed her head.

He'd called her in to his office to tell her about the will Hempel had, but the thought of her moving out to Ashton's was nauseating. She'd be in too much danger. There were simply too many things that could go wrong. "Angel," he said, drawing his daughter's needs forward was his saving grace. "Angel is used to a less formal environment, and we must both do everything we can to aid her education. Don't you agree?"

"Yes, of course."

"Ellis," he added, wanting to hear her say his name.

"Ellis," she repeated.

It was ridiculous for a grown man to experience such joy from someone simply saying his name, Ellis knew that. Yet the wave rippling over him was like nothing he'd ever known. More so, it gave him an excitement for the future he hadn't had for years. Her cobalt-blue eyes met his, and the glimmer in them increased his enthusiasm for life tenfold. Sent his heart somersaulting, and other parts of his body heating up.

Her cheeks grew rosier, but she didn't pull her gaze away. Neither did he. The world seemed to go quiet; he heard nothing but the soft sound of her breathing and the thudding of his heart pulsing against his eardrums. It hadn't been a dream. He'd felt those lips on his, tasted their sweetness. And he wanted to do so again.

She gasped slightly, he heard it, and it made him pull his eyes from hers. Catching his breath was difficult. When he finally did, he picked up the piece of paper in front of him. "I—ah—I came up with an amount I hope you'll agree is fair."

The paper fluttered as she took it. "That's more than agreeable." She sounded as breathless as he felt.

"I left the time span open. Hard to say how long it'll take—teaching Angel manners."

She chewed on her bottom lip, which merely increased the thudding in his chest. When the silence lasted as long as he could take, he asked, "Do you have anything you want to add?"

She shook her head. "Would you pass me the ink," she asked as she set the paper down, "so I can sign it?"

Mind whirling, Ellis flexed his fingers before reaching for the inkwell. He had to tell her about Ashton's will before she signed the agreement. It was only fair. Perhaps it all could wait until tomorrow, when his thinking was clearer. Right now he couldn't distinguish between dreams and reality. Whether that was true or not, never before had he withheld information from someone, especially not information that could hold a bearing on their decision-making. It was as if he were becoming a different person. Still Ellis Clayton, ranch owner, father, widower. The shiver rippling him from head to toe had him leaping to his feet.

"There's no need to sign it." Moving toward the door, he added, "I have to get out to the barn."

Chapter Nine

Ellis brushed the snow from his coat sleeves and stomped his boots before entering the house. The welcoming heat of the kitchen was a wonderful reprieve from the blizzard once again blanketing the ground. In the three weeks Constance had been at the ranch, it had snowed almost continuously. He pulled his hat from his head, and his heart started to drum as he wondered when he'd started marking time by her arrival. Seems lately everything he referred to was either before Constance arrived or after.

"Here, I'll take that," she said, holding her hand out. "You take your stuff off." She frowned at the snow caked around his ankles. "Or do you have to go back out?"

"Thanks." He gave her the hat, watching as she spun to hang it on one of the hooks beside the closed door. Her breasts strained against the material of her dress, and the chill the weather had instilled in his loins was instantly replaced by a bolt of heat. "No, I don't have to go back out. What can be done in weather like this is done."

She took his coat as he shrugged out of it, hanging it beside his hat while he sat down on the chair below the hooks to remove his boots, focusing his gaze on the rug that had been placed under the chair to catch the water that formed as the snow melted.

Graceful as always, she moved from his side, walking to the stove where the coffeepot perked merrily. He couldn't help but wonder, in moments like this, how things had been before she'd come to live here. He and Angel had gotten along fine, never missing the little things like rugs and coffee already made.

There was always a pot brewing in the bunkhouse, and he'd consumed gallons of the black brew over the years, but now he didn't. When the chores were done, he headed straight for the house, knowing Constance would have some of her delicious coffee ready, along with a cookie or other such treat to warm his insides.

The routine had started the day she'd read their contract, legally binding her to stay at the ranch for the next six months. Maybe that was when he'd started counting the days, for it certainly had been when his mind had started badgering him for not telling her about Ashton's will. Could it be guilt sending his pulse racing?

One boot hit the rug with a thud, and Constance glanced his way. He stood the boots side by side, and brushed at the snow still clinging to his pant legs. She turned back to the stove and his mind took off again. That had been the reason he'd called her into his office that day—to tell her about her inheritance. But it hadn't happened. And in the weeks that followed, it still hadn't.

It wasn't that he didn't believe she had the right to know, he knew she did, but truth be told, he didn't want her to leave. That, he told himself, trying to justify his thoughts, would break his daughter's heart.

"Where's Angel?" he asked, moving from the chair to the table.

"Where do you think Angel is?" Constance grinned, setting a plate holding a piece of chocolate cake on the table.

His blood was racing again, sent that way by her smile, or the way strands of hair fell from her bun, or just about anything else about her. "Reading?" he asked teasingly, while taking a seat.

"Yes." She set a steaming mug of coffee in front of him. "Reading."

A repartee had developed between them, a teasing banter of sorts, that he enjoyed and looked forward to each morning; the want to touch her, just brush his skin against hers, grew stronger every day. Every hour. Today, right now, it was too intense to ignore, and he caught her hand as it slipped off the mug. The warmth of her palm closed around his chilly fingers. Not willing to admit why he felt the need to touch her, yet not willing to let her go, he focused on their conversation. "*Little Women* again?"

Her eyes flitted from their hands to his face. "No, I think three times was enough. Today she's reading *Around the World in Eighty Days*." A smile brightened her face. "For the second time."

There were times, like right now, when he pulled forth in his memory the days he was ill, wondering all over again if they had really kissed. She acted as if they hadn't, yet he no longer believed it had been a dream. With regret, he let her hand loose. "Angel does know we have a full library?"

"She claims she gets more out of a story the second time around." Constance walked across the room and gathered a rag to wipe the snow he'd left upon entering. "Perhaps," she said, kneeling in front of the door, "you'd like to read the report she writes on this one."

The familiarity of her simple actions awed him. They'd grown companionable over the past weeks, conversing as they'd gone about their individual tasks. She often dusted his office while he worked on ledgers, and they talked then, too. About nothing ever too serious, and it often was him that left the room, escaping before he had to think too deeply about the effect she had on him. It was here again now, this heated stirring inside him whenever she was near. "I will," he answered. "Tell me when she's done, and I'll grade it."

"Oh, and what gives you the authority to hand out book report grades?" she asked teasingly.

The heat inside him picked up a notch. Instilled an urge to cross the room and pick her off the floor by wrapping both hands around her slender waist. He clenched the coffee mug beneath his fingers. "I'm her father."

Constance stood slowly, and the coy smile on her lips made her entire face glow. "Oh, and that's enough?" Keeping one eye on him she moved to the sink. "Have you read *Around the World in Eighty Days*?"

"One doesn't need to read the book to recognize a good book report." He finished his sentence by poking a forkful of cake in his mouth.

The gleam in her eyes could charm a snake as she challenged, "How would you know if her assumptions are correct?"

She had the uncanny ability to make the simplest conversations stimulating, and today, right now, her teasing had him wound tighter than a cheap clock. He pushed away from the table at the same time she left the sink. They met in the middle of the room. Eye to eye, nose to chin. Something flashed deep in the depths of her sparkling blue eyes. Excitement? Desire? The thrill of that hit him dead center.

"I've read the book."

"Have you?" she asked softly.

"Yes. Have you?"

"Of course." Her breath tickled his chin and made his lips quiver with anticipation.

It was like playing with fire. Dangerous. Challenging. Exhilarating. "Then," he said, working hard to keep the topic foremost in his mind, "we shall both read the report, and compare notes." His gaze slipped to how her breasts gently rose and fell with each breath, making him think of other things he'd like to compare. Like how perfectly the round mounds would fill his hands.

"Compare notes?"

He tugged his eyes upward to meet blue ones that had gone from sparkling to smoldering. A bolt of heat shot into his loins, but it was the tip of her tongue wetting her bottom lip that drew him forward.

"Yes," he whispered, lowering his face. "Compare notes." Her sweet breath flowed between his lips, entering his mouth with tender, sensitive heat that made his lungs expand, begging for more. The time had come. The urge to kiss her had been with him for weeks. Only a fool would fight it any longer.

The softness of her lips was delicate and fragile, making him wonder what they were made of. Their honey-dipped taste had him pressing his lips to them a second time. This time he tilted his head sideways, to fully engulf her mouth and experience the full effect. It was like dancing with an angel, completely impossible, yet the ultimate accomplishment.

Her fingertips clutched onto his shoulders, as if she needed him to brace her stance. Pleased—he wanted her to need him as he'd grown to need her lately—he spanned her waist with both hands and brought the firmness of her hips against his thighs.

Some things in life shouldn't be pondered, but merely experienced, and this—kissing Constance—was one of them. Finding the gracious curve at the small of her back, he secured the connection of their lower bodies as she cupped his lower jaw with one hand. The tiny fear that she'd reject his advance, or perhaps his own reluctance holding him in check, dissolved as their kiss deepened.

He never thought it possible, to feel this deeply, to want an embrace to last for hours upon hours. There was more, he knew that, as did his throbbing body, but right now, just holding her, kissing her, was heavenly.

"Constance!" Angel's voice, though muffled by the door, had his eyelids flying open. The startled expression on Constance's face was so adorable the urge to kiss her one more time almost won out.

She pushed at his chest as her cheeks turned bright red. He took a step backward, and let his hands slip off her hips. She immediately turned about face. Her shoulders heaved as she drew in short, fast breaths. The desire to grab her and tug her back into his arms made him clench his hands into fists when the door flew open.

"Oh, hey, Pa," Angel greeted.

"Hey," he croaked while walking to the table— as stiff-legged as a British solider. "How's the book reading coming?"

"Good. You ever read *Around the World in Eighty Days*?" Angel asked, stopping near the table.

"Yes, I have." He picked up his fork, but the chocolate cake had lost its appeal. "So," he asked his daughter, "what were you yelling about?"

Angel twirled to face Constance, who'd busied herself at the stove. "I was wondering how long it took you to get from London to New York."

Constance carried the coffeepot to the table, and Ellis was amazed. Not only by how easily she crossed the room—his loins were still throbbing to the point that sitting was difficult—but by how innocent she appeared. Other than a slight tinge of pink on her cheeks, there was no indication she'd been in his arms moments before.

"Oh, why?" Constance asked, refilling his cup.

Why had she been in his arms? Because he'd lost control, could no longer fight the desire that ate at him night and day. He'd known what he was doing, yet at the same time, it had been as though he was someone else, watching the scene from afar.

"Just fact checking," Angel replied.

"The book is a novel, a work of fiction," Constance said, carrying the pot back to the stove. Ellis found it impossible to keep his eyes off her backside and his hands from tingling, wanting to cup one particular cheek again.

"I know." Angel pulled out a chair and sat. "But don't you think the author needed to make it as real as possible, so people would believe it?"

Ellis waited for Constance to answer. For some reason he wondered if she knew what they shared was real, understood the underlying sizzle of the air whenever they were in the room together. Surely the embrace moments ago had had some effect on her.

"What do you think?" Constance reiterated while slicing another piece of cake.

"I think he'd have to. The story wouldn't be as interesting if it didn't seem possible." Angel turned to him. "Don't you think, Pa?"

His mouth was full, thankfully. He gave an

agreeable nod, and chewed. Possibilities certainly made things more interesting. Constance had yet to meet his gaze. Was it possible she was afraid? Didn't want him to know just how deeply the kiss had moved her?

Constance set the cake, along with a glass of milk, in front of Angel, and then she pulled out the chair on the other end of the table. "Actually," she started. "The story was first published as a serial in a very popular publication, and therefore, some people thought Mr. Fogg was real and his journey was actually taking place."

"Really?" Angel asked, frowning.

Ellis still watched Constance, wanting to see a reaction to their earlier action.

"Yes. It was the topic of conversations everywhere, whether he'd make it in time or not," Constance said. "It was also said that railroads and ship lines contacted Mr. Verne, the author, requesting Mr. Fogg and his valet, Mr. Passepartout, travel exclusively on their lines."

Was kissing him so unmoving a novel held more interest?

"They thought it was really happening, too?" Angel asked.

"Yes," Constance assured. "My Aunt Julia was quite taken by the adventure, and gave us an update every day during afternoon tea."

The tiny bit of English accent she still carried

came through loud and clear as she spoke. Ellis couldn't help the chuckle it evoked. Constance glanced up, and the soft blush upon her cheeks made him want to kiss her again. And again.

"I wish I could have met your aunts. They sound so wonderful," Angel said.

"I wish you could have met them, too." Constance patted Angel's arm. "They were delightful, and would have loved you."

Angel remained quiet for a moment before she said, "I bet you miss them a lot, and wish they hadn't died."

Ellis took a sip of coffee, waiting for Constance's answer. His mind had circled about, made him wonder what she wished. Did she still want to be in England?

"Yes, I do miss them," Constance admitted. "But it was time for me to leave England." She flicked the end of Angel's nose with the tip of one finger. "If I hadn't, I would have never met you."

"Or Pa," Angel added.

Constance grew thoughtful, and Ellis's heart quickened. He pressed his heels into the floor, bracing for her reply.

"Or your pa," she answered shyly, but the way her eyes settled on him shouted the words into his heart.

"And that would have been awful." Angel let out a silly snicker.

Simultaneously, he and Constance turned to look at her. The humor emitting from his daughter was contagious.

"Yes," he agreed, chuckling. "Awful."

"Downright dreadful," Constance added with that lifting giggle that had his insides flipping again.

That evening as they sat in the parlor, books in hands, the only sounds were the snapping of the fire and the wind as it knocked every now and again against the window. It wasn't all that different from any other night they'd shared over the past few weeks. They gathered here each evening, sometimes playing cards, or discussing Angel's studies, or simply talking, sharing stories or even gossip from town. It was Constance's favorite time of the day—prior to this afternoon.

Tonight Ellis held a thick book whose title she couldn't make out from where she sat next to Angel who was devouring the last few pages of *Around the World in Eighty Days* with renewed force. The book in Constance's hand was unimportant. Her mind wasn't interested in reading. The memory of the kiss she and Ellis had shared in the kitchen had consumed her all afternoon, but now, in the quiet, cozy time of evening, the actions played out so vividly she could almost feel his lips again. The after-effects, both on her insides and in the air when she'd catch Ellis looking at her, seemed almost magical.

She sighed, and let her eyelids close. Kissing wasn't new, Byron had kissed her. Not a lot, but then again, they'd only been married two days before he left England. Her brows tugged tight. His lips had always been hard and his movements harsh. The frown on her brows relaxed. Whereas Ellis's had been gentle and... She sighed again. Amorous. That's what his lips had been. The kind of kiss written about in books, the kind girls dreamed about.

She'd dreamed about kisses lately, almost every night. The past few weeks she'd felt an energy inside her every time Ellis was in the same room, it was as though an invisible rope stretched between them and kept trying to pull her closer. It left her pondering little else except him.

Prior to coming here, she'd never dreamed of kisses. Taking care of Julia and Theresa had been too consuming to think about such things. Besides, neither of her aunts had held very high opinions of men. They assured her an unmarried woman was by far better off than a married one. Perhaps that was part of the reason she'd never taken their dislike of Byron too serious. They hadn't been rude to him, nor refused her to see him, but they'd warned her to be wary. In all actuality, if the poor dears hadn't died, she'd never have married him.

Angel's earlier question slipped forward. Constance was sorry her aunts had died, and she did miss them, but she'd spoken the truth: if they hadn't died she'd never have met Ellis and Angel. A long, appreciative, contented sigh escaped her lungs.

An obvious throat clearing had her opening one eye, directing it at Angel.

A petulant expression sat upon the girl's face as she glanced from Constance to the book she held.

"Sorry," Constance mouthed.

As Angel turned back to her book, Ellis set his on the table with a thud. "If our company is disturbing you, perhaps you'd like to read in your room."

"No, you're fine," Angel replied, never lifting an eye.

Constance bit her lip. Sometimes she couldn't help but laugh at Angel's conduct, while other times she cringed. Ellis's gaze was on her, had her senses peaked. Biting her bottom lip, she chanced a glance his way.

Humor danced in his eyes. "Angel," he said expectantly.

The girl let out an exaggerated sigh. "I only have five pages left."

"You've read it before," he stated.

"So?"

Constance was going to giggle. She shouldn't, but for whatever reason, the happiness filling her heart wanted out. Not willing to do it in front of the others, she stood and carrying her book, walked toward the doorway.

"Where are you going?" father and daughter asked simultaneously.

Without turning around, she told them, "I have things to see to. Enjoy your books."

The fit of giggles contained themselves until she entered Ellis's office. Muffling the sounds by keeping her lips tight, she crossed the room and stuffed the etiquette book on the shelf with the half dozen others.

"Coward."

She spun about. Ellis leaned against the door frame, arms folded across his chest. It was there again, that invisible rope tugging her toward him, stronger than ever. "Why do you say that?"

He grinned, but it was his eyes that held her attention. "As her tutor, shouldn't you have reprimanded her?"

Constance bit the tip of her tongue. He was teasing her, with both his words and eyes. It was fun and enticing, and she didn't want it to stop. "For what?" she asked, moving to stand behind one of the chairs.

"Perhaps for speaking to me so rudely?"

She shook her head.

"Why not?"

The cheerfulness inside her wasn't done being

released. It also gave her a keen sense of courage. She moved, letting her hand trail along the back of the chair as she walked away from it. Stopping a few inches from where he stood she said, "Because as her father, you are her first and foremost teacher. I'll reprimand her if and when she misbehaves around others…." The air between them was intensely warm, causing her to pause for a breath.

"So you're saying I'm in this alone?" His arms fell to his sides as he straightened his stance.

Constance shook her head. "No, I'm not saying you're in this alone."

"Then what are you saying?" He took a step. Just one, that caused the tips of their stocking-covered feet to touch.

A bold, hot heat flared inside her. She wouldn't be able to keep up the conversation much longer. The need to touch him had her trembling and was hampering her ability to think. With the end of one index finger she tapped the center button of his shirt, the one closest to his heart. "That your daughter already knows how far she can go with you, and how far she can't."

"Do you?" His whisper floated next to her ear.

"Do I what?" Spicy and fascinating, his scent filled the inside of her nose, leaving her breathless while a million little tingles raced about inside her body.

"Know how far you can go?"

She looked up, knowing what he'd see in her eyes, but not caring. Her ability to hide how badly she wanted him to kiss her was nonexistent. She'd never craved something like this before. No longer able to recall his question, her gaze went to his lips. He filled her mind, nothing except him. "Ellis," she whispered.

Everything happened within a split second—him stepping forward, grasping her arm as the door closed, and the room spinning while he twirled her around, pressing her back against the door.

His hands held both her upper arms, and his gaze bored into hers. "I'm going to kiss you, Constance."

Excitement shot through her veins, and she nodded.

"You want me to kiss you?" he asked, leaning closer.

She cupped his jaw. "Yes," she whispered. "Please kiss me, Ellis."

His lips landed on hers, and the kiss was nothing like the soft and gentle one of this afternoon. This one was hot and frantic, and made her arms fly around his neck. Their lips, moving upon each other's as if searching for a place to land, was sweet torment and left her pulse echoing in her ears and beating in unique, special places.

It wasn't just one kiss, but a series of them, short and fast and long and deliberate. A restless, wild ache sprang forth within her. She stretched on her toes, pressing her body against his.

As if he understood exactly what she needed, Ellis gripped her hips and lifted. Her spine inched up along the solid door until their hips met. His body, firm and taut, held her there as her toes dangled near his ankles and the fire in her center danced hotter by the delightful, intimate fusion of their bodies.

When his tongue ran between her lips, instinct had her mouth opening. Another profound thrill was released as his tongue engaged hers in a wild, sensual game of hide and seek. He pressed her deeper into the wood, and she grasped him tighter, overwhelmed by the excitement flaming inside her core. She'd never known her body could ache there. Ache and throb and swirl to the point she wanted to scream. It came out as a moan, rumbling deep in her throat.

Ellis deepened the kiss, opening a world of feelings and sensations so amazing she followed every swirl of his tongue, felt every touch of his fingers, wanting to experience each moment to the ultimate fullest.

When his mouth left hers, she rolled her head against the door at how the muscles between her legs contracted with sharp spasms. He kissed her cheeks, her nose and closed eyelids. The trail of his kisses went up and down her neck next. It was divine and heavenly, the way his lips danced along her skin, awakening sensations that had her gasping for air and craving more.

Ellis's breathing was hard and laborious as his lips lingered in front of one ear. "Constance," he whispered in such a way the need inside her soared hotter. "This could get dangerous."

A flash of fear that he'd step away had instincts she hadn't known existed taking over. She hooked one leg around the back of his knee, tightening her thigh muscles that twitched frantically. "It already is."

His mouth caught on her neck, suckling her skin as he brought his hip to grind against her center. She felt his arousal, and her body bucked at the connection, meeting his with a forcefulness that had her senses reeling. An inner drive had her yearning for more. She buried her face in his neck, kissing and nipping his skin.

He grasped the bottom of her thigh and lifted it higher. Her body slid downward while he brought his knee up, planting it between her legs. Arching against the door, she heaved for air as the pressure of his knee ignited an inferno inside her tender folds. The fire and desire was enough to drive her mad. She tightened her hold on his shoulders, pressing her body against his as tightly as possible.

His lips found hers again. In between deep, wild

kisses, he whispered, "We...shouldn't...be...doing this."

The heat of his palm penetrated her pantaloons and played havoc on the underside of her thigh as he gently caressed the area. She shivered at the delectable sensations. "I...know," she admitted, returning every kiss he gave. "But we are."

"Do you want me to stop?" he asked in a rush, stealing her lips before she could answer. The intensity of his kisses, of his hands and body, had her tingling from head to toe. Every touch, every kiss, made her want more, need more.

Gasping for air, she responded, "No, I don't want you to stop."

Ellis groaned and pressed her deeper against the door. The pressure was intense, heavy and the most wonderful thing she'd ever known. His kiss lasted until she thought she saw stars dancing in her head. He drew his lips away, and rested his forehead against hers.

"I don't want to stop, Constance," he said hoarsely. "You know what happens next."

"Yes, Ellis," she whispered. "I know what comes next." Her mind knew, but her body shouted it didn't. It had never been to these heights, had never craved the things Ellis's touch promised.

The sigh that left his chest was so thick and mournful she pressed the back of her head against the door. His hand slipped from her thigh, and he gently eased his knee away. Grasping her hips as her toes bumped the floor, he held her tight as he shifted them around so his back was now against the door. He folded his arms around her, creating an embrace that allowed every inch of her body to press against his firm, hard frame.

"We can't do it here. Not with Angel reading in the parlor."

Constance rested her head on his shoulder. "No, we can't." Disappointed by the knowledge, knowing what he said was true, she groaned. The tidal wave deep inside her raged on, burning and begging for release.

Ellis held her close, running his hands along the length of her hair and along her sides, while kissing the side of her face in a gentle and soothing way. She lifted her head, caught the sincerity in his eyes.

"Shh." He pressed her head back onto his shoulder. "Just stay right here. Let me hold you." His hands, now soft and tender, continued, stoking and calming the commotion inside her. As it ebbed, he continued to cradle her in his arms, lightly rocking until the last flame dwindled into little more than a deep and honing ache. Then he wrapped her in an embrace that was so tender and endearing, tears pressed against her closed lids. She'd never felt so cherished. A profound sigh of contentment flowed easily from her lungs.

Ellis laid his cheek against her temple. "Better?"

She nodded.

His hands ran down her back and cupped her backside, holding her center against his. "Later, when Angel's asleep, may I come to your room?"

The unsatisfied ache inside her flared like a struck match, ready to rise to the surface again. She lifted her face. The feel of him—hard and pressing against her stomach—told her, but still she asked, "Do you want to?"

His lips twitched with an endearing smile. "You know I do."

Her cheeks flamed.

He chuckled softly and one hand caressed her cheek. "I want you, Constance, like I haven't wanted something in a very long time." There was a glint in his eyes she'd never seen before. She couldn't read it, couldn't decipher exactly what it was, but it made her heart beat with elation.

"Then I'll be waiting," she whispered. "I'll be waiting."

He kissed her again, and this time, his tender actions held so much promise she swayed. The way he smiled, and caught her, had Constance swooning against him and sighing with a great longing.

Ellis held her until he felt her spine stiffen with resolve. His hands shook as he ran his fingers through the long mass of silky hair a final time. Fighting the urge to keep her right where she was, he kissed her temple before he opened the door, and then watched as she glided out of the office as if they'd simply been talking instead of attacking one another in a heated exchange of frantic kisses.

The door closed beneath his fingers, and he leaned heavily against the solid wood. Just as he feared, the heavy hand of reality slapped him as soon as he was alone. What had he done? Furthermore, what had he promised? Threading his fingers together behind his neck, he pressed his tension-filled body into the hard wood of the door. God, he wanted her. Wanted Constance with every ounce and inch of his being.

But it wasn't right—no matter how strongly he desired her or how willing she was. He'd hired her to cook and clean and educate his daughter, not to satisfy the hunger tearing apart his insides. It had been building, this want that had overtaken him, all day, and watching her hips sway as she'd walked out of the parlor earlier had jolted his desire into mammoth proportions. He'd never craved something so fiercely. Never felt it so keenly in each cell of his being.

He pushed off the door and walked to the window. The moon shone down on the snow-covered earth. A few flakes still fell from the sky, but nothing like earlier in the day when they'd tumbled down with the ferocity of a stampede. His gaze went to the single oak tree that stood inside the small wrought iron fence. He'd chosen that spot to put Christine just for this reason. So he could stand here and look at her.

He grew still. The lingering pain he'd grown so accustomed to was no longer. Hadn't been there, gnawing at his insides, since he'd awakened after being ill. He'd carried it for years, wanting Christine back. He still loved her. Always had and always would.

The calluses on his hands scratched his face as he rubbed his palms over his cheeks. Pressing his fingertips against his eyelids, he searched for the lost pain, wishing it would engulf his body and ease the throbs pulsating in his britches.

The pain didn't come, and his body still ached.

Is that why he kept Constance here? Almost held her prisoner—since she could move out to Ashton's place—because she made him forget?

Frustrated, he leaned against the windowsill. To hell with his needs. What about hers? He couldn't bed Constance because it wasn't fair to her. She'd come west looking for a husband, not some cowpoke who'd been without a woman too long. They were a dime a dozen out here. And not what she deserved. She deserved a man to love and cherish her until death—or beyond. His gaze went back to the fence.

Running his hands through his hair, he rubbed at his scalp. His brain hurt from all this thinking. "You, Ellis Clayton, are one sorry-ass critter," he chided aloud. "You are doing exactly what you told the group of men sitting in your front parlor less than a month ago not to do."

He took a seat then, not behind his desk as usual, but in one of the arm chairs, and hopped the chair around until he faced the fire. There, he stared at the flames, wondering how Constance would react when he didn't show up in her room as promised.

Nothing good could come of it. He couldn't marry her. Not that she'd necessarily expect it—though she'd have every right to—but he would. That's the kind of man he was. Or had been until sparkling blue eyes had led him astray. He pinched his lips together, refusing admittance to the smile pressing forward as her image formed in his mind. It wasn't her fault. It was his, and no matter how dire his need, he couldn't—wouldn't—bed her just to appease himself. Besides, she wasn't ready for that. Still needed time to get her bearings after all she'd been through. Even though her kisses and body said otherwise.

A log rolled, spitting sparks through the mesh gate. He stretched forward and grasped the poker, but didn't nudge at the log. Twirling the rod between his fingers, he watched the tiny sparks on the hearth fizzle and become nothing but tiny spots of ash.

What if he did bed Constance, and marry her? There was the chance she'd become pregnant, a very likely chance, the way his body still throbbed. His throat swelled and a raw tightening happened in his chest. She could die in childbirth just as Christine had. His gaze went over his shoulder to the window. He couldn't take that again. He'd be even more bitter and lonely with two graves to stare at instead of one. Matter of fact, this time it might just kill him.

The poker fell to the floor, thumping on the carpet. He should have told Constance about her inheritance. That's what he should have done. She'd be living out at Ashton's place now.

With no protection and most likely freezing to death.

He twisted, first left then right, wondering where the words had come from. Emptiness surrounded him. His mind did that every once in a while. Shot a thought out of nowhere. In the past, he'd assumed it was Christine, since the thoughts were more sensible than the ones he created.

Grabbing the poker, he stood and pushed aside the grate. She wouldn't be here now, telling him what to do about Constance.

Why not? Someone has to.

He jumped this time, spinning around in mid-air. Bookcases, a closed door and furniture. Not another living soul in sight. Without banking the fire, he pushed the grate back into place and stuck the poker in its holder.

Ellis left the door open and strolled down the hall, ignoring the urge to look over his shoulder. The lamps in the parlor had been doused, and no glow came from beneath the kitchen door. Cautiously, he pushed the door open and, noting the room was indeed empty, made a dash for the back door, where he donned his boots and coat and then met the freezing wind of Wyoming with hopes it would clear his spooked mind.

Chapter Ten

Constance fought heavy eyelids until the ability to do so left her exhausted. Then she tumbled into a deep, depressed sleep that didn't lift until sunlight filled her room and a clatter echoed in the house.

Tossing the covers aside, a squeak caught in her throat as icy air bit her naked flesh. Little good it had done to worry whether she should wear a gown or not last night. Ellis had never come to her room. The desire to be in his arms remained as strong as it had been last night. Had he come and found her asleep? Perturbed, she completed her morning necessities within minutes and left the room, all the while wondering how one goes about apologizing for such a thing.

Slowing in her rush down the back stairs due to the soft thuds echoing from below, she eased off the steps.

"Morning, ma'am," Thomas Ketchum greeted. "Hope I didn't wake you. I dropped an armload of wood." He finished filling the box and then brushed his gloved hands together over the logs.

The rest of the room was empty. "You didn't wake me," she lied, walking to the sink to fill the coffeepot.

"You up most of the night, too?"

"Excuse me?"

Thomas paused by the swinging kitchen door. "Nothing to fret about. Coyotes can't get in the house."

"Coyotes?"

"Yeah. A pack of them moved in last night. Ellis and a few other men were out all night keeping them off the young stock. With the snow coming so early and all, the coyotes are already getting brave. Gonna make for a long winter." Thomas tipped his hat as he pushed open the door. "G'day, ma'am."

Constance squeezed her temples. No wonder Ellis hadn't come to her room, he'd been out in this weather all night. The poor man must be frozen. She'd been warm in her bed, acting like an expectant bride, while he'd been outside fighting snow and ice and wild animals.

Fueled with determination, she quickly prepared the beans and set the coffee to perk. A thud came from somewhere in the house. It was probably Thomas, but it could be Ellis, up in his room. Then again, he may already be seeing to the morning chores. Glancing between the stairs and the back door, she chose the stairs. With her skirt hitched to her knees, she raced up the steps and down the hall.

At his door, she paused to catch her breath and tap lightly. When there was no response, she eased it open and noted the still-made bed. Within a minute, she was back downstairs, cutting strips of bacon for breakfast.

Two hours later, what she and Angel hadn't eaten sat cold and limp on the counter.

"Pa probably ate in the bunkhouse," Angel said from where she sat at the table writing her book report.

Knowing he had reason to be out all night didn't ease the frustration eating at Constance's insides. The desire their actions had instilled last night was still alive inside her, churning and sputtering in a way that filled her with a keen disappointment. "I suspect you're right." She tried to sound like her unfulfilled cravings weren't irritating her, but knowing that was impossible, she changed the subject. "How's the report coming?"

"Fine." Angel nibbled on the end of her pencil. "You never did answer my question yesterday."

"What question was that?"

"How long your boat ride from London was."

"Well," Constance began, her mind only half on the answer, "London is inland a short distance, so I had to travel overland to Southhampton and there I boarded the steamer to New York. All in all it took me about thirteen days, I believe."

"You believe? You don't know?"

The days had meshed in Constance's mind, forming a few months of little more than awful, yet significant events, all of which were better left forgotten. "Yes, I know," she replied. "It was thirteen days." Not up for conversation, she pulled a towel from the hook near the sink. "I'm going to go do some dusting."

"Well, don't wear yourself out," Angel muttered. "Come summer there'll be enough dirt to dust three times a day."

"Finish your book report." Constance marched to the door.

"Sheesh, someone has a bee in her bonnet."

"I heard that," Constance replied as she pushed open the door.

"I know," echoed behind her as the door fluttered shut.

Constance slapped the rag against her thigh. She had no to right to snap at Angel. It was just that she wanted to see Ellis, make sure coyotes had been the reason why he hadn't come to her room.

The big windows in the office filled the room with sunlight. Standing in the rays, she took a deep breath. The aromatic fragrance she treasured filled her nose, and she drew in air until her lungs threatened to burst. Letting her breath out slowly, a small slice of tension slipped from her shoulders.

"That's better," she assured herself, moving toward the window to wipe the wide sill.

Nothing looked purer than a fresh layer of snow, and the white span outside the window caught her full attention. She took in the scene, accepting the simple beauty of the rolling mounds of fluffy white, until her gaze locked on a single image.

The rag fell from her fingers.

Ellis, on one knee, knelt near the headstone inside the little wrought iron fence. His hat was pressed to his chest and his head bowed. The wind whipped at his hair and jacket, yet he remained statue still.

Constance grew shaky. She'd been out to the grave with Angel shortly after the first big snowstorm. Closing her eyes, she covered her mouth and nose with both hands. The sight out the window tore at her chest. Words shouted at her back in New York sprung into her mind with as much venom as they'd held months ago. *Husband stealer.*

Constance spun around and hurried from the room, closing the door tightly behind her.

In her own room, she paced the floor. What a malady she'd caused. She couldn't bed down with Ellis—no matter how badly she wanted to. What had overcome her to the point her thoughts were blundered? That first week—the days following

Ellis's illness—she'd feared the men would return, expect her to choose a husband. Knowing Ellis would step in had been her saving grace. He wasn't like the rest of them. Had that been it? She'd been so thrilled at his friendship and companionship that she'd turned it all around. Was her life so futile she'd do anything to have a home? It appeared so. She'd married Byron, and then accepted a stranger's marriage proposal, and now...

Plopping onto the bed, she hung her head. Though she'd planned to, and started to once or twice, she'd never told him about Byron. It had just never seemed to be the right time, and the way snow continuously fell from the sky, impeding travel, the urgency that the authorities might be looking for her must be diminished. Well, that and how the camaraderie she and Ellis had formed had given her an invisible security blanket. There were times she'd half imagined she and Ellis were married and Angel was their daughter, and life was as wonderful as it had been all those years ago back in Virginia.

A sob mushroomed in her throat. She didn't belong here. Never had. Never would. He'd never understand why she'd lied—withheld the truth from him for so long. He'd never understand about Byron, not after the way she'd behaved last night.

The sob threatened to suffocate her. He'd hate her for that, too. Pretending she could replace

Christine, the mother of his child. Something she could never be, no matter how hard she wished. It was as if a great fist of fire squeezed her chest.

For a few weeks she'd had everything she'd ever wanted. Ever dreamed of. But it had been a farce. She was a farce. There had to be someplace she could go. Where she wouldn't impose her selfishness on others.

A rap sounded on the door and before she could respond, it opened. "Constance?" Angel poked her head in. "You are up here. What are you doing?"

Constance balled her hands, searching for an ounce of control. "Oh, just straightening up," she lied, jumping off the bed and jutting across the room as chaotically as a bumblebee trying to fly in the rain. It would break her heart to leave Angel, but it couldn't be helped. She fluffed the curtains, and the brilliant white out the window had her eyes burning.

"Pa's back. He's ready for lunch."

Constance's heart went crazy. First it leaped to her throat, screaming with the joy his name had instilled, and then it hit her toes, pouring dread all over her feet.

"Are you coming?"

"Yes," Constance managed to say. "I'm coming."

By the time she reached the bottom few steps, she had her emotions under control—at least that's what Constance thought until her feet refused to move. How could a simple brown hat, creased with wear and hanging innocently on a hook, stop someone dead in their tracks? Praying she wouldn't stumble, she forced her feet to glide off the last step and across the kitchen floor.

Without glancing left or right, she walked to the counter. Ellis didn't say anything, but she knew he was there. Her senses tick-tocked faster and louder than the mantel clock in his office. Every tick saying *he's here*. Every tock saying *right behind you*.

Angel, on the other hand, hadn't yet learned the act of silence. "What are we having for lunch? I'm about as starved as a spring bear. Thought you'd never finish dusting."

Constance closed her eyes, drawing an ounce of fortitude that would prevent her from snapping at the child—or swooning at Ellis's feet. Moving to the ice box, she asked, "Have you finished your book report?"

"Yup."

"What are you working on now?" Ellis asked.

The sound of his deep voice had the bowl slipping from Constance's hand. She set it back on the metal shelf, and clenched her fingers momentarily before attempting to carry the leftover stew to the counter.

Luckily she set the bowl down seconds before

Angel answered her father, "A schedule for Constance's intendeds."

"A what?" Constance and Ellis asked at the same time.

Constance spun around, keeping herself upright with a hold on the edge of the counter. The frown on Ellis's face had his brows almost touching.

"Hank brought these from town last week. I've finally read them all." Angel pointed to a stack of letters on the table. "I figure I'll do most of the interviewing during the holiday party this weekend. That way the men won't have to make two trips to the ranch."

For the past week, Constance had been embedded in the plans for the party only three days from now, but that had been before Ellis's kiss, and last night. Complacent and content—up until yesterday—she'd forgotten Angel's plan to interview the men.

Ellis remained as silent as she. When he did speak, it was a question to Angel. "When did you send a post to Link?"

"I didn't. The men just started writing."

Constance shot away from the counter. Her mind fought her every step of the way—to the pantry and back to the counter with a pot. It might be a way out. Accepting one of the men's offers would get her out of Ellis's life. The word he'd teasingly called her last night rang through her head. She was a coward. Furthermore, she didn't want to wed anyone. Leastwise no one that wanted to marry her.

After setting the pot on the stove, she moved back to the counter and lifted a loaf of bread wrapped in cheesecloth out of the cupboard. The authorities were never there when she needed them. Not in England, and not now when she wished they'd arrive and haul her off to a prison. It really didn't matter if she was innocent of Byron's murder or not. She just had to leave—as soon as possible.

The knife handle wobbled in her hand as she drew the blade through the top crust, and the slight weight that settled on her shoulder was enough to make her jump. Quick pain had her dropping the knife and wrapping her fingers around her opposite thumb.

"You cut yourself."

Constance stepped back, out of Ellis's reach, squeezing her thumb to stop the blood trickling between her fingers.

"Here, let me see."

"No." She skirted around him. "Where's Angel?"

"I asked her to leave us alone for a moment." Ellis took her clutched hands, but she twisted from his grasp.

Thrusting her thumb into the sink, she pumped water with the other hand. Blood mixed with the water, but remarkably, there was very little pain. Probably because it was all in her chest.

Ellis took her hand with a hold too strong to break. She gritted her teeth at the way her skin betrayed the will she conjured up to ignore his touch. Instead of aching from the injury, even her thumb quivered with delight as he dried it and wrapped a strip of cloth tightly around the gash.

Drawing a hidden ounce of reserve, she pulled her hand from his grasp and secured the bandage by tucking in the edges.

He took her elbow. "We need to talk."

The image she'd seen earlier filled her vision, as if she was looking out the office window at the grave again. The pain in her chest created a crust around her heart. "Yes, we do, Ellis." She feigned interest in the stew. Retrieving a long spoon, she stirred the pot, watching the bubbles disappear and assembling her wayward thoughts.

"Constance, I—"

Not willing to listen, she interrupted, "I locked my bedroom door last night."

He stiffened, nothing but his eyes moved, and they intensely searched her face. "What?"

Concocting tales was not common for her, but the desperation gnawing at her gave little choice, seemed to create the tale on its own. She pushed the pot to the back of the stove. "What happened between us should never have happened."

"I—"

She had to continue before she lost her nerve. "It was my fault." That much was the truth, but the rest was conjured straight out of thin air. "I—I've been missing my husband lately. We met during the holidays last year, and with Christmas being next Tuesday, our short time together has been on my mind." Unable to meet his gaze, knowing he'd catch her lies, she covered her face with both hands. "Last night I was imagining you were him." The sob burning the back of her throat let loose, and the tears forcing their way forward were real. That much she couldn't pretend. "I'm sorry."

"Constance."

His touch was too gentle. "I just loved him so much," she lied, stumbling backward.

The grip he had on her arm increased. "Then why'd you agree to marry Ashton?"

She should have known one lie would lead to more. "I thought I could pretend with him, too."

His eyes narrowed. "I don't believe you."

Long fingers of fear, or perhaps anger, gripped her heart. "You don't believe me? You, the man who's still in love with his dead wife?" Instant regret sent a groan rolling up her throat that threatened to choke her.

His hand left her arm, and the anguish on his face made her spin around and dash toward the stairs. "Please tell Angel lunch is ready." Without looking back, she ran up the staircase and didn't stop until she was behind her locked bedroom door.

In the kitchen, Ellis stared at the staircase that had swallowed Constance until his eyes blurred. His insides had grown as hollow as a log infested with termites. Every breath he took stalled between his throat and chest.

All of a sudden he wanted to yell and hit something until it hurt as bad as he did. The urge was foreign. He'd never turned to violence, not even in the darkest days following Christine's death.

Damn, he was a fool.

He twisted and, pulling his hat and coat from the hook, stormed out the door. His fury-filled growl sent the dog on the porch yelping and tearing down the steps.

Ellis slapped his hat on his head, but the coat, he whacked against the porch rail. It didn't help. Neither did the cold air stinging his lungs.

Only a fool would fall in love this hard. This fast.

The coat hit the porch rail again, but this time when it flayed in the air, he caught it and thrust a hand in an arm hole as he barreled down the steps with no particular destination in mind. He ended up in the barn, where he saddled a horse.

"Mr. Clayton, where you going? You need help?" one of the hands asked.

He didn't bother to look to see which ranch

hand, and not holding an ounce of trust in his burning throat, waved the man away.

Whoever it was held the barn door open. Kneeing the horse, Ellis rode out, daring the wind to freeze his face and hands. Then they'd match his heart.

Three days later, Ellis was no worse for wear. That's what he'd convinced himself anyway. Leaning against the tree near the headstone, he watched a wagon glide into the yard. The holiday party was an annual event that brought visitors from far and near. This year there'd be even more, with every man in the territory wanting the chance to ask Constance for her hand.

His heart hitched up a notch, but he ignored it. Bracing the bottom of one boot against the tree trunk, he folded his arms and pressed his back against the thick bark. The past few days they'd barely spoken.

A ranch hand jogged across the yard and took the visitor's team, then led the horses and wagon toward the barn. Ellis let out a gust of air. He couldn't blame Constance for not talking to him. In all honesty, he'd kept his distance, even taken his meals in the bunkhouse, telling Beans Constance had her hands full getting ready for the party. A smile attempted to grace his lips. She had her hands full all right. The decorations Angel had ordered and strung around the parlor had the place looking like someone had tarred and feathered it. Paper lanterns and bells and balls of all colors had hung in a disorderly fashion around the room when he and Thomas had carried in the tree.

Constance must have worked her magic on Angel, convinced the girl too much was sometimes worse than none. The smile won this time, making a small chuckle bubble in his throat. He could almost hear Constance's sweet voice explaining things in the remarkable way only she could do that must have made Angel understand how elegant the room would look with fewer gaudy things swaying about. And elegant it did look. He'd taken a quick gander of the room this morning, as he'd made his way out the front door without peeking into the kitchen where he'd heard the clatter and clang of last-minute preparations taking place.

The ranch house was impressive, he knew that. It was how he'd meant it to be while nailing every board together. Lately, with Constance's subtle touches, the place had become more than just a house, it was a home. The kind he'd always wanted. He hadn't completed the house until after Christine died. There had been a few months where he wondered if he'd ever finish it.

His brows tugged. The melancholy he'd carried in his chest the past few years had left, but there was another hole there now.

A ray of sun bounced off the headstone. When he blinked a faint whisper touched his mind. *It's about time you moved on.*

Eyes back on the house, he whispered, "I know that, now. But she's not ready. May never be."

Give her time.

He nodded as the rattle of harnesses echoed across the frozen ground. "I will."

Another wagon with thick wood and iron gliders in place of wheels slid over the snow, coming to stop in front of the house. Link jumped off the side and then turned, lifting both arms up to aid Lula Mae as she stepped down. Several other people climbed out of the back of the wagon, all carrying packages and bundles.

Ellis pushed off the tree. As much as he'd rather just stand out here and freeze to death, he'd best make his way inside. With the toe of his boot he kicked a fluff of snow and watched it dance and twirl while falling back to the earth. Yeah, he was putting off the inevitable. He really didn't want to be anywhere near the house today. Not because of the holiday party, but because he didn't know if he could watch all those men begging for Constance's attention.

His fingers curled into his palms, and he squeezed, hoping the action would give him a bit more control. How long would she need? How long would it be before he could ask her to be his wife? Now that he'd made up his mind, impatience had set in. He understood time healed all wounds, and he'd give her all she needed, but the way she'd responded to his kisses contradicted his rationalization.

Two more vehicles glided into the yard, and letting out air until his lungs screamed to be refilled, Ellis trudged his way over the snow.

A few yards from the house, he planted a smile on his face and returned a wave from those climbing out of the wagon.

"Ellis!" Mr. Homer shouted. "Help me with this, would you?"

Ellis arrived at the side of the wagon and took a large basket from the banker as the man rolled his round shape over the tailgate. Once they'd climbed the front steps, waiting in line for their turn to enter the house, Mr. Homer reached over. "Here, I'll take that now." The man lifted the edges of the red and green plaid covering, peeking inside.

Ellis's curiosity was piqued. "What's in there?"

"Oranges," Mr. Homer whispered as if it was the secret of the day. "Link bought them off the army wagon master. He said Miss Jennings really likes fruit." Homer's eyes took on a hopeful glint. "She does like oranges, doesn't she?"

Ellis's molars locked top to bottom.

"Hey, Pa!" Angel greeted, holding the door wide as the line of guests entered. "Constance was wondering where you went."

Of its own accord his heartbeat increased.

"Where is Miss Jennings?" Homer asked, glancing around the area.

"She's in the parlor," Angel answered.

Ellis elbowed his way through the standing-room-only-crowd. There were faces he'd never seen before, had no idea who they were or where they'd come from. Ninety percent of the guests were men—a fact that made his teeth clench harder. He searched the room, finding Constance on the far side, accepting a large package from a thin man. Ellis couldn't decipher if he knew the man or not. Constance nodded her head agreeably and turned to place the package on the overflowing table beside the tree.

Making a beeline for her and the tree, Ellis was roughly nudged aside by Mr. Homer barreling across the room like a boulder rolling down a mountain slope.

"Ellis," Link said, stepping in Ellis's path. "Happy holidays."

Tugging his eyes from Constance, Ellis turned to the storekeeper. "Happy holidays, Link." He gave a slight nod to include the man's wife. "You, too, Lula Mae."

"The house looks wonderful, Ellis. So festive and homey," Lula Mae said while sipping a frothy mixture out of a tiny glass cup. "This is delicious." She nodded at the cup before she continued, "And the house is bursting with so many people. You must have invited the entire state."

As far as he knew invitations hadn't been issued. It was just the annual holiday party, and anyone that heard about it was welcome to attend. His gaze roamed the room. Half the nation must have heard and decided to attend.

A tingle racing along Ellis's neck had him turning back to the tree. The sounds of the room faded, as if his head was stuck in a hole. Constance's eyes were on him, and the trepidation glistening in them had him glancing to her surroundings. John Hempel stood beside her, and the look of distress on the man's face told Ellis all he needed to know.

The lawyer had told her about Ashton's place. Something Ellis had never gotten around to mentioning. A log formed in his throat and his stomach sank to his knees. Without offering an excuse to Link and Lula Mae, Ellis shoved his way forward.

"Call me Buford, Miss Jennings, that's my given name," Mr. Homer offered as Ellis drew closer.

"Well, thank you, Mr. Homer for the oranges," Constance replied sweetly. "Now, if you will excuse me, I have some things I need to see to." She stepped around John Hempel, the opposite direction from where Ellis approached.

He angled across the room, heading off her trail. "Constance." He caught her arm near the doorway.

She tugged from his hold. "Wonderful party, isn't it?" Her tone held no delight. "Excuse me. I have things to see to."

Physically restraining her wouldn't solve anything. Reluctantly Ellis let her maneuver away, watching as she smiled and nodded at guests along the way.

He followed on her heels though, weaving his way through the crowd and biting his tongue. Once they arrived in the kitchen, he opened his mouth, but the room was as full as the parlor had been. The table was laden with food and a crowd circled it, filling their plates as they stepped from platter to platter.

The widow Wagner caught Constance's arm, pulling her to the counter and pointing to several pies. They were her meat pies, which he'd grown quite fond of. A couple other women crowded closer, intently listening as Constance explained the contents.

A hand landed on Ellis's shoulder.

"Why didn't you tell her about Ashton's property, Ellis?" John Hempel asked. "You said you would."

Ellis sucked in air. He had no excuse, leastwise, none he could admit to the lawyer.

"If I'd known you hadn't, I'd have ridden out before now."

Chapter Eleven

The pie Constance attempted to cut into wedges was nothing but a blur. She closed her eyes and willed the tears to stay behind her lids. Why hadn't Ellis told her about Ashton's will? Furthermore, why would Ashton, a man she'd never met, will his property to her? She should be pleased. It could provide the escape she'd told herself she wanted. The past few days had been a nightmare, but even that didn't make the thought of leaving any easier.

She completed cutting the pie and set the knife aside. None of it made sense. Ellis hadn't said more than three words to her since she'd lied to him about locking her door. But before then, there'd been plenty of opportunities for him to mention Ashton's will. She pressed a hand to her cramping stomach. Yes, there had been plenty of time for him to tell her, just as there'd been plenty of time for her to tell him about Byron.

A tit for a tat as Aunt Julia used to say.

The next few hours brought her twisting and turning stomach little relief, and no remedy formed in her guilt-ridden mind. Guests rolled in until barely a path was left open to walk from room to room. Most brought food or other gifts of the season; there were enough oranges to feed the entire territory twice over. Constance cut several and arranged them on a plate to sit amongst the vast array of food covering the table, including a few loaves of banana bread she'd taken out of the icebox on the back porch. The tasks of uncovering or slicing other dishes kept her occupied and in the kitchen, where she didn't have to face the fear of encountering Ellis.

However, she managed to disgrace herself further by conjuring the notion that Ellis had considered swindling her out of Ashton's property the way Byron had her aunts'. Which was ridiculous. Ellis was a rich man. Ashton's few acres would mean nothing to him, not to mention the distance between it and Heaven on Earth.

The crowd lessened a bit when the children, and a few young adults, layered on clothes and went to slide down the large hill. The extra space gave room for people to mingle, but Constance, thankful for dish duty, maintained her solace in the kitchen.

A few women were among the guests, and she was glad to make their acquaintances, but despite her attempts to be cordial, she couldn't muster up the ability to partake in small talk—her mind was consumed with how soon Ellis would send her to Ashton's place. He didn't need money or land, but he had needed her to prepare the food and house for the party. Angel said the entire territory looked forward to the annual holiday gathering. Now that the day had arrived, there was no need for Constance to remain at Heaven on Earth.

Link's wife, Lula Mae, was quite charming and talked nonstop. She'd hovered near the eggnog in the hall since arriving, and Constance wasn't overly surprised when the woman set the empty punch bowl next to the sink.

"Can we mix up another batch of this?" Lula Mae asked. "What did you call it again?"

"Eggnog," Constance explained. "And, yes, I can make more."

"I'll help. I want the recipe." Lula Mae wiped her hands on a cloth. "Tell me what to do."

Thankful for anything that would take her mind off Ellis, Constance slid a basket of eggs across the counter. "Separate out a dozen yolks from their whites."

"Will do," Lula Mae said, already cracking an egg. "So, how are things for you out here? Angel's absolutely blooming. She's a good girl, but did need a woman's touch, that she did."

"Yes, she's a good girl," Constance agreed. "You'll need to whip the yolks lightly, and then add this bowl of sugar."

Lula Mae gave Constance an inquisitive look before she picked up the fork and started to stir the yolks. "Eggnog, that's what this is called?"

"Yes." Constance answered. It was clear Lula Mae comprehended Constance had sidestepped around the other question. She wasn't ready to talk to anyone about how she was doing, especially since she didn't know herself. Pouring one glass of brandy and another of whiskey, she set the two near the bowl. "I read once that President George Washington was known for his eggnog. He made it year round to serve to visitors." Her attempt at small talk seemed a bit off kilter even to her ears.

"Really?" Lula Mae poured in the sugar. "I figured it was a recipe you brought from England."

"This one is. I don't know what the president used in his recipe. My aunts enjoyed eggnog and always served it over the holidays."

"Well, I've never had it before." Lula Mae pointed at the glasses. "Do I add both of those?"

"Add that one first. It's brandy and will cook the eggs." Constance pointed to one glass before she moved to the icebox where she kept the milk she hadn't separated just for this reason. "Then add the whiskey."

"You certainly have a lot of recipes from England. I tried the bread you made out of those bananas. Had I known about that, I would have had Link keep some," Lula Mae commented as she continued to work on the eggnog.

The memory of Ellis bringing home the bags of bananas was strong enough to make a smile tickle Constance's lips. "The banana bread was an experiment. I honestly didn't know what I was going to do with all those bananas." She set the milk on the counter and started to whip the egg whites.

"I'd never have thought to bake with them. They didn't look like much to me, and they were so soft, I wondered if they'd gone bad," Lula Mae replied.

"They would have in another day or so," Constance agreed. Her mind was back on the night when she and Ellis had baked bread. It was such a simple, silly thing, yet the memory was planted in her head like a mighty oak, with roots that went clear to her heart.

"Now what?" Lula Mae asked, looking at the mixture in the bowl.

Constance nodded toward the pitcher. "Add the milk, and then grate a bit of that nutmeg over the top. Once the egg whites are frothy, we'll add them and it will be done."

"He's a good man, you know," Lula Mae said thoughtfully.

For a split second, Constance's hand stilled. Clutching the fork tighter, she continued to whip the whites. No one had to tell her Ellis was a good man, she'd known that from the moment she'd met him.

"Losing her mama at such a young age was tough for Angel, but right from the day his wife died, Ellis put everything second to that girl. Poor man's going to have a hard time when the day arrives for her to leave this house. He'll take that mighty hard."

Constance bit her lip. What Lula Mae said was true, and Constance agreed, but right now it was impossible for her to talk about Ellis, or anyone leaving. She gave the whites a final good whipping.

"He needs more children. That's what Ellis needs," Lula Mae said, scraping the nutmeg. "That's why he built such a large house. He and Christine wanted half a dozen children. Talked about it all the time. It was sad when she passed, along with their baby boy. The son he wanted to inherit all this someday." Lula Mae smiled brightly. "But there's still time. He's young enough to—"

"Here, these are done," Constance interrupted, trembling from head to toe.

Lula Mae frowned slightly before she said,

"Well, dump them in. Folks are waiting for it in the other room."

Constance had a lump the size of an egg in her throat. She didn't mean to appear rude and really could use a friend right about now, but her mind and heart were just too heavy. Fighting against the pressure forming behind her eyes, she folded the egg whites into the mixture in the large bowl.

"I'm going to run out to the outhouse," Lula Mae said. "Before I have another cup. Do you mind carrying the bowl back into the other room?"

Constance nodded, loathing the scars on her stomach with newfound hatred. "Thank you for helping," she had to whisper due to the burning sensation bubbling in her throat.

"Anytime. And anytime you want to talk, you know where to find me." Lula Mae turned to make her way to the back door followed by the swirl of the lacey bustle of her dark green gabardine dress.

Constance picked up the heavy bowl and walked toward the swinging door that had been propped open for people to mingle freely between the parlor and the kitchen. The front hall was packed. Carefully selecting a path around and between the guests, she prayed her trembling hands wouldn't drop the bowl, and was almost to the small table she'd set out just for the eggnog when the front door flew open.

"Mr. Clayton!" a young boy shouted. "Mr. Clayton!"

Ellis appeared in the midst of the crowd. "What is it, Jonathan?"

"It's Angel! Her sled hit a tree, and we can't wake her up! You gotta come quick!"

The punch bowl slipped from Constance's hands, hitting the floor with a glass-breaking crash and spewing a tidal wave of eggnog.

Ellis grabbed her hand, and without care to the mess or broken glass, as one they dashed out the door.

They ran across the porch and down the steps, closely following the child tearing across the snow in front of them. She searched the field for the group of children, and clutched Ellis's hand tighter when the deep snow attempted to slow her down. By the time they arrived where a crowd had gathered around the base of a large tree several yards away from Angel's little barn in the backyard, Constance could barely catch her breath.

Panic clawed at her chest as she landed on her knees beside a still form wearing a bright red stocking cap. Ellis was right beside her, brushing the snow from Angel's arms and legs.

"She opened her eyes a minute ago," someone said.

With trembling hands, Constance pushed the thick, knitted hat from Angel's forehead and after a quick search for injuries she patted the girl's cheek. "Angel?"

The girl's eyes fluttered open.

Ellis was next to her, hovering over Angel. One of his arms was wrapped around Constance's shoulders, and he squeezed her upper arm. The touch released the tears pressing on her eyes.

"Angel," he said softly, "where does it hurt, honey?"

Angel's face scrunched as she gestured toward her left leg, which was twisted oddly in the deep snow. "My leg, Pa. It hurts something awful."

"Let me through," a gruff voice demanded. "Let me though, I say." The man made his way to Angel's other side. "It's Doc Neely, Angel. Where's it hurt, girl?"

"Her leg," Ellis answered.

"Don't move, Angel, let me take a gander first," Doc Neely ordered.

Angel lifted her hand. Constance wrapped both of hers around the thick mitten. "It's all right, just lie still."

Ellis's hand, big and warm, covered both of theirs. "Does anything else hurt, honey?"

Angel shook her head slightly. "No, Pa. Just my leg."

"It's broke all right," Doc Neely said. "Let's get her inside so I can set it before the swelling starts."

The doctor pushed off the snowy ground, rising to his feet. "I'll need a couple of straight boards."

"I'll get them," someone said.

It sounded like Beans, but Constance didn't take her eyes off Angel to see if it was or not. The pain on the girl's face was eating a huge hole in her heart, and overriding her now insignificant worries. "It's going to hurt to move her," she whispered.

"I know," Ellis answered, squeezing her hands still clutching Angel's. "But it can't be helped." The cold wind swirling around them set in, making Constance shiver and jerk. "Come on," Ellis said close to her ear. "We have to get you inside, too."

Constance accepted his help, and once she was standing, she stepped back, giving Ellis the space he needed to lift Angel off the ground. The girl groaned and then a wrenching screech emitted as Ellis hoisted her upward. Constance cowered at the sound, but hurried around Ellis's other side and used both hands to support Angel's legs hanging over his arm.

"We'll take it slow, honey," Ellis said, kissing Angel's pain-twisted face.

He set an unhurried pace, walking around the larger drifts. Constance stayed at his side, keeping her arms beneath Angel's ankles and shins.

Doctor Neely shouted orders as they arrived at the house, clearing a wide path that led straight to the staircase. Constance stayed at Ellis's side, all the way up the stairs and down the hall to Angel's door. There he paused, turning sideways. "You go in first," he instructed.

Constance did so, sidestepping all the way to the bed. Lula Mae was already there, pushing the covers back and shoving the pillows aside. As the woman moved out of the way, Constance realized she and Ellis needed to make a half circle so he could lay Angel on the bed. When she glanced his way, he nodded, reading her thoughts.

Taking slow, jutting steps, they maneuvered about. While Ellis held Angel over the mattress, he looked at Constance. She nodded. As one, they slowly lowered Angel until she lay flat on the bed.

The girl was taking short, shaky breaths, and her face, eyes closed, held a tight grimace. Constance leaned past Ellis and pressed a hand to Angel's cheek.

Angel opened her eyes. "It really hurts, Constance."

"I know it does, sweetheart." Constance brushed past Ellis to pull the hat from the girl's head, and then began to unbutton her coat. "But Doc will have it set in no time." She attempted to sound reassuring, but the ache inside her had the words breaking apart so hard they burned her throat.

"I can help her, you go change your clothes,"

Ellis said, settling his hands over the top of Constance's.

"No," she insisted. "I'll stay in case the doctor needs assistance." She didn't glance up. One look into his knowing eyes would shatter the measly amount of strength she held on to. "You can go."

"No," he said. "We'll both stay." After giving her hand a tiny squeeze that had her scrounging for control, he moved toward the foot of the bed. "Angel, I'm going to take your boots off."

Angel had her eyes closed again. "All right, Pa," she said, clearly trying to be strong.

The tiny yelp Angel released had Constance pressing a kiss to her forehead. "You're a brave girl, Angel Clayton, and I'm very proud of you."

Angel bit her bottom lip and gave a slight nod.

By the time Ellis had Angel's boots off, Constance had slipped the coat out from beneath her, and Doctor Neely had arrived with his sleeves rolled up to the elbows. He gave a nod toward Ellis, and then bent his head, running both hands over Angel's leg.

Something bumped the back of Constance's knees, and she glance around. Ellis laid a hand on her shoulder. "Sit down."

Never releasing the hold she had on Angel's hand, Constance complied. A blanket fell over her shoulders before Ellis leaned over and brushed Angel's hair away from her temple. "You doing okay there, Angel girl?"

"Yes, Pa."

"You hold on to Constance's hand and don't let go." His tone was gravely somber. "Don't let go."

"I won't, Pa," Angel agreed.

The concern filling Ellis's eyes had Constance's heart thumping. She clutched on tighter to Angel's hand, and gave him a slight nod, assuring him she wouldn't let go of Angel, no matter what. He bowed his head, and then turned to the doctor who was cutting the leg of Angel's bloomers in two. Their voices were low and hushed.

Constance couldn't hear what the men said, but knew it didn't matter. Her focus was on Angel. Leaning next to the girl's shoulder, she started to whisper. She talked about the weather, what a beautiful job Angel had done in decorating the front parlor and how the guests had eaten all of the banana bread. Constance kept the one-sided conversation flowing, leaping from subject to subject, attempting to hold Angel's attention or at least draw it off what the doctor and Ellis were doing. It worked for the most part. Angel whispered a few replies and nodded a few times, but when the girl let out a scream that filled Constance with piercing pain, she pressed her cheek to Angel's.

"Shh," Constance whispered.

Angel's grip tightened as she muffled another agonizing screech.

"Shh," Constance repeated. "I'm right here, honey. I know it hurts, but it'll feel better soon." She lifted her head. "Look at me, Angel," she coaxed. "Look at me, honey."

Angel let out a little sigh and lifted her lids. Tears streaked her red cheeks and trickled from the corners of her big brown eyes.

Constance delved up a smile. "That's my girl."

Angel touched Constance's cheek. "You're crying."

Resting her cheek against the girl's palm, Constance nodded. "It hurts me to see you in pain."

"I'll be all right," Angel assured.

A soft smile came straight from Constance's heart. "I know you will be." She leaned down and kissed Angel's temple. "I love you."

"I love you, too," Angel answered.

The bed shifted slightly as the men worked, and Constance started whispering again, talking about things that really didn't matter, but came to mind. When a hand tugged on her shoulder, she twisted to glance up. Ellis stood beside her chair. The gratitude in his eyes renewed her tears.

Soft and tender, he wiped the tears from her cheek. Constance drew in a breath to keep from leaning into the touch. Ellis's fingers slipped away as he bent down to caress Angel's face. "It's all set, honey. How are you doing?"

"Better," Angel answered. "It still hurts though."

Ellis kissed her forehead. "I know it does. It will for a while."

"I have something to help with that," Doctor Neely said.

Ellis stepped aside, and Constance had to move as well. Ellis moved the chair, giving the doctor room to sidle up next to the bed.

"Here, Angel, it's kind of bitter, but swallow the entire spoonful," the doctor instructed, filling a spoon with a thick glob from a small brown bottle.

Lula Mae appeared at the bedside. "Here's a glass of water for her to wash it down, Doc."

The shivers came with an expected rush, encompassing Constance until she shook and trembled from head to toe. She pressed her toes against the floor and folded her arms across her chest to rub her opposite elbows.

As if he knew her every need, Ellis responded. He resettled the blanket over her shoulders, and draped both arms around her from behind. His chin nestled into the top of her head. The gentle hold beckoned her to lean against him. She thought she could fight the urge, but when he tugged softly, bringing her back against his chest, she went willingly, and closed her eyes for a moment, forgetting the agony filling her heart and soul.

"That's a girl," Doctor Neely said.

Constance pulled her eyes open half believing the doctor spoke to her, for Ellis's hold had healing powers.

"You did a good job there, Angel," the doctor continued. "I just want to take a look at your head now, make sure you don't have a lump from hitting that tree."

Constance clutched onto Ellis's forearms wrapped around her breasts, praying the doctor found no other injuries. She hadn't seen or felt anything, but then again, in her hurried examination, she may have overlooked something.

Eventually, the doctor moved away from the bed. "You're gonna be fine, Angel," he said as Constance stepped closer to the bed. "But if something else gets to hurting, you tell Miss Jennings or your pa right away."

Ellis had stepped forward as well, still had his arms around Constance. Angel noticed, and a sleepy smile covered her face. "I will," she whispered.

"There's no bump on her head," Dr. Neely said. "I think she must have blacked out from the pain of the break. Sleep is the best thing for her right now."

"Thanks, Doc," Ellis said.

Constance's throat didn't want to work. The comfort his touch provided was too great to ignore, as was the relief of knowing Angel hadn't been more seriously injured.

"I gave her a good dose of medicine. She'll sleep for a fair while." Doctor Neely rolled one sleeve down and buttoned the cuff before switching to the other sleeve. "Miss Jennings," he nodded toward her, "you'll want to go get out of that dress. You're soaked clear through. Don't need you coming down sick with Angel to take care of."

Beyond the edges of the blanket, yellow splatters of eggnog covered the front of her dress, and the bottom of the pale blue velvet had turned purple where she'd knelt in the snow. Constance held no concern for the gown, but knew she should follow the doctor's orders, if for no other reason than to demonstrate to Angel how important it was to comply with what the man said.

"I'll be back in a few minutes," she said, patting Angel's hand.

Angel closed her eyes and nodded. "Take your time, I'm fine." Her voice held a touch of her usual grit and determination.

Ellis couldn't contain a grin, but when his gaze went to Constance, guilt raised its ugly head, instantly filling his insides and erasing the smile from his lips. Her shoulders slumped forward, making his hold feel unwelcome and irritating. He eased his arms from around her and stepped aside.

Pain for Angel still filled her blue eyes, but he

saw more. Disgust. Betrayal. Loathing. All the things he imagined filled her soul. He couldn't blame her, he had betrayed her. He'd attempted several times to speak with her since he'd seen her and John Hempel near the tree, but every time he got close, she'd scooted away. Even while concerned for Angel, Constance held a large portion of his attention.

He loved his daughter, and had been truly alarmed by her accident, but once the initial shock had grown into deep parental distress knowing she was injured but would be fine, his thoughts had once again returned to Constance. Both her learning about Ashton's will and how deeply Angel's accident had affected her.

"Constance," he started, not really knowing what he wanted to say, but wishing he could somehow ease her pain and clear the tension between them.

She dropped the blanket on the chair and stepped away from the bed. He turned to follow her, but Angel's weak voice stopped him.

"Pa?"

His gaze bounced between Constance and his daughter. This had never happened before. He couldn't remember a time when he'd had to make a choice between his daughter and anything else. His heart went both ways, splitting right down the middle.

As if she understood the battle going on inside him, Constance pointed to the bed, and then walked out the door.

He took a hold of Angel's outstretched hand. "Don't worry, honey, I'm here."

Angel grinned. "It's you who shouldn't worry. She'll be back as soon as she changes her clothes."

Sometimes Angel was more forthright than any child should be, and twice as loveable. "You need to rest," he told her.

"I am," she said.

Ellis pulled the chair next to the bed.

"You know you'll have to tell her," Angel said.

"Tell who what?" he pretended ignorance.

Her eyes were cloudy from the medicine, and the little smile on her lips was tranquil. She let out a gentle sigh. "You know who, silly." Her eyes closed. "And what."

Ellis laid a hand on her forehead. The smooth, peachy skin was warm, but not feverish. "Go to sleep, honey."

"Why didn't you tell her about Ashton's will, Pa?" she asked groggily.

He continued to stroke her forehead and brush the curly tendrils from her temples. "Shh," he whispered.

"You know, Pa, when you love something, you have to let them choose. You gotta give them the chance to decide if they stay or leave. That's what you tell me about my animals."

He knew that, but nonetheless was afraid. The door to Angel's room was open and his gaze locked onto the space, while his heartbeat increased. Not so much as a shadow flickered in the hall, yet his gaze remained transfixed, refusing even a blink of an eyelid, waiting for Constance's return.

"She loves you, Pa. She loves us both, and she'll stay. But you gotta give her the choice."

His daughter was right in more than one way. But that was a conversation he and Constance needed to have. He bent down near the bed. "What would you say if I told you I want to ask Constance to marry me?" He'd made the decision a few days ago, and couldn't bypass the opportunity to ask for Angel's approval—wanted everything in place when Constance was ready.

Angel's grin grew. "I'd say it's about time. When are you going to ask her?"

His chest grew heavy. "I don't know. It won't be for a while. She needs a little time, yet." A flicker of hope it could happen soon, had him asking, "But you'd be okay with it?"

"You don't need to ask my permission. It's your choice. Just like it'll be my choice when I find who I'm going to marry." She closed her eyes. "I'll be all grown up then and won't need permission."

He kissed the top of her. "Yes, you'll be all grown up then."

Burrowing her cheek deep into the pillow, she mumbled, "I'm going to sleep now, Pa."

"You do that, Angel girl," Ellis whispered past the tightening in his throat and chest. His insides were a tangled mass of emotions he couldn't decipher. Angel's leg would be fine, it was a clean break that set quickly, and as long as she stayed off it so the bones could heal she'd be as good as new in a few weeks. He on the other hand, had doubts if he'd ever be fine again. Leastwise not until he had a chance to explain things to Constance.

Constance did love Angel, and he'd grown accustomed to the laughter and lightheartedness they filled the house with. It was the aching inside him he'd silently battled. At first, he'd struggled with the fact it was no longer his dead wife he wanted, but, as hard as it was for him to admit, he'd never desired Christine as profoundly as he did Constance. It had been that admission that made him understand he was no longer content in his life as a widower, hadn't been since he'd discovered the intense love he had for Constance.

He bowed his head, and let his eyes flutter shut. Could Constance forgive him? Not just for Ashton's will. He'd hurt her when he'd said he didn't believe she was still in love with her husband. He'd been where she was at, knew denial was a person's first reaction. He hadn't believed he no longer loved Christine at first, either. Given the choice to stay or leave, Constance would leave. Whether he loved her or not, she'd leave. Just as he would have, not so long ago.

Chapter Twelve

"Is she sleeping?"

The whispered words might as well have been shouted, the way Ellis bolted out of his chair.

Constance stood at the foot of the bed, running a hand along Angel's uninjured leg. The gown she wore was olive green with rows of tiny bits of lace running up and down the front, and made her look even lovelier than she had earlier.

Ellis took a breath to calm the racing in his chest. He glanced to his daughter, watched the way her chest rose and fell evenly before he replied, "Yeah, she's sleeping." His quivering voice box made his whispered answer scratch his throat. He coughed to relieve the pressure. "Constance."

She didn't turn his way; instead she closed her eyes with an agonizing slowness that made the swirling of his insides almost painful.

The chatter of the party below entered the room. Lost in his disheartened world, he'd forgotten about the holiday guests. Not that it mattered. Constance needed him, and he needed her. If only he could tell her how much.

He moved to her side. Tears rolled down her face. He wiped them away, and then drew her to his chest, where he held her tight. "Angel's going to be fine," he whispered.

"I know." She sniffled and snuggled in deeper.

The sweet, vanilla scent wafting around him had the ability to make him lightheaded. Or maybe it was simply holding her. He kissed the top of her head. This was how things were meant to be, Constance in his arms. His love was so different this time. With Christine it had developed slowly over years of growing up and maturing, but with Constance, love had hit him like a train barreling downhill. The force and intensity had him unable to think of anything except her. He'd tried to fight it, had been since he'd seen her sitting on the chair outside of Link's, but the battle was over.

He understood how precious the prize was, but he couldn't claim it. Not right now. Constance needed time, and he had to give it to her. He folded his arms tighter around her slender form, absorbing the bliss of simply holding her.

Her arms around his waist tightened, and her sniffles grew stronger.

Ellis forced his mind to go beyond what he felt, and concentrate on her. Her crying continued to escalate instead of decline. He leaned back, cupped her chin with one hand. "Hey, there," he whispered, while wiping at the steady trickle on her cheeks. "Angel's fine. The worst is over."

She nodded, squeezing her eyes shut.

His heart balled into a hard knot, making every beat raw. In the brief moment he'd looked into her eyes, he'd seen a pain so deep he started to tremble. "Constance—"

Shaking her head, she stepped back, pushing on his chest. He let her go, reluctantly, and watched for a glimpse of her next move. She spun and headed toward the door. He followed, laying a hand on her shoulder.

Shrugging, she whispered, "Ellis, please."

"Please what?" Confusion clouded in his mind. "Where are you going?"

"To pack."

Incapable of moving, of even breathing, he watched her race out of the room. It seemed like an eternity before his wits returned. He ran then, out the door and down the hall. The door to her room was closing. He caught it before it shut.

She spun around. Her chin was thrust forward and her spine stiff, but it was a show. He saw deeper, into her very soul. It was like a slap in the face. The pain and loss were beyond anything he'd ever known, and there was more, a battle ensued inside her. He was the cause. He had pushed her too far, too fast.

The validity of it all stung his spirit. Deeply. Profoundly.

"Where are you going?" he asked, when capable. She was leaving and he had to let her. He loved her too much not to.

She glanced to the trunks stacked along the wall. "I've asked Jeb if I can ride to Ashton's place with him this evening."

Another day, another time, he'd watched one of those dome tops rock back and forth across the floor. In an odd way, the memory drew strength from the pit of his being. Someday, somehow, she'd be able to love him; he'd be here, waiting for her with open arms. His hands curled into fists so tight his knuckles stung. He could do it. He'd wait for years if that's what she needed.

"Just take what you need for a few days." It was amazing how normal he sounded, since his insides were blubbering. "I'll fix the hinges on your broken trunk and have it delivered to you."

With those pain-filled eyes, she stared at him for several quiet moments before she whispered, "Thank you."

His control was ebbing, fading with every second. He stepped closer and laid a hand upon her cheek. "For what it's worth, I'm sorry."

She shook her head, but then leaned into his touch, pressing the softness of her cheek deep into his palm. "I—I'd like to come and see Angel in a few days." She sniffled and caught her breath with a little sob. "If that's all right."

The desire to pull her close ate at his mind and body until he trembled. He had to swallow the log in his throat in order to answer. "Of course it's all right. Anytime, night or day, and for as long as you want to stay."

Her struggle was fierce. Confusion, fear, pain and a list of other things he could only imagine. It was on her face, in her shaky breathing, pouring from the depths of her eyes, and wrenching him in two.

This was by far the hardest thing he'd ever done, letting her go. But for her sake, he had no choice. In time she'd understand it was all right to move on, to love again, just as he had. Leaning forward he placed a kiss on her forehead. His lips didn't want to leave her skin, and it was a combat of inner will to make them.

"Let me know when you need someone to haul your trunks down." He was breaking from the inside out, and had to leave before he shattered.

Without looking back, he crossed the room, pulled open the door and grudgingly forced his feet over the threshold. He didn't go downstairs, instead walked down the hall to his room. There he shut the door and moved to the window where he stood, gazing at the snow-covered hill with blurred vision.

Three days later, Constance wondered how her body was able to function. Her heart hung so heavy in her chest, walking across the room made her breathless. Every part of her body hurt, making even the simplest tasks laborious.

After adding a log to the fire, she made her way back to the bed where she'd spent the majority of her time since arriving at Ashton's home. The house was a one-room cabin, with the bed along one wall, the fireplace and table with two chairs in the center, and a large cook stove and newly built cupboards along the wall opposite from the bed. Upon arrival, Jeb had told her how Ashton had installed the stove a few days before he'd died. He'd also built the cabinets—all for her.

Ironically, the stove was the exact one Ellis had. Every time she looked at it, tears blistered her eyes. She'd done little more than cry for the past few days, and today, Christmas Day, would be no different. Sleep was the only thing that helped, for when she slept, she dreamed. Visions of Ellis refusing to let her leave Heaven on Earth filled her sleeping mind. In the far-off world of dreamland he proclaimed to love her, and she admitted her love for him. Nothing else mattered there. No memories haunted them, no past or present indifferences separated them. They just loved and laughed and lived. Her and Ellis and Angel.

Constance laid her head on the pillow, ready to go to that world again. Beckoning dreamland to ease the pain engulfing her, she closed her eyes and waited for the visions to come.

A knock on the door startled her lids open. She stared at the rafters that held the roof overhead, wondering if they'd go away when she didn't respond. It was likely Jeb or Miles—the two of them lived in a partitioned-off room in the barn—coming to check on her as they did two or three times a day.

The knock sounded again, and she swung her legs off the bed. She didn't bother to straighten the covers, for as soon as she told them she was fine and didn't need anything they'd leave and she'd return to the comforting dreams.

She did run both hands over her hair, to smooth it down and then push the front clumps behind each ear. Mustering a smile was impossible, so she simply pulled open the door.

Lula Mae's eyes widened, going from Constance's head to her stocking-covered toes. "Good Lord, girl!" The woman propelled into the house, kicking the door shut behind her. As soon as she set a large basket on the table, her hands were all over Constance's face. "Are you ill?" Lula Mae continued to pat and probe. "You don't seem to have a temperature, but it's so cold in this place it's hard to tell."

Constance could do little more than stare. Seeing Lula Mae reminded her of the moment her heart had shattered. Similar to the punch bowl full of eggnog, her heart had hit the floor so hard it had splinted into a million pieces, leaving nothing except painfully sharp shards. It had happened when she'd walked out of Angel's bedroom, accepting she couldn't put off leaving any longer.

She was still numb, probably would be for the rest of her life.

"Here, sit," Lula Mae demanded, leading Constance to the table. A blanket was draped over her shoulders before Lula Mae piled log after log into the fireplace. The woman then turned her attention to the cook stove. In no time, she had a fire blazing there, too, and a kettle of water sitting on the front burner.

"We're going to have some tea," Lula Mae said, opening the flap on the basket and pulling out a dainty porcelain pot decorated with yellow roses along with two matching cups and saucers.

Staring at the tiny flowers, Constance asked, "What are you doing here, Lula Mae?"

"Making tea," the woman answered still bustling about.

Constance didn't want tea. She just wanted to return to the bed. "Why?"

Lula Mae wasn't a large woman, nor was she tiny, just average, with a few tiny lines around her eyes and impressions near her mouth that grew deep as she smiled. "Why?" She placed a finger below Constance's chin, holding her gaze. "Because you need a friend, and by the looks of things, I arrived just in time."

To Constance, it felt as if an eggshell surrounded her and someone had just cracked it on the side of a pan. It was an odd sensation, quite inexplicable, and accompanied by another realization. "I've never had a friend," she admitted.

Lula Mae's gaze grew soft and tender. "You do now."

Believing she didn't even deserve a friend, Constance shook her head.

Lula Mae smiled sweetly as she moved to the stove. After filling the teapot with hot water, she dropped in the steeper and sat down on the other side of the table. "I was out to see Ellis and Angel yesterday."

A thrill zipped up through Constance, snagging on her heart. "How are they? How's Angel's leg?"

"Fine. Ellis had her sitting on the divan in the front parlor." Lula Mae patted the large basket. "They sent some things for you."

Something inside her burst, made her want to cry again. "They did?"

Lula Mae tested the tea by pouring a small amount in a cup. "Not quite ready." Her hand ran along the top of the kettle as she added, "Ellis bought this tea set for you a couple weeks ago."

Constance's throat locked up.

"He'd ordered Angel a new saddle for Christmas some time ago, and stopped in to pick it up. This set had just arrived. Quick as a whip he told me to wrap it up. Said you talked about having afternoon tea with your aunts back in England. I'd never seen Ellis that giddy. He was downright excited to give it to you." Lula Mae tested the tea again, and this time filled both cups. "I brought along some cookies, but I have some other things I think you need more than sweets."

Bread and cheese, along with ham slices, came out of the basket next. Constance watched the unloading, while her mind danced with visions of Ellis buying the tea set. He was such a thoughtful man, and she missed him so terribly much. The blistering tears came again. "Lula Mae, it's Christmas Day, you should be with your family," she half blubbered. The desire to climb back into bed and let the tears roll was overtaking her. "Thank you for coming to see me. It was very nice."

Lula Mae laughed. "You aren't getting rid of me that easy, girl. I said I'm your friend." She set a plate of food in front of Constance. "Friends are there for us when we need them, no matter what day of the year it is."

She didn't have the strength to stand, and the bed looked a mile away. The trip to Ashton's place from town wasn't a short one, either, and it had to be bitterly cold outside, as it was inside. Another lump formed in her throat. "Lula Mae, you shouldn't have…." She choked up. "I don't deserve—"

"Deserve?" Lula Mae shook her head, and then leaned across the table to gather Constance's hands. "You deserve a life full of happiness and love and friendship. We all do."

That's what she'd had at the ranch, with Ellis and Angel. It had been so wonderful. If only it could have lasted. But that had been impossible from the beginning. She shook her head, chasing away the notion she'd been sent away again, like when she was a child. She'd harbored that excuse for years, believing if she'd remained in Virginia she could have saved her family. Not so unlike Angel and her animals—except Angel put her beliefs into use, whereas Constance had just wallowed in self-pity. Furthermore, she hadn't been sent away this time—she'd run, all on her own accord. Life was life. Past, present or future, it was time she admitted her shortcomings—without blaming others.

"It's Christmas Day. You should be with your husband," she told Lula Mae.

"Link knows where I'm at, and we'll have our Christmas celebration when I get home." Lula Mae sat back in her chair and her expression grew thoughtful. "I'll never forget the day I met him. It's been ten years now. I was on my way to California."

The sip of tea Constance took left her stomach growling. She picked up a slice of cheese to nibble on while waiting for Lula Mae to continue. The woman appeared to be in no hurry to leave, and had traveled a long way. The least she could do was listen.

"My folks owned a saloon back in Abilene—Kansas that is—during the cattle drive days. There was a group of us girls that were pretty good at singing and playing the piano, and decided we'd head west to the gold country and make us some real money."

Constance washed the ham in her mouth down with a sip of tea. "What happened?"

"Link happened," Lula Mae answered with a laugh. "The girls and I were part of a wagon train that stopped in Cottonwood to replenish supplies before heading over to Gooddale's Cutoff. The minute I walked in his store, I was lost."

"Lost?"

"Uh-huh," Lula Mae mumbled while sipping

her tea. She let out a laugh then. "Head over heels and cut off at the knees. It took that man less than a day to talk me out of heading to California and staying here instead. 'Course, anyone that's met him knows he can talk a rattle off a snake, and he sure enough did it to me."

"He asked you to marry him?"

Lula Mae chuckled. "No, I was the one that told him we'd be getting married as soon as the preacher made his rounds."

"You were?"

"Yup. You know how it is, when you can't think of anyone else, when you can't keep your hands to yourself no matter how hard you try, and all you want to do is snuggle up next to them and let the world roll on by."

The cup in Constance's hand clattered as it landed on the saucer. The food she'd eaten grew heavy and thick in her stomach.

Lula Mae eyed her. "You do know what I'm talking about."

Constance had no control over how her head nodded in agreement.

"So what are you doing here?" Lula Mae asked. "When the man you love is over at Heaven on Earth, as miserable as you."

"He's miserable?"

Lula Mae pointed a finger across the table. "He looks about as worn out and wretched as you."

The image of Ellis bowed over his wife's grave flashed before her eyes like a lightning bolt. "He's missing Christine, not me."

A barrel laugh echoed over the room. Lula Mae covered her mouth, stifling her laughter. "Christine's been dead a long time, and I've never seen Ellis looking the way he did yesterday." The woman refilled Constance's teacup. "Why don't you start at the beginning, back in Europe, and tell me what's happened. Sometimes saying things aloud makes us understand them better."

Constance bit her bottom lip. She hadn't shared her tale with anyone. Was she even able to do so? Parts of her past were buried so deep she doubted she could recall what had happened.

"Trust me, Constance, getting it all out will make more sense, and let you find your next steps."

The past was best left forgotten, she'd determined that years ago. Yet she did have to move on. Couldn't stay in the cabin, crying her eyes out for years to come. The yellow roses on the teacup glistened as Constance spun the tiny cup about on the saucer. Aunt Theresa would have loved the flowers, while Aunt Julia would have said the cups were too dainty to be serviceable.

"I know you lived with family in England, why was that?" Lula Mae asked.

"My parents sent me there when the war broke out. It was only supposed to be for a few months, but my father, mother and brothers died in the fighting. I most likely would have died, too, so I guess in the end, I was the lucky one." An unexpected sense of resolve washed over her. She'd never considered the outcome of her leaving Virginia as lucky. Leaving Heaven on Earth as she had made her understand how deeply her parents had loved her—sending her away meant, saving her life. When you love someone you want the best for them, no matter what it is and how badly it hurts you. Her aunts had loved her, too, she'd never doubted that. She hadn't been able to save them, no more than she'd been able to save her family, but she could save Ellis and Angel. Perhaps telling Lula Mae everything would help. Make her broken heart understand Ellis and Angel were better off without her.

"That war was an awful thing. Hurt a lot of families," Lula Mae said softly. "When did you return home?"

Home. One little word that means so much. "I wanted to go home so badly," she admitted, "even after my parents and brothers died. Not just Virginia, but the United States. When I met Byron I couldn't ask enough questions about America."

"Byron?"

"My husband."

"Oh?" Lula Mae's eyes were wide.

Constance waited for fear or dread to trounce

upon her like it had in the past, but nothing happened. Evidently she was too numb for even that. "I met him on Christmas Day last year. My aunts lived several miles outside of London, and Byron stopped at our place to ask directions to a party he'd been invited to. My aunts had several friends over, who invited him in, all giving him different directions as to where the party might be."

Aunt Julia had been the only one skeptical about his arrival. She'd wanted to chase him off the front porch with the broom. "The family he searched for was a few miles up the road. I'd tutored their children during the summer months, so I gave him the proper directions and he left. But the next day he came back, and the day after. Each time he brought little treats for my aunts, tea and fancy crumpets, and he'd tell me all about America. When he arrived on the third day, Aunt Julia had become ill, so I met him at the door and said he couldn't enter, not knowing if what she had was contagious. He insisted on seeing her, and even brewed a pot of tea for her. The poor dear couldn't drink any though, nothing stayed down. She died the next day."

"Oh, my, she was really ill."

"Yes, Aunt Theresa as well. Byron brought a doctor out to see her, but nothing helped, and ten days later, she died."

"How dreadful." Lula Mae leaned her elbows on the table. "But you never became ill?"

"No."

"And then?"

"Byron asked me to marry him, and I said yes." Constance shook her head, trying to recall exactly how it had happened. "There were so many things to see to. A solicitor was at the door when we returned from the funeral, and other people, needing papers signed and payments for things...." It was no clearer now that it had been then. "I was so confused. Byron took care of most of it."

"He did?"

"Yes, he even packed my trunks, since I was quite overcome with grief. I barely recall the ride to London. We were married there and bought our passages to America." Something cold and chilling tickled her spine. "It was costly and I was uncomfortable spending my aunts' monies, but Byron assured me once we got to America he'd have access to his funds again. It was as though I was in some kind of a fog. A dream really, and wishing I could wake up so it would all go away."

"Did you leave then? For America?" Lula Mae asked.

Pain grew inside her head, and Constance pressed a hand to her forehead. "No. There was a performance Byron wanted to see. I'd had a headache for days, and the music was so loud we left early. Instead of hiring a coach, we walked back to the hotel. We were in the alley, not on the street, and Byron said it was so he could kiss me." A sudden lurching happened in her stomach. "But instead, he shot me," she whispered.

"What?" Lula Mae gasped.

Constance hadn't told anyone the entire story, not even the authorities when asking about Byron. Then again, they hadn't asked. She ran a hand over her stomach, feeling the scars as tears pinpricked her eyes. "He shot me. The next thing I remember was the surgeon telling me I'd never be able to have children. He'd extracted the bullet, but the damage had been too extensive."

"Good heavens, girl. Does Ellis know all this?"

"No."

"How'd you get to America?"

"I had some money that I hadn't told Byron about, and I used it to stay at the hotel until I was able to travel. I left for New York as soon as I could. To find him."

"Who? Byron?"

"Yes. He'd sailed for New York the day after I was shot. I believe he left me in the alley to die. The surgeon said two boys found me—saved my life." Anger of what she'd uncovered before leaving England returned with renewed force. "I had to find Byron, not because I loved him, but to get my aunts' money back. He'd even sold their cottage. He had no right to do that."

"Did you find him in New York?"

"Not really. I thought I saw him a couple of times, but…" Constance shook her head, chasing away the quivers rippling her shoulders. "I finally found his widow."

"Widow? You got my head spinning, girl."

"I know," Constance agreed. Hers had been spinning for months. Still was. "His widow claimed Byron had been shot in England and died shortly after retuning to America. She said she was going to turn me into the authorities for trying to kill him in England. I went to the police station, asking who was investigating the case so I could share my side of the story, but no one knew anything about it. I went back to her house several times, but she was never home, or if she was, she didn't open the door. I went back to the police, too, but they said without a body there wasn't a case. Eventually, I ran out of money. I could no longer pay for lodging and started doing laundry at the boarding house in exchange for room and board. That left me little time to continue my pursuit."

"How long were you in New York?"

"About seven months. I didn't know what to do. I didn't believe Byron was dead, and continued to search for him, until the night his widow came to the boarding house and took me to the cemetery. She showed me his grave and said Byron had told her all about me on his death bed. She knew about my aunts and their deaths. She called me a husband stealer, and claimed I'd shot and robbed Byron in the alley. She said all he'd wanted was to return home and die in her arms. Their children were with her. Two boys and a girl. The boys looked just like Byron, and the oldest one asked me why I had killed his father." The child's innocence tore at Constance's heart all over again.

"Oh, Good Lord, girl. My heart's just a-breaking for what you've been through." Lula Mae leaned across the table. "What did you do then?"

Constance shrugged. "I had no choice but to believe her, the grave already had grass growing on it. She said she'd gone to the police—told them all about me, not just that I'd killed her husband, but how I had ruined their entire family." Constance met Lula Mae's gaze, begging for someone, anyone to believe her. "I never knew he was married. I didn't particularly want to marry him, it just happened. And I didn't kill him. I don't even know how to fire a gun. I've never touched one."

Lula Mae wrapped her hands around Constance's. "Of course you didn't kill him. No one could believe you did."

"I thought about going to the police again, but I was scared. If they believed her and not me, I'd be arrested."

Lula Mae frowned. "So you became Ashton's mail-order bride?"

Constance nodded. "The day after seeing Byron's grave, a girl I knew showed me Ashton's letter. She wasn't interested in traveling to Wyoming, and traded the letter for a dress. It seemed my only hope. I had no money and I thought the authorities were looking for me. I wrote to Ashton that afternoon, and when his reply and funds arrived two weeks later, I left New York." Now, here she was, a mere month after arriving in Wyoming, in worse shape than when she'd left New York. This time she'd managed to include a broken heart in the tangled mess her life had become.

Lula Mae sat quietly for a moment, and then after giving Constance's hands a tender squeeze, she let them loose and pressed both hands to her bosoms. "Dear Heavens, I never imagined your tale would be so…so tragic. I don't even know what to say."

"You don't need to say anything. I need to say thank you. You have no idea what a relief it is to have told someone. I feel as if I just lost a hundred pounds." It was true, telling the story had cleared out space inside her. Left more room for her heart to wallow in pity. Constance rose and walked to the fireplace. She stirred the flames and added a few logs.

Lula Mae had spun in her chair; as Constance replaced the poker, Lula said, "It's a tragic story, Constance, a truly tragic one, but I still don't understand why you are here, and Ellis is at his ranch."

"Because I love them," she admitted. "I can't put him and Angel in danger."

"Danger?"

"Yes, if the authorities find me—"

"*If* the authorities are looking for you, and *if* they find you, you'll tell them the truth. That you didn't kill anyone."

"Which is worse." In spite of the flames, Constance was chilled to the bone and went to the cook stove to add a few logs to that fire as well.

"Worse?"

The authorities had been a ruse she used upon herself, lessening the threat of her real fear. "Byron's still alive, Lula Mae. I don't know how I know, but I do. And he'll find me."

Lula Mae jumped to her feet. "We need to get you back to Heaven on Earth."

"I can't go back there."

"Why not? Good heavens, girl—"

"There's no reason for Ellis to protect me from Byron." Constance returned to her chair. Not even the fear of Byron overrode her broken heart. "I don't have anything to give him in exchange. I don't have anything Ellis needs. Now that the holiday party's over, he doesn't even need a housekeeper."

Shaking her head, Lula Mae sat down. "Honey, Ellis has put on that holiday party for years without a housekeeper. He loves you. You love him. That's enough reason right there."

Pain came forth as strong as ever. Constance squeezed her eyes shut, holding the tears at bay. "He wants more children. I can never give him that."

"Did he tell you that?"

Constance bit her lip, dredging up enough fortitude to continue. "No, you did. At the par—"

"I should never have said that," Lula Mae interrupted, "about Ellis and more children. It wasn't my place, and I don't believe it holds any bearing on his love for you."

Constance shook her head. "Ellis still loves Christine, not me. I'd hoped…" The words burned too hard for her to continue.

Lula Mae took her hands. "Ellis may still love Christine, may always love her as we all do those that have passed on, but he's *in* love with you. I saw it the day he bought you this tea set, but more so, I saw it at the holiday party. His eyes never left you, and when he had his arms around you, and you were holding on to him while the doctor saw to Angel, I knew for certain. The two of you were right where you should have been. I could feel the love, not just pouring out to Angel, but to each other."

Constance pressed a hand to the ache in her

chest. The memories were too painful. The loss too great.

Lula Mae wouldn't give up. "There's a certain look a man and woman share when they're in love. It's there. I saw it. Ellis loves you. Angel loves you. And you love them."

"Even if that were true, I can't give him more children," Constance whispered.

Lula Mae knelt down in front of her. "Link was married before me," she said. "His first wife died, too. But it's never made me question his love for me. Actually, it's made our love stronger, because we both know how precious it is, and how lucky we are to wake up next to each other every morning." Another protest rose in Constance but Lula Mae continued, "Link and I haven't had any babies. Can't say why. Guess it just isn't meant to be." Her whisper grew softer. "You and Ellis are lucky, you already have Angel. Don't befuddle your good fortune by wanting more than you need."

Lula Mae's perspective hit, jarring the splinters inside Constance heart. Could it be true? Ellis had never mentioned more children. Of course he still loved Christine, as did Angel. They had a right to, just as she'd forever love her aunts and brothers and parents. Furthermore, even though he'd known of Ashton's will, he'd never spoken of her leaving. Not once. Nor had he penned anything about it in their agreement. And when he'd kissed her, he'd made her feel like the only person in the universe. Yes, when he kissed her. Though she'd wanted it, he had always been the one to initiate their kisses, their embraces. If she knew anything about him, it was that he didn't do anything without careful consideration.

Constance's heart, just starting to pull itself back together, bounced off the pit of her stomach and landed on the floor, splintering into a million pieces all over again. After all the kind and wonderful things he'd done for her, she'd betrayed him. Told him she'd pretended he was Byron. "Oh, dear Lord," she sobbed. "What have I done?"

Chapter Thirteen

Ellis paced his office like a caged bear he'd once seen at a circus in Cheyenne. *Give her time. Give her time.* Repeating it over and over didn't help. Didn't make the minutes, hours or days go faster. Didn't ease the agonizing desire to see her. Didn't calm the fears she was cold or hungry or scared out at Ashton's place all alone.

"Damn it!" He slapped the top of his desk so hard several papers flew off. Ignoring how they fluttered to the floor, he leaned heavily on the wood. It had been a week, seven days, since she'd left. Had that been long enough? His gaze went to the window and the little fenced in area covered with new fallen snow.

"No, it hasn't been long enough," he muttered. It had taken him six years.

He twisted his neck, flinching as the tension

popped along the top of his spinal cord. He'd perish if she needed that long. The gut-wrenching misery he was in would flat-out kill him long before six years were up. Perhaps he could just ride out and see her. Make sure she was all right. Hank would keep an eye on Angel while he was gone. But would seeing her make the waiting easier or harder?

He picked up the envelope near his foot that had been delivered at the holiday party. The trip would give him a chance to tell her about Eli's letter. His brother had said the property near Richmond was known as Royalton. A land agent from New York named Byron Carmichael had tried to sell it earlier in the year, but was having a hard time proving who owned it. The letter didn't mention their names—the elderly women who had been overseeing the property for their young charge in England—but Ellis knew they were her aunts. Had to be. The letter did say that Eli felt he'd uncovered a conspiracy and would send more information as soon as possible.

A knock on the front door had Ellis spinning about. The rap sounded again as he made his way down the hall. He paused near the parlor where Angel was reclining on the sofa, reading a book. Mustering up a grin was tough, but he managed to pull one together. "How you doing, scamp?"

"I'm fine, Pa. Who's at the door?" she asked.

Someone knocked again. "I don't know," he admitted, "I'm on my way to answer it."

"Well, get going before they knock the door down," she suggested.

Her smart mouth lifted his spirits a touch, but apprehension set in when he opened the door to find Link and Lula Mae standing there.

"Good afternoon, Ellis," the storekeeper greeted.

"What's happened?" His insides said it pertained to Constance.

Lula Mae reached behind her and tugged someone forward. "We brought Tanna out to visit with Angel for the afternoon. Hope that's all right."

The young girl, one of Angel's friends who lived in town, waved. "Hi, Mr. Clayton."

He sighed, though not totally convinced Constance was fine. "Hi, Tanna." Stepping aside he gestured everyone over the threshold. "Angel's in the parlor. She'll be glad to see you."

"Thanks." The girl buzzed past and as soon as she turned the corner, excited squeals emitted.

"Thanks," Ellis said, feeling a bit uneasy. He should have thought about finding company for Angel. For Link to have driven Tanna out was a bit odd. "Who's minding your store?"

Lula Mae hooked Ellis's elbow with hers. "No one is minding the store. We—" her gaze went to Link "—decided it could be closed for one afternoon. Didn't we?"

"Yes, we did," Link agreed. He pushed the door to the kitchen open. "Got a cup of coffee to share, Ellis?"

Ellis cringed at his lack of manners. "Of course." With Lula Mae's elbow still hitched with his, he led the way into the kitchen. The space wasn't messy, since Beans brought meals in for him and Angel, but it didn't have the glow it had had while Constance had been home.

Home. The word hit him like a branch falling off a tree in a storm. Would she ever consider this her home? Why should she? She not only had Ashton's place, from the sound of Eli's letter, she also had property in Virginia. He moved toward the stove. "It'll take a few minutes to get a fire started." One hadn't been built in the stove since Constance had left.

"I'll do it," Lula Mae offered. "You sit down with Link. He needs to talk to you."

"What about?"

Link sat down and patted the back of a nearby chair. "Have a seat, Ellis."

An eerie sensation traveled along Ellis's spine. "What's going on? As long as I've known you, I can count on one hand the number of days your store has been closed."

Link patted the chair again. Ellis sat, glancing from Lula Mae building a fire and back to Link, who was looking much too thoughtful.

"Quite a storm we had again, the past couple of days," Link started, folding his arms across his chest.

"Yeah," Ellis agreed, feeling as if another storm was about to hit.

"It's done now though," Link said. "Sun's shining. The sleigh made it out here with no problems. Traveling ain't too bad at all."

Ellis was ready to snap. "Are you trying to irritate me, Link? I gotta warn you, it won't take much. I'm not in the mood for small talk, so spit out why you came, and don't try to make me believe it was so Tanna could visit with Angel."

Lula Mae answered from her position near the stove, "We aren't trying to irritate you, Ellis. We have something to talk to you about, and Link was just trying to break the ice."

"Consider it broken. What do you want to tell me?" He had no patience left. Between the weather, being cooped up, worrying about Angel and Constance out at Ashton's—too far away for him to check on—he was at the end of his rope.

Link laid a hand on the table. "Lula Mae made it out to see Constance."

Ellis's heart cartwheeled.

"She's fine," Link hurried to say. "Jeb was in this morning, they made it through the last storm just fine, too."

"Does she have enough to eat out there?" Ellis

asked Lula Mae. "Did you give her the basket I packed? Is it warm enough? How's her wood supply?" His mind then went in another direction. "Are men lining up at her door?"

Lula Mae set the coffeepot on the stove. "She has everything she needs right now. And I posted a note that said there wouldn't be any interviews for her hand. Ever."

Ellis had already said as much on the night of the holiday party, which had had men leaving faster than they had arrived. But he hadn't known if it had kept them from her door.

Lula Mae walked to the table. "Ellis, she told me about her first husband, and I'm wondering what you know about him?"

Ellis didn't so much as know the man's name. A tightening happened deep inside him. "Nothing. Other than he's dead."

"His name was Byron Carmichael," Link said.

Lightning shot up his backbone. "Byron Carmichael?"

Lula Mae pulled out a chair. "Normally, I wouldn't repeat what a friend told me in confidence. I've held a lot of secrets over the years, and most I'll carry to my grave, but this one I just can't. That man did Constance wrong, Ellis. Real wrong, and I just can't sit around and not do something about it."

The contents of Eli's letter, so fresh in his mind, had his hands balling into fists. "What did he do?"

"He shot her for one," Link said, quite disgustedly.

Too stunned to react, Ellis repeated, "Shot her?"

"Back in England," Lula Mae added. "And then left her for dead in an alley after he stole all her aunts' money."

"The hell you say." Ellis jumped from his chair. The image of Constance lying hurt in an alley had his heart racing and temples pounding. "Why didn't she ever tell me any of this?"

"Well, I suspect it ain't something she's too proud of," Link said.

Ellis glared. The urge to punch someone had never been stronger.

"Constance has nothing to be ashamed of," Lula Mae said, casting a shameful look at Link.

The man bowed his head in a way Ellis had never seen. "No, she don't," Link agreed. "She surely don't."

"Anyway, that's not the reason we're here," Lula Mae said.

"Then what is? What more do you know?"

"The man's not dead," Lula Mae said.

Ellis knew the man wasn't dead, leastwise not from the sound of Eli's letter. Why would Constance have claimed he was? The coffeepot boiled over, filling the room with sizzling spits and spatters—just like his insides. Was she running from the man? The one who'd shot her? Had she claimed her husband was dead to stop his advances?

"I don't think she should be living out there with just Jeb and Miles," Lula Mae said, lifting the pot off the stove. "Don't take me wrong. I like them both, but Jeb's little more than a kid, and Miles is an old man. Neither of them would be much protection if her husband comes looking for her. And I think he will. I don't believe he's done hurting her yet."

Ellis was already moving toward the back door, to where his coat and hat hung, but Lula Mae intercepted him, blocking his reach. "Where you going?" she asked.

"To get her," he stated the obvious. "Husband or not, he's going to have to go through me to get her." Ellis turned to Link. "There's a letter on my desk from my brother Eli. Take it to John Hempel and ask him to hire a Pinkerton man to investigate Carmichael."

Link nodded and Lula Mae, as quick as a bee, snatched his hat and coat from the hook. "That's a good plan, Ellis. But…"

Ellis struggled for self-control, he wanted to rip the coat and hat from Lula Mae and ride to Ashton's, yet the way she paused had his nerve endings popping beneath his skin. "But what?"

"That girl's been through a lot between England

and here—and she did it all alone. She's experienced a lot of pain and suffering, and needs someone to understand that."

Ellis shivered, as if a goose walked over his grave. He'd known her past was grim. Had since that first night in his office. Yet not once in all the weeks he'd known her had she ever appeared weak or powerless. The day Beans had stormed through the door with his iron spoon waving and ranting about the banana bread, the only one who'd remained calm and unalarmed had been Constance.

Regret fueled his ire like oil on a fire. Why hadn't he asked her about her past? Talked to her, let her know he'd help in whatever way he could. His body, as if able to answer for him, hummed with memories. That's why. Most days he'd been too infatuated with her to think clearly. His mind had been jumbled with his own problems, his own issues. His own needs.

"*Ask* her to come home, Ellis," Lula Mae said softly. "Constance needs to be asked, and she needs to be wanted and loved. She hasn't seen love since her parents sent her to England." Lula Mae handed him his coat. "She's forgotten what it is. What it looks like. What it feels like. And how nothing else matters."

First Angel and now Lula Mae. Why hadn't *he* figured out to *ask* her? Well, he would now. Most definitely. Ellis shrugged into his coat, but wondered if he'd need it with the way his heart pumped hot blood through out his body. "I'll ask her, Lula Mae. And I'll tell her just how much I love her."

Lula Mae's face softened. "She loves you, too, Ellis. She just didn't know what to do about it."

He grabbed the door handle, but realization hit. "Angel—"

"Tanna's mama said Tanna could spend the night with Angel, and I think I'll hang around and spend the night, too," Lula Mae said. "If that's all right with you of course."

Ellis was so downright excited he wanted to kiss her, so he did. Flipped around and planted a big kiss right on Lula Mae's grinning lips.

"Ellis," Link said as Ellis pulled open the door. "I got that letter from your office, I'll head back to town and talk with John Hempel, see what he can do to get that investigation started."

At this moment, Ellis took back every frustrated thought he'd ever had about Link. The man was a true friend. The excitement of seeing Constance had him glowing inside. "Thanks, Link, I appreciate it. Tell him to spare no costs, none at all."

Link nodded. "I'm on my way."

"Go on," Lula Mae encouraged, pushing him out the door. "You got a long ride ahead."

He moved, but spun around before she closed the door. "Tell Angel—"

"I'll tell Angel you went to see Constance. She'll be happy. Now scoot!"

He nodded and leaped down the steps in one bound.

"Don't break your neck before you get there!" Lula Mae shouted in his wake.

He waved a hand, but never turned around, making his way to the barn at a dead run. He hadn't run this fast in years and damn if it didn't feel good. If he didn't feel good.

Constance lugged the bucket of water along the snowy trail. The weight pulled on her arm, but she trudged forward. Jeb and Miles had hauled so many gallons of water this morning, she wasn't about to ask them to carry more. She'd waited until they both had ridden away, out to check on the cows, before she'd made her way to the well.

Her hair was still damp from the thorough washing she'd given it, and the brisk wind made a few frozen tendrils snap at her cheeks. She didn't mind. This was the last bucket, would be more than enough to last her through the rest of the day and night.

The water the men carried in this morning she'd used to take a long hot bath in preparation for tomorrow's journey. She'd wanted to go long before now, but the weather hadn't cooperated. The days of being snowed in had given her time to clean the cabin from top to bottom, hence the reason she needed a bath. The cobwebs had been thick enough to cut with a knife. How she hadn't noticed them the first few days was beyond her.

Then again, with the way Jeb and Miles constantly checked in on her, it was amazing she'd got as much done as she did. They were kind men, but acted as if she couldn't even wipe her own nose. No one had ever coddled her—thankfully—because she really didn't like it.

She shifted hands, carrying the heavy bucket on the other side for a while. It wasn't much further, but with the deep snow, she had to keep the bucket hefted nearly to her waist. If a shovel had been near, she'd have cleared a path, but her quick glance in the barn hadn't discovered one, and the condition of the barn didn't show evidence one might be anywhere about.

Frowning, she gave herself a chiding. Who was she to criticize how Jeb and Miles chose to live? It was truly none of her business. She was just edgy, that's all. The desire to see Ellis and Angel had her ready to snap at whatever came in her path.

The thought of Ellis had her heart skipping across her chest. She sincerely couldn't wait to see him. Or Angel. She hadn't known she could miss people so profoundly. Lifting her face to the golden sun lighting the earth with a glorious blaze, she grinned. Tomorrow. She'd see them tomorrow no matter what. If Jeb or Miles couldn't take her, she'd walk all the way to Heaven on Earth.

Maybe that was part of why she loved Ellis so much, he not only didn't coddle her, but not once in all the weeks she'd known him had he told her what she could or couldn't do. He trusted her to make her own decisions. He'd even been willing to learn from her. It had only been a bread recipe, but it made her love him all the more.

She arrived at the house. After kicking the snow from her boots, she opened the door and set the bucket down with a thud. It took a few minutes to brush the snow from the hem of her skirt, and then empty the bucket into the larger crock near the cooking stove. The golden brown crust said the meat pie baking in the oven for Jeb and Miles was done, and she set it on the counter before moving to hang her coat near the door.

The men would be surprised. She hadn't cooked for them before today, but hoped the action would persuade them to give her a ride to Heaven on Earth first thing in the morning. It was time she faced up to Ellis, told him about her past and that she'd lied to him. She was nervous; he hadn't deserved to be treated so, and she had no excuse other than that she'd been afraid. The days and nights since Lula Mae's visit had given Constance plenty of time to evaluate the things that mattered and the things that didn't.

Ellis mattered. Angel mattered. In reality, that was it.

The thoughts lifted her spirit, and she floated across the room to where she'd stacked the books from Ellis's library back in the big basket. Amongst several others were *Little Women* and *Around the World in Eighty Days*, telling her Angel had helped pack the basket.

A noise outside the cabin had her moving to peer out the one small window the cabin boasted next to the door. The dark opening of the barn revealed the shadowy figure of a man leading a horse into the darkness.

Jeb and Miles no doubt. She moved to the cupboard to find a plate for them to carry the meat pie to their room. As anticipated, a knock sounded on the door within minutes. One or the other always checked on her as soon as they arrived.

Leaving the pie on the counter for the time being, she moved to the door.

A moment of pure shock rendered her speechless, motionless. Then her heart slammed against her rib cage so hard and fast she thought her chest might break open.

"Hello, Constance."

The voice, though not heard in some time, sent her instincts rearing. In one swift motion, she slammed the door shut and dropped the heavy lock in place.

"Open the door, Constance! Open the door!"

She shouted the only words racing in her mind. "You're dead! You're dead!"

Byron pounded harder. "Do I look dead to you?" The door rattled against the long board bracing it closed. "Open the door, Constance or I'll break it down."

"Go away!"

The bottom of the door bucked, making her jump back. He kicked at it again, and again. The wood was weathered, and wouldn't hold for long. "Go away, Byron. You've already taken everything I had. Go back to New York."

He pounded at the top again. "Open the door, Constance!"

A rifle shot sounded, and Constance cowered, clutching her stomach with both hands. It was a second before she realized it had come from far off. Heart racing in her throat, she bolted to the window. Byron ran for the barn. Another shot sounded but she couldn't see where it came from, and seconds later an iron-black horse with Byron in the saddle tore out of the barn and disappeared beyond her vision.

Constance moved to the door, but fear kept her from lifting the heavy latch board. She stood, trembling from head to toe, and half questioning if Byron had been real or a product of her imagination.

"Miss Jennings! Miss Jennings!" Jeb's shout had her lifting the lock and peeking out. His horse spun in a wide circle, tramping the snow near the door. "Who was that? What did they want?"

Her mind went blank, or was so balled with information it was unable to complete a coherent thought.

"Who was that?" Jeb repeated.

"A m-man," she managed to eke out. "A man I knew in New York—I mean England."

"Friend or foe?" Miles asked in his gruff voice.

"Foe," she admitted. "Most definitely foe." Her stomach erupted, sending a ball of fire to the back of her throat. She made it out the door and to the corner of the cabin before she heaved, over and over again until nothing was left to come out. The spasm continued though, and she leaned against the house, holding her burning stomach.

"Here, ma'am, drink this." Miles handed her the dipper from the house water bucket. "Just rinse your mouth. Don't swallow or it'll come back up."

She did as instructed. It helped, not only in removing the nasty taste from her mouth, but in grounding her. "Thank you." She gave him back the dipper.

"Let's get you inside." Miles led her all the way to the bed along the wall. "Lie down for a few minutes. There's nothing to worry about. Jeb went to make sure the man's gone. And I'm here to look out for you."

The softness of the mattress sucked her in, and she went willingly, closing her eyes as her head sank into the pillow. Something cool was pressed to her forehead. She opened her eyes and took the wet cloth from Miles's hand. "Thank you," she said. "And thank you for arriving when you did."

"You just rest for a few minutes. You can tell us all about it when Jeb gets back."

She placed the cloth over her entire face, hoping it would block the image attempting to plant itself behind her eyelids. Byron's blond hair and faded blue eyes had looked ghostly with all the white snow glittering behind his image. Had he always looked so evil, or was it just because she now knew how wicked he was?

The thunder of hooves sounded outside, but she didn't move. Miles was still in the house and it was just Jeb returning. Soon enough they'd want to hear who'd been at the door and what he'd wanted.

A click echoed as the door opened, followed by footsteps. She pulled the cloth from her face, wondering why Jeb was rushing toward her bed. The image coming at her was the most wonderful thing she'd ever seen. A sob exploded in her throat and tears gushed from eyes. She flipped her legs over the edge of the bed and held up her arms, catching Ellis around the neck as he knelt down beside the bed.

His arms wrapped around her, and filled her with such emotion she buried her face in his neck and did the one thing she sworn she wasn't going to do again. She cried her eyes out. It was what she'd done the last time she'd seen him, the night she'd left Heaven on Earth, and she didn't want him to see her crying again.

He held her, rocking her until the storm inside her slowed. "Shh," he whispered. "Everything's all right."

"You're here," she sobbed into his coat collar. "You're here."

"Yes, I'm here, darling." He hugged her so tightly she was lifted off the edge of the bed. "I'm here."

She folded her knees, planting them on the floor near his, refusing to let even an inch separate them. "I missed you so much."

"I missed you, too."

The gaze in his eyes stole her breath, yet somehow she managed to ask, "You did?"

"I did."

His lips met hers then, in a merger so sweet and precious she closed her eyes and thought of nothing but him. The power of his kiss, the magic of being in his arms was unparalleled, inexplicable.

It was as if a part of her had been missing, and was now back.

The kiss, fully engulfing her senses, lasted a great length of time, but still ended too soon. However, the enchantment of his lips upon hers went on and on. She laid her head against his chest, never wanting to move.

She had to though, when Ellis whispered, "Come here. Let's get you off the floor." He helped her onto the edge of the bed. After he pulled off his coat, and set it aside, he sat down and wrapped an arm around her shoulders. "That's better."

Leaning against him, she whispered, "I can't believe you're here." Then a shiver pinched her spine. "Angel?"

"Is fine." He pressed his forehead against hers.

"Her leg?"

"It's healing." He kissed her chin and the tip of her nose, teasing her lips in an almost wicked way. "I'd have been here before now, but the weather didn't cooperate."

"It didn't cooperate for me, either," she answered, catching his lips. It was in the middle of that kiss her mind chose to suddenly recall the day's event. She hurled herself out of the kiss, glancing around the room. "Where are Miles and Jeb?"

"They must have thought we needed some time alone."

The word *alone* had her clutching his shoulders. "Ellis," she whispered. "I don't want to be here anymore. I want to go home."

Chapter Fourteen

Constance held her breath, waiting for his response. She hadn't meant to sound so desperate, but she was. Being away from him had been torture, excruciating and numbing anguish.

Ellis lifted her chin. "Home?"

She nodded.

"To Heaven on Earth?"

She nodded again.

His fingers combed into her hair, drawing her closer. "I want you to come home more than anything in the world."

Her lips met his at the same time, equal partners in the merger. She gave all she had, parting her lips to deepen the kiss intimately, and sharing all the devotion boiling in her chest. Maybe she pulled him down, or perhaps he led the way, regardless, they reclined onto the bed, scooting across the mattress without breaking their kiss until they lay side by side.

When the kiss ended, she tugged his hat off his head. "I should never have left Heaven on Earth."

He took the hat and tossed it on the floor. "Why did you?"

Constance took a moment to contemplate her answer. It had only been a week, yet seemed so long ago. "I don't know. I didn't want to go, but I was so afraid you'd send me away...."

"Send you away?"

She swiped a clump of his hair off his forehead while searching for a way to say what she had to say. As much as she believed her reasoning, doubt still trickled in. "With the holiday party completed, you wouldn't need a housekeeper any longer."

He shook his head. Heart pounding, she continued, needing him to believe her. "That's what our agreement was for, and when I left Angel's room to change my dress, Jeb was in the hallway—"

"You've always been more than a housekeeper," he interrupted, gently kissing her forehead. "I'm sorry I didn't tell you about Ashton's will. I meant to, but—" he shook his head "—I was afraid you'd leave if I did."

There was such love and sorrow in his eyes her head practically spun. "You were afraid I'd leave?"

"Yes." He cupped her cheek. "I'd never send you away. What made you think that?"

She had to tell him the truth, everything, but it wasn't easy. The bits of fear mingling in her heart twisted into a knot. "History. For years I thought my parents sent me to England because they didn't need me. I was too little, and a girl. Couldn't fight in the war like my brothers—couldn't do anything to help them. It wasn't until lately that I realized they did it for my own safety."

"They did it because they loved you."

"I know that now, but…" She rested her head on the pillow, stared at the ceiling for a moment trying to come up with a way to describe how she'd felt. "I never felt like I *belonged* in England. My aunts were wonderful, but I saw the pity in other people's eyes, heard them whisper how Theresa and Julia were burdened with me."

"Aw, honey," he whispered, slipping his arm beneath her neck and tugging her close.

"I felt at home at Heaven on Earth. As if I had a purpose. A reason for being there."

He ran a finger along the side of her face. "You did, and do. It's where you belong." His lips brushed hers briefly. "I wish I had known. I'd have—"

Shaking her head, she pressed a finger to his lips, unwilling for him to take any blame. "I didn't know. I didn't understand it all until a few days ago." It was time to tell him everything. Delving up an ounce of courage, she began, "I was in your office, and saw you out the window." Ashamed of spying on him, she pulled her eyes from his. "You were at Christine's grave, kneeling in the snow." The image was so clear in her mind she could almost see it in the rafters overhead. "You looked so sad." She fought to hold the tears at bay. "I thought it was because you regretted what had happened between us the night before—wh-when we kissed in your office. I—"

He made her look at him. "I've never regretted kissing you, and never, ever will." His eyes were somber, serious. "I was telling Christine about you. I had been standing guard against the coyotes all night, and that had given me plenty of time to think, to realize what had happened." His fingers combed into her hair. "That morning, I told her I'd fallen in love with you."

She gasped at the eruption in her chest.

"It's true. I love you."

The knowledge had her heart soaring, but remorse burned her throat. "I behaved so foolishly." She'd get on her knees and beg his forgiveness if necessary. "Please forgive how I lied to you that day. I hadn't locked my bedroom door. I was upset you hadn't come to my room, and when I saw you out the window—" Shame tore at her. "I—I've never imagined you were someone else. I should never have said that."

Her emotions were so raw and close to the surface, the hesitancy she sensed in him tore at her. Pressing a hand to his face, praying he believed her, she whispered, "I never loved Byron. I've never loved anyone the way I love you."

He grinned, and kissed her slowly, softly and so sweetly her heart began to sing. As his lips left hers, he whispered, "I've been in love with you since the night I was ill and we kissed."

The gasp in her throat turned into a whimpering moan as her cheeks heated. "You remember that?"

"I'll never forget it," he answered, kissing her brow.

"I thought you were asleep."

"And I thought you'd discover just how much I wanted you then."

She frowned, not comprehending what he meant.

He chuckled and ran a finger playfully down her side. "You were washing me with a cloth, and coming very close…" His palm, floating over her lower stomach, ignited delicious sensations. The mischievous glint in his eyes gave her full understanding.

Enticed, and more than a touch excited, she trailed her hand down his side, over his ribs to where his shirt was tucked in his pants. "Really?"

"Really," he said, capturing her mouth once more.

All sorts of things were zipping to life inside

her. Wants and needs and desires, but when Ellis drew out of the kiss and cast a very somber look upon her, she squirmed a touch, growing fearful of what he was about to say.

"There's something I need to know you understand, Constance."

Almost paralyzed, she nodded.

"The morning you saw me out the window?"

She nodded again.

"I told Christine I was in love with you. I also told her there would always be a part of me that loves her. We had a good life together. She gave me Angel. I'll always be thankful for that. Always love her for that."

The pleading look in his eyes tore at her heart. "Of course you will. I'd expect you to."

He caressed the side of her face with a single fingertip. "But I also want you to know that I never loved her the way I do you. Christine and I knew each other for years. She grew to become my best friend and then my wife. You—" he grinned and touched the end of her nose "—hit me like a snowstorm. You blew in so fast and tied my heart up so quickly I get dizzy just thinking about it. I can't go a minute without thinking about you. I can't look at something without wondering what you'd think about it, if you'd like it. I don't even need a calendar, I mark time using the day you walked into my life."

Her heart could barely hold all the love rushing into it. "That's how it is for me, too."

"You, Constance Jennings, are my world. You are my Heaven on Earth. Not the place, but the feeling."

If a person could melt, she did, into a puddle on the mattress. Ellis joined her, kissing her lips and caressing her body until Constance swore they'd melded into one. He was lying on top of her, but his weight wasn't crushing, instead it was a part of her. She ran her hands over his hard yet supple back, and explored the inner regions of his mouth with her tongue.

Intimate, swirling sensations raced through her veins, making her shift beneath him, so his body could press against her most sensitive points. The ache that lingered inside, the one she knew only he could satisfy, roared into life.

Ellis broke the kiss with several tiny ones as he lifted his face from hers. She ran her hands down the curve of his backside to keep his hips pressed into hers.

He grinned. "Not yet, darling, we aren't done talking."

She wiggled, pressed her hips into his, loving the teasing friction. "I'm done talking."

After a swift kiss, Ellis moved off her. "No you aren't." He sat on the side of the bed and took her hand, pulling her upward.

Even though she'd have rather had him back on top of her, she went willingly, flipping around to sit beside him. The disappointed look she flashed at him said more than words could have.

Chuckling, he wrapped an arm around her shoulders and pulled her close. "I do love you, Constance. More than anyone can imagine."

Smiling, she leaned her head on his shoulder. "And I love you, Ellis. You make me so happy… so…oh, I don't know…I can't describe how wonderful I feel."

"I know," he whispered. "Loving you is like a destination I always wanted to go to, but never knew how to get there. Now that I've found it, I never want to leave."

The room grew still as Constance savored Ellis's declaration. His love was so precious it felt as though she held a delicate crystal ball in her heart. When he shifted to gaze upon her, a glorious wave washed over her. It was there—boldly in his eyes—for her to see. His love wasn't delicate, but solid and rich. Like gold. It would never break, nor tarnish or perish, no matter what.

"Constance?"

She smiled up at him, extremely content, but the seriousness on his face stole a piece of it.

"I'm sorry I never told you about Ashton's will. That was wrong, and not something I'm proud of."

"I understand."

"Do you?" he asked.

She nodded, wondering how to prove it. "I wondered if it was because you wanted the land, but I couldn't imagine why. You already have so much land, and…" She shook her head. "All I could come up with was that you wanted me to stay long enough to host the holiday party."

"The holiday party had nothing to do with it. It was me. All me, and my inability to believe you'd stay if you had somewhere else to go. I felt as if I coerced you into working for me. That's why I didn't have you sign our agreement." He shook his head. "Thinking somehow that made it better. I want you to know, and understand, whatever you own, whatever you bring into our union, is yours. Now and forever."

Seeing how serious he was, she nodded instead of insisting she wanted to share everything she had with him. That could come later.

He bent down and picked his hat off the floor, after setting it on the bed beside him, he asked, "Now, what was Byron Carmichael doing here?"

The swift change of subject stole the gust from her sails. "How did you know it was him?"

"I don't. I'm assuming."

His nearness—his love, kept fear at bay and allowed her to speak and think coherently. "I don't know what he wanted. When I recognized him I shut the door and told him to go away."

"I need you to tell me everything, Constance. I can't help if I don't know what I'm up against."

"I was told he was dead," she said. The fact Byron had been at the door seemed impossible. "Did you see him?"

"No. Jeb lost him in the woods. When I met Jeb on the trail, he said there had been a man pounding on the door that you knew in New York and England."

Still confused, Constance shook her head. "How did he find me? What does he want?"

"I don't know, but I need you to tell me everything you know so we can figure it out. Start with the first time you met him."

It took a moment for Constance to push aside all the wonderful things Ellis stirred inside her and go back to the past she didn't want to recall, then she began to tell him the exact tale she'd told Lula Mae—almost.

Ellis had listened to her every word, asking questions when needed, and digesting all Constance said. His guts churned. Lula Mae was right. There were too many things that didn't add up, and the idea of Constance being left, injured, in a London alleyway had his jaw locked tight and his fingers itching to get a hold of Byron Carmichael by the throat.

He spun around, facing the table where Constance now sat. The way she chewed on her bottom lip said she had something more to say, but didn't know how. It was amazing how he knew so many little details about her. Some were probably things she didn't even know about herself. That's how habits are. Others see them, whereas the person who has them doesn't.

"What haven't you told me?" He wrapped a hand around the one she was tapping on the table. Even years from now, when he was old and feeble, he'd have the desire to touch her.

She continued to chew on her lip. He knelt down, looking directly into those adorable blue eyes, which right now were full of anxiety. "What is it, honey?"

"When…" She wrapped her other hand around the one he still held. "When I told you I was shot…"

"Yes," he softly encouraged her to go on.

"Well, the surgeon—" She swallowed. "The surgeon said I'd never have children. He removed the bullet, but the damage had already been done."

The wave of anger engulfing his system was quickly overshadowed by her distress. "Aw, sweetheart." He drew her from the chair and held her close. "I'm sorry. So sorry." Ellis folded his arms completely around her and wished he could absorb her pain.

Constance wasn't weak or frail; other than the two times she'd cried in his arms, he'd barely seen her upset, let alone shed a tear. But it did surprise him that she wasn't crying now. Was she too distraught over her loss? He leaned back and used both hands to tilt her head up. Her eyes were misty, but not teary.

"I'm sorry, Ellis. I just have to be honest with you. You have the right to know in case someday you decide—"

"I decide?" he interrupted, somewhat taken aback.

"Yes, if you decide to remarry and want childr—"

"I've already decided to remarry," he interrupted again. "You." He held her face firmer, so she couldn't do anything but look at him. "And I don't want anything but you." He kissed her forehead. A sense of loss bit at his heart. He'd never wanted more children, didn't want to take the chance such an event could steal Constance from him, yet the knowledge they'd never share a child rolled painfully around in his chest. "I love you, and if someday we decide we want children, there are plenty around that need good homes. We'll find a couple, or a dozen, or however many you want." He met her gaze again. "I'll share Angel with you. I know that would make her very happy."

Her smile filled her eyes with stars. "That would make me very, very happy."

His hands slid over her shoulders and grasped

her upper arms. He should have asked her before, and wasn't about to wait any longer. "Constance Jennings, will you marry me? Will you be a mother to my daughter, a wife to me and the one person I want beside me until the day I leave this earth?"

A sparkling droplet slipped out of the corner of one eye. "Yes, Ellis Clayton, I'll marry you. I'll love Angel like a daughter, you as my husband, and I'll never want to be anywhere but at your side, until we both leave this earth."

The emotions he'd felt today—the excitement of seeing her, the thrill of holding her, the anguish of hearing her story or the fury he held for Carmichael—couldn't compare to what he experienced at this moment. None of it had gone as deep as the devotion overtaking his heart. It went beyond his mortal presence. Encompassed his very spirit. "I love you, Constance. From this moment on, don't ever doubt how very much I love you."

"I've never doubted you, Ellis, and I won't start now. I love you too much for that. I'll always love you too much to have any doubts."

His lips had barely touched hers when a knock sounded on the door. He wanted to ignore it, to kiss her deeply, thoroughly, and then carry her to the bed along the wall and show her how genuine his love for her was, but, there was business to attend to first.

"It's probably Jeb and Miles. It's been a long

time since they left us alone." Her hands roamed up and down his sides as she spoke, leaving him begging for more.

"Yes, I suspect it is Jeb or Miles." He kissed the tip of her adorable little nose. "But I'll never have enough time alone with you."

"Nor I with you." As the knock sounded again, she added, "You get the door. I'll warm up their meat pie."

"Sorry to interrupt," Jeb started as soon as Ellis pulled the door open. "But that fella might be all the way to Montana by now."

He hadn't forgotten about Carmichael, or the fact the man still had a hold on Constance. "He's not in Montana," Ellis said. His guts told him the man hadn't gone far. "Come on in, Constance has supper about ready." He nodded through the open doorway. "You, too, Miles."

"You don't want us to see if we can pick up his trail?" Jeb asked, removing his coat.

"No, we aren't going to chase him." Ellis shut the door. "He'll be back, and we'll be waiting."

Miles glanced to the table where Constance set plates down. "I'll go get a couple more chairs. If that's all right?"

"Yes, Miles, please get two more chairs. The food will be ready soon," Constance answered, with a gleam in her eyes that renewed the excitement in Ellis's veins.

He followed her to the stove and laid a hand in the small of her back. "What can I do to help?"

"Eat fast," she whispered.

It was downright hard not to wrap his arms around her and hold her tight—until the end of time. "I will," he assured, picking up the plate of bread she'd sliced. "I will."

The hour that followed was extremely long. Jeb and Miles were intent on talking about Byron Carmichael. Concern the man would return weighed heavy, but the idea of lying Constance down on the bed and her soft body merging completely with his held precedence on Ellis's thoughts. He still had to tell her about Eli's letter, and would as soon as Jeb and Miles settled into watch duty in the barn.

As if she read his mind, Constance gave him a shy yet excited glance out of the corner of her eye. "I'll pack up the leftovers for the two of you," she said to Jeb and Miles. "You can take them out to your room."

"Thank you, ma'am," Jeb replied. "That meat pie sure was good. Is there any of that left?"

"I'm afraid not, but there is cheese and bread and oranges, besides a few cookies." She stacked the empty plates from the table upon one another.

Ellis leaped to his feet so fast the legs on his chair bounced, and moments later, saw the men to the door. They spoke, told him their plan of action for the night, and he must have responded—

habitually, because his mind was across the room, where Constance was quickly cleaning, and on the other side of the cabin, where the bed rested along the wall. His insides were full of tiny bits of lightning, striking specific spots fueled with anticipation.

When he shut the door, he moved to the sink. She glanced over her shoulder, and the quiver tugging at her lips made his insides pitch. Covering the swell of her hips with his palms, he nuzzled the side of her head. "Hey."

She trembled, and he massaged the gentle curves beneath the material of her dress.

"I'm scared, Ellis. What if Byron returns tonight?"

"I'm here," he whispered, kissed the tip of her ear.

She leaned against him. "I'm so thankful you are, but—"

"I'm here," he repeated, running his lips down the side of her neck, nipping at the skin. "Even if he makes it past Jeb and Miles, he'll never make it past me. I promise." He caressed the flatness of her stomach and the firmness of her rib cage.

She sighed and tilted her head, giving him more precious skin to kiss. "You're making me forget what I'm doing," she whispered. "Making me forget about—"

"Good. I don't want you to think about anything...." He nibbled on her earlobe and trailed his hands along her arms until his fingers met hers in the warm soapy water. "Except the dishes we're washing," he whispered.

Her fingers intertwined with his, and she swayed, burrowing her back into his chest, and her charming backside against his groin. "Do you know how to wash dishes?" she asked teasingly.

"Yes," he mumbled against her neck. He knew how to make her forget all about Carmichael, and was more than willing to do so. "I even know how to bake bread."

Her giggle rumbled the skin beneath his lips. "That was one of the most amazing nights of my life."

"Mine, too," he admitted, pressing her forward, trapping her hips between his and the counter. She arched, intensifying the divine connection and indulging the intensive swirl of desire building between them. As one, their hands washed and then dunked the dishes in the rinse water before setting the dripping items on the towel she'd laid on the counter. The simple actions became a game of sharing and teasing that quickened his breath and had the air around them sizzling with anticipation.

When the last dish was washed, she used a towel to wipe his and her hands simultaneously, and then gracefully twisted around to face him. No trepidation lingered in her eyes. He lifted her until her pelvic bones slid between his with perfection.

"I need to dump the water," she whispered, looping her arms around his neck.

"Later," he said. "I'll dump it later." His lips found hers, not in a heated rush, but in a slow perfection of mutual bonding. Her sweet essence flowed through his veins as their waists rolled in tune with majestic inner music. They had all night, and he planned on loving her the entire time. No rushing, no quick, hot explosions that would leave them gasping for air. That could come later, after he'd shown her exactly how precious and adorable she was to him.

Walking backward, he towed her across the room, never taking his gaze off her face. She was so beautiful, and the adoration filling her eyes had his heart tripling in size. "I love you," he whispered several times as they maneuvered across the room.

The backs of his knees bumped the bed. She folded their clasped hands beneath her chin. "I almost feel like I'm dreaming. Like I'm in a land far, far away where everything is perfect and wonderful."

"Everything *is* perfect and wonderful."

She tilted her chin. "Kiss me."

"You want me to kiss you?" he teased, hovering his lips above hers.

"Yes." She arched, pressing against him.

The effect she had on him was amazing, extraordinary. He had every sense ticking and his pulse pounding. "A delightful thought," he whispered, barely brushing his lips over the tip of her nose. "What will you do if I kiss you?"

"Kiss you back," she answered, breathlessly.

"Mmm," he mumbled, loving the sparks dancing between them. "You will?"

"Yes." She tried to catch his lips as he brushed them over her cheek.

The teasing was driving him crazy, to heights unbeknownst, but he wanted to make sure her thoughts were on nothing but him. Them. "Right now?" he asked.

Her whimper, and the way she moaned, "Ellis," told him exactly where her thoughts were.

He gave in, and as he'd known it would, the kiss led to another and another, each more commanding. The thrill racing through him said he'd soon be too far gone to take it slow and easy. Constance's needs were on the surface, too. She'd wrenched his shirt out of his britches and was now kneading his skin, growing as impatient as he.

She stretched, following his lips as he pulled them from hers. Finding an ounce of restraint, he slowly unfastened the buttons at her throat, taking time to kiss her glistening skin before moving to the next button, and the next. Admiring the wonders being revealed, he eased the material off her shoulders. Let it fall to the floor.

"Shouldn't we douse the lights?" she whispered.

"No," he answered. "I want to see you."

"But I—" She held the material tight across her stomach.

Understanding flooded his mind, and a fierce bitterness erupted over her previous suffering. He couldn't erase her past, but he could release her from it. "You are the most beautiful woman on earth," he said. "And I love you. With all my heart and soul." Tilting her chin so he could see deep into her blue eyes, he continued, "No one has ever been more beautiful, nor will they ever be."

Her lids fluttered shut and an adorable blush tinted her cheeks. "It's the truth," he said between kissing her brows. "Everything about you is beautiful."

"I love you," she whispered, kissing his chin.

"Then let me see you. All of you."

She took a step back, and with a deft tug, let loose the pink ribbon bow on her camisole. His breath caught as the edges fell and the laces parted, exposing the flawless, creamy flesh of her breasts. He all but groaned as the peaks, lovely, perfect in every way, came into view, but remained still, waited, as she pushed the straps off her shoulder and shrugged out of the garment.

His heart wrenched at the way she swallowed

before untying the band holding up her pantaloons. She drew an audible breath as the silky garment fell over her hips. The scars marring her skin, proving the pain she'd experienced, tore at him, but it was the torment in her eyes, the bits of fear she was trying to hide that he reacted to.

Placing his palm on her stomach, he kissed her forehead. "We all have scars, Constance. They make us who we are. And yours—" he stroked the scarred skin softly "—make you more beautiful. They demonstrate your strength, the will you have to survive against all odds. They prove to me you are the woman I want to spend the rest of my life with."

"Oh, Ellis," she whispered, covering his hand with hers.

He knew he loved her, had for some time, but the emotions bubbling inside him grew stronger than he'd known they could, and he kissed her. Let the depths of his devotion spew between them.

A delicate, delightful moan sounded as his fingers brushed the underside of her breast, and again when he ran the pads of his thumbs over her nipples.

"You have no idea how you make me feel," she said between tiny gasps.

Nuzzling her neck, kissing her collarbone, he answered, "I hope it's good."

"Oh, yes—" She shivered and her nails dug into

his arms as he licked the tips of her breasts. "Very good."

He tasted her thoroughly, reveled in how the hardened nubs teased his tongue with a charm that was downright wicked. The sweet torment was pushing him to the limit.

"Ellis," Constance whimpered. "I can't take much more." She pushed at him, yet tugged at the same time.

His breathing was as ragged as hers. Her fingers were tearing at his buttons, and he straightened, gave her leave to unfasten each one. His hands went back to her breasts, cupping the weight and plying the tips.

"Ellis," she chided, though her tone said differently. She shoved his shirt over his shoulders, making his hands momentarily leave her breasts. Her hands were on his chest, flesh upon flesh, and teasing him with a hunger a thousand lonely nights had never caused. Taut and hard, he ached and throbbed, and when her hand slid downward, inching toward the part of him that begged to be released, he could bear no more.

Ellis caught her hand. Excitement and anticipation had her eyes glowing with a smoldering light. He kissed her gently. "I want to take it slow, pleasure you—" His hoarse whisper caught as her other hand tugged at his waistband.

She unbuttoned his britches, and found him so

quick and deftly he jolted. "We can take it slow next time," she whispered. "We've waited too long as it is."

"You're a minx," he growled between short, quick breaths as he grasped her wrist.

"Do you mind?" she asked, scooting onto the bed in a way that fully displayed the ultimate beauty and perfection of her body.

He stepped from his pants, kicked them aside. "I love it." He crawled onto the bed, in full pursuit.

She giggled sweetly, and her fingertips played over his skin like a piano player teasing the ivory keys into a soul-searching ballad. "I love you," she whispered into his mouth as she parted her legs.

He lowered his hips, resting against her downy softness. He needed her. His breath tore at his lungs and his throat was swollen with raw emotion.

Constance arched her hips. "I've never—"

Bemused, Ellis stiffened from head to toe.

She grabbed his taut backside, pressing him downward. "I've never wanted something so badly in my life," she finished, and he heard the smile in her words besides reading it on her face.

"You—" he started. "Tease." It was the only word that came to mind.

A pleading grimace overtook her face. "Please, Ellis, I can't wait any longer."

"Well," he said, attempting to sound casual.

She let out a painful sounding groan.

He reached beneath her. "I can't wait any longer, either," he admitted, lifting her bottom as he glided into her moist, welcoming heat.

Her cry of delight completed a perfection he'd never known. A homecoming of his heart and soul merging with hers. He withdrew slowly, and entered again, luxuriating in how she moved with him, up and down, in and out.

"Oh, my," she whispered.

He drove in deeper. "Is that what you wanted?"

She arched, wrapped her thighs around his. "Yes, and this," she whispered, moving her hips, gliding her velvet softness along his length.

"Damn, you're good," he groaned, as close to heaven as he'd ever been. Their pace, a complete union of two becoming one, grew steadily. Teasingly at times, serious at others, and ultimately gratifying, taking him to tremendous heights.

Clutching his arms, her breath quickening as fast as his, she gasped, "Good heavens!"

The world as he'd known it must have changed, for nothing had prepared him for the extreme fulfillment engulfing him. He caught Constance's lips as they raced up his chin. Their kisses became as wild and hungry as the need peaking in his veins. He guided her movements with his hands on her hips, bringing her with him in the hard, fast drive to the destination of love everlasting. The thunderous eruption of completion loomed and he couldn't hold the ecstasy filling his chest as they merged with a final unified drive. "Constance," he all but shouted, holding her hips tight against his.

Then, almost as if suspended in time, rapture exploded between them. A riot of tiny aftershocks left them both sighing. Constance, gasping his name, and shuddering with a sweet, divine surrender, sank into the mattress, tugging him with her. His body, heavy and moist from exertion, covered hers as she wrapped her arms around him.

"Oh, Ellis."

He rolled, dragging his weight off her and tucked her to his side. She snuggled in, and the warm, satisfied smile on her lips made his spirit soar. Ellis ran a finger along the curve of her chin. "Next time, we'll take it slow, minx."

She giggled and nipped his shoulder. "Just tell me when you're ready."

Chapter Fifteen

Constance opened her eyes, blinking at the lingering mist of sleep. The wonderful bronze skin creating the pillow she rested upon made her heart skip a beat. She ran a finger along the gloriously defined contours.

"Good morning, minx."

Happiness spread over her. "Good morning."

"Sleep well?" he asked.

"Divinely." She sighed, never having known such bliss. "You?"

He rolled her onto her back. "I thought you'd never wake up."

His hand stroked her stomach, over the scars he'd kissed and caressed so tenderly last night. They'd loved, hot and furious one minute, slow and cherished the next, until the sun had streaked the sky, leaving her ensconced in a pleasure-filled world. "Oh and why's that?" she asked, her heart soaring with anticipation of his answer.

"I don't know, maybe because I have a strong desire to kiss you from head to toe." His fingers brushed the underside of her breasts.

The touch made her nipples harden and her breasts grow heavy as if swelling with passion. "Then why didn't you wake me?" Her fingertips slid along the smooth flesh of his lean side, and then worked their way across his abdomen. Smiling as the muscles tightened beneath her touch, she declared, "I have that same desire."

Amazed yet thrilled to accept he'd released a boldness she'd never imagined she'd harbored, her fingers found what they sought. Her hand folded around him with the expertise she'd acquired last night, and she giggled at the growling sound he made. Knowing her touch affected him as keenly as his did her had her heart hammering with joy.

"Think it's funny, do you?" he asked huskily as he dipped his head.

The jolt of excitement racing through Constance had her arching her back, giving his parted lips direct access to her eager breasts. As Ellis took one throbbing peak into his mouth, she let out a sound that could easily have compared to his growl.

Already half crazy with desire for him, his tongue, lapping and teasing, had miniature spasms bursting between her thighs.

"Still think it's funny?" he asked, moving to suckle the other peak with ultimate perfection.

Unable to take much more, her body reaching its limits, Constance scooted beneath him as he rose. Using the hand still folded around him, she guided him toward the throbbing juncture of her parted legs. "I never…said it…was funny," she gasped.

His entrance into her, hot and slick, was so gratifying she moaned aloud. Not caring what it sounded like or who heard.

"You didn't?" he asked.

Quickly catching the swift rhythm he set, Constance, on the verge of losing herself in the mystical world he carried her to, could barely speak. "Not funny. Fun," she whispered. Wrapping her arms around his neck, so she could hold on and enjoy the journey, she added, "So irresistibly fun."

Focused solely on the pleasures shooting through her body—wave upon wave of glorious sensations that stole her breath yet had her begging for more—Constance cried out his name as she reached her final point of destination with startling awareness. He stiffened and groaned so pleasurably that tiny offshoots of pure bliss spewed from her heart.

The ultimate union of their bodies was so profound, even the ability to move left her. Limp but utterly fulfilled and happy, she closed her eyes. "Will it always be this perfect, Ellis?"

He rolled onto his back, pulling her languid body to collapse against his captivating flesh. "Yes, Constance, our love will always be this perfect."

She opened her eyes, wanting him to understand just how she felt. "I never imagined when I left New York that I'd find this." She kissed his chin. "How could I? I never knew it existed."

"Me neither, darling, me neither."

She loved the sound of his husky whisper. Loved him. She took his lips in a slow, unhurried kiss laced with the pure devotion she felt. It was a miracle that she'd found him, the perfect man, the one she'd dreamed of thousands of miles away in England. There must have been a supreme being, a mastermind above all others, behind every decision she'd made to bring her here, to the wilds of Wyoming, where cupid blessed her with his mystical arrow.

Giggling, she buried her face into the pillow next to his ear.

Nipping at her shoulder, Ellis asked, "Now what's so funny?"

Constance pushed up until she was sitting, straddling his torso. Unabashed by her nakedness or the scars on her stomach, she stretched her hands overhead. "I was just imagining cupid's little arrows."

Ellis ran his hands up her sides and caught her arms before she completely lowered them. He scooted upward on the bed, until his back was propped against the pillows and her open center sat upon the very part of him that gave her great satisfaction. He let loose her arms then, and his fingertips gently fluttered over her breasts. "Cupid?"

The quickening inside her had her biting her bottom lip. She nodded.

He rolled her nipples between the tips of his thumbs and fingertips. "Enchanting little character, isn't he?" he asked, leaning forward.

The anticipation already pulsing in her veins made it impossible for her to even nod as his mouth covered one aching nipple. "Again?" she asked.

"Again," he agreed.

It was sometime later when they finally crawled from the bed. Ellis helped her dress, briskly rubbing his hands over her arms and legs to chase away the chill before he held her garments up, one at a time, and endearingly fastened the many bows and buttons.

"Your little friend…" he said as he buttoned the last button.

Constance spun around, waited for him to continue. When he didn't, she asked, "What little friend?"

"Cupid." Ellis cupped her cheeks and kissed her soundly on the mouth before saying, "He paid me a visit, too."

Laughing, she wrapped her arms around his

waist and basked in the durable, solid shelter of his
protection and love. He was hers. Now and forever.

"You keep looking at me like that, and I'll drag
you back to bed," Ellis said, roaming his hands
down to cup her hips.

She'd never understood flirting until last night.
Lifting one brow, she asked, "Promise?"

He kissed her, and between his glorious teasing lips and the way his fingers fluttered over her
body, Constance was ready to drag him back to
the bed when he lifted his head to say, "I better get
the fires going before we freeze to death in here."

Half dizzy with want all over again, Constance
had no idea if she was cold or not.

He winked. "Jeb and Miles have been up for
hours, minx."

She'd never have imagined a single word could
become an endearment that would spark such joy
in her. While he built fires, and then hauled out
the cold dishwater from the evening before, she
gathered ingredients for breakfast and set a pot of
coffee to perk.

Jeb and Miles followed Ellis into the cabin. "Everything will be ready in a few minutes," she said.

"Thanks, ma'am, but we've already had breakfast. Just thought we'd haul your trunks to the
wagon. Figured you two would want to head over
to Heaven on Earth as soon as possible," Miles
said, strolling across the room.

Ellis placed a hand on her lower back. "We'll drive the wagon home. Jeb will follow on my horse. Is there anything else you need loaded up?"

All of a sudden fear knotted her stomach. Byron was out there, possibly waiting for them. She shook her head, half afraid to speak. "J-just the basket of books."

As soon as Jeb and Miles carried her trunks out the door, Ellis took her shoulders. "There's nothing to worry about."

"Byron's out there."

"And I'm here to protect you."

She had more to lose now than ever before in her life. "He's evil. He'll hurt you and—"

Ellis's lips pressed against hers. After kissing her deeply, he said, "Trust me, Constance. Byron Carmichael isn't going to hurt me, and I won't let him hurt you, either."

He was so strong and caring, and she loved him so much. Couldn't imagine life without him. A wave of terrible shame hit her. The pain was strong enough to drop her to the floor, had Ellis not been holding her upright. "I'm married to him, Ellis."

He shook his head. "No, not if he was already married to that woman in New York."

"But—"

"Constance," he interrupted. "We'll talk about Carmichael once we get to Heaven on Earth. We'll work it all out. Just trust me."

Before she could respond, Jeb door opened the door. "Just the basket, ma'am?"

"Yes," Ellis answered.

The fear shrouding her remained long after breakfast was consumed and they climbed onto the wagon seat. If anything it increased when Ellis tucked her close to his side and covered their laps with a heavy wool blanket kept under the seat.

Blue sky and fields of untouched snow surrounded them as they glided along, the rudders running smoothly over the trail. Yet none of it, or even Ellis's charming attempts to converse, eased her qualms.

Jeb trotted up to ride close, his firearm resting across the pommel of his saddle, as they traveled through a thick grove of pines so tall they darkened the sky. She wrapped her hands around Ellis's thick forearm, as if that could keep him safe.

He laid a gloved hand on her knee. "We're almost to Cottonwood."

"Are we stopping there?" She just wanted to get to Heaven on Earth, where the big house and bunkhouse full of men would provide more protection. The home had been a fortress against her fears before, and she wanted that again. She needed to know Ellis and Angel were safe.

"I have to stop in town, but it won't take long."

She clutched his arm tighter as the trees gave way to a wide-open prairie that was dotted with small buildings on the horizon. A foreboding hung in the air, one that had her insides knotted and trembling.

Link barreled out of his store before the rudders on the wagon slid to a stop. "Ellis! Ellis, you got a mess going on out at your place! The marshal's out there along with that Carmichael fella." Link leaped over the sideboard behind the seat. "Hank," he shouted toward the man in the store doorway. "Lock the door." Link then slapped Ellis on the back. "Get rolling! My Lula Mae's out there!"

Fear gripped Constance's spine at the vision of Byron pounding on the door back at Ashton's place. Hatred had filled his face—that's what had made him look so evil and sinful. The image of Angel with her leg bound with boards had Constance grabbing Ellis's arm. "Hurry, Ellis! We must hurry!"

He whipped the reins over the team of horses, and Constance clung to his coat to keep from bouncing off the seat. The pounding of hooves and clanking of harnesses echoed in her ears as her heart raced in her chest.

"What's happened, Hank?" Ellis shouted as the man caught up to them on horseback.

"I don't know. The marshal showed up last night, looking for Miss Jennings. Lula Mae invited him to spend the night. She said the two of you would be home today." Hank steered his galloping horse around a drift. Once back beside the wagon, he added, "Bright and early this morning, I found that Carmichael man snooping around. And then John Hempel showed up, needing to speak to you. I was on my way to Ashton's place to get you, and stopped at Link's to tell him just in case I missed you along the way."

"Ride on ahead," Ellis yelled back. "Make sure Carmichael doesn't get away!"

"And make sure my Lula Mae's all right!" Link yelled over Constance's head.

Hank nodded, but glanced toward Constance briefly, then his gaze landed back on Ellis. "That Carmichael fella claims he's Miss Jennings's husband."

It felt as if an iron first clamped onto her heart.

"I know," Ellis shouted. "Just make sure he doesn't get away!"

Hank spurred his horse, leaving a shower of snow made by the animal's hooves in his wake.

Jeb, still riding beside the wagon, shouted, "I'll ride ahead, too, Ellis. Tell the marshal how that fella tried to knock down the door at my place."

Ellis nodded, and though a mountain of questions swirled in her head, Constance remained silent, not wanting to distract his attention from the horses laboring to race through the deep snow.

It seemed like hours before they arrived on the plateau overlooking Heaven on Earth, but even then, as they began to descend the steep hill, Ellis didn't slow the team. He stood though, to see over the backs of the horses as he steered them down the knoll.

Link grabbed Constance's shoulders, pressing her tightly in the seat. "Don't fret, missy, I won't let you bounce out."

Constance had the blanket balled in her fist, and ducked behind it when the snow flying off the horses' hooves flew in her face.

"Whoa! Whoa!" Ellis shouted. Snow spewed the air, and before the wagon completely stopped, he spun about and lifted her from the seat. He jumped over the edge with her in his arms.

Constance's feet barely hit the ground before she was running up the steps at his side. The door opened, and in a blur, Link flew past them, gathering Lula Mae in his arms.

"I'm fine, I'm fine," the woman repeated, hugging her husband.

"Where's—" Ellis started.

Lula Mae pointed. "In the front parlor."

Ellis propelled Constance down the hall. They turned the corner, and she saw no one but the girl sitting on the sofa with her leg propped on a pile of pillows.

"Constance!" Angel shouted.

The joy of seeing Angel overshadowed the dire

circumstances. She rushed across the room. "Are you all right?"

"I'm fine." Angel wrapped her arms around Constance's neck. "I'm so happy you're home."

Constance folded Angel to her breast. This was her daughter. The only child she'd ever need. Ever want. No one was going to take her away from Ellis or Angel. Not now. Not ever. There and then, over and over she gave prayers of thanks for Angel being unharmed, letting the thankfulness build in her chest until she felt strong enough to turn and face the rest of the room's occupants.

Her gaze went from John Hempel near one of the armchairs, to a tall, brutish looking man wearing a badge and resting a hand on the mantel, to Byron tied in a rocking chair with Hank and Jeb leaning against the wall behind him, to Ellis shrugging out of his coat in the doorway. Her gaze settled there, on her true strength.

He handed his coat off to Lula Mae and moved forward. Constance accepted his assistance to remove her coat as an eerie sensation had her turning around, back to Byron. The glare in his eyes sent sour bile flipping in her stomach.

"Jeb," Ellis said, "help Angel into the kitchen."

The girl didn't protest, which increased Constance's fear. Ellis eased her onto the couch and sat himself, keeping one arm wrapped around her shoulders. "What's happening here?" he asked.

The marshal gestured toward John Hempel. "You want to start?"

The lawyer leaned forward, picking up a stack of papers. "I have a letter here from a solicitor in Virginia. It says a land agent by the name of Byron Carmichael attempted to sell some property that didn't belong to him." John gave a brief glance toward Byron. "The solicitor, Mr. Parsons, has been in charge of the property since the original owners perished during the war, and was quite surprised when Mr. Carmichael claimed Constance Carmichael, neé Jennings, had died in England."

Constance glanced toward Ellis, already befuddled. His eyes held an odd glimmer, looked almost shameful. "The property John is referring to used to be known as Royalton."

Her heart threatened to choke her. "Royalton," she whispered, "was the name of my father's plantation."

"I was going to tell you last night," Ellis said. "But—"

"Tell me what?" she interrupted, fighting the shivers tickling her skin. "I don't understand."

Ellis gestured toward John Hempel.

"Ellis," the man said, "contacted his brother Eli in the Carolinas, asking about your family's plantation." He held up a single piece of paper and glanced at Ellis. "This letter from Mr. Parsons arrived before Link dropped off the letter from your brother." The lawyer addressed her again, "Mr. Parsons explains that after Mr. Carmichael approached him about the property, he traveled to England. What he discovered there was very disturbing. He followed your trail to New York, and eventually learned you left New York for Wyoming as a mail-order bride. Eli, Ellis's brother, met with Mr. Parsons and confirmed that you, Constance Jennings, were living here—" he gestured with one hand "—at Heaven on Earth." He then gathered up the entire stack of papers. "Mr. Parsons then sent this packet of legal documents to me, to act as your lawyer if you so choose."

Constance didn't realize she was shaking until the man held the papers toward her. "It's all in here. For you to read," John Hempel said.

She balled her hand into a fist, but the trembles wouldn't ease. Ellis took the papers and laid them on her lap.

"She can't be someone's mail-order bride," Byron said bitterly. "She's already married." He paused, waiting for her to look his way. "To me."

Her shivers increased tenfold. Ellis's hand, still gripping her shoulder, tightened.

"No, I don't believe she is," John Hempel answered. He pointed at the papers in her lap. "Mr. Parsons discovered you were already married to a woman he met with in New York."

"That woman and I divorced," Byron snapped.

"Do you have any proof?" John Hempel challenged.

"I don't have to prove anything to you." Byron struggled against the ropes binding him until Hank planted a heavy hand on his head.

"Yes, you do," the marshal, a tall man with a thick black mustache, stated. Pushing off the fireplace, he stepped forward and touched the brim of his wide hat. "Hello, ma'am. My name's Newton Adams. I'm the territory marshal."

"Hello," Constance managed beyond the lump sitting in her throat. Confusion still muddled her mind. The only thing she knew for sure was Ellis was beside her, sheltering her, and Angel was safe. Everything else was a thick whirlwind swarming inside her head.

The lawman nodded toward Ellis. "I've known Ellis for years, and when Mr. Carmichael visited me the other day, claiming Ellis was holding his wife hostage, I didn't believe a word he said, but since I hadn't been out to Heaven on Earth for a while, I decided to pay a visit." His gaze went to Ellis. "It appears my timing couldn't have been better."

"Good to see you, Newton, it has been a while," Ellis said.

After he gave Ellis a nod, the marshal looked back at her. "I've read everything in that packet of papers Mr. Hempel brought out. I'd like to ask you a few questions, if you don't mind."

She shook her head, and then nodded, not sure which was the correct response.

He waved a hand around the room. "Witnesses make my job easier. Is it all right if I ask you now, with everyone here?"

Her hand clutched Ellis's knee, not wanting him to leave. He rubbed her shoulder, assuring he wouldn't. "Yes, that's fine," she answered.

"The first few might sound silly, but bear with me."

She nodded.

"Do you know that man in the rocking chair?"

"Yes, his name is Byron Carmichael," she answered.

"Where did you first meet Mr. Carmichael?"

"In England, last December."

"And who were you living with in England?"

His tone was kind and his questions simple, easy to answer, which eased the trepidation that had been making her stomach churn. "My elderly aunts, Julia and Theresa Jennings."

"What happened to them?"

"They took ill and died. Julia in December and Theresa in January." Their deaths still tugged at her heart. "It was quite shocking since they both had been very healthy."

"What did you do after they died?" the marshal asked.

She bowed her head, not wanting to answer.

"You have nothing to be ashamed of, Constance," Ellis whispered near her ear. "Nothing at all."

She nodded, but the guilt in her chest didn't lessen. "Byr— Mr. Carmichael asked me to marry him, and I did."

"Did you travel to America with Mr. Carmichael?"

She shook her head.

"Why not?"

Anger found a way to break through, flared across her stomach. "Because he shot me."

"Mr. Carmichael shot you?" Marshal Adams asked.

Byron spoke before she had a chance to. "That was an accident."

"And I suppose it was an accident that you left her there to die in the alley while you jumped on a ship to New York." The fury in Ellis's voice showered the room, and his knee beneath her hand had turned as hard as cast iron.

"No comment, Mr. Carmichael?" Marshal Adams asked.

"I thought she was dead," Byron said, with a dull stare that held no remorse.

"So you just set sail for America?" the marshal

questioned. "No funeral for your new wife? No time of mourning or sorrow?"

Byron shrugged.

Constance's fury rushed forward. "You sold everything. Stole everything they had."

"That was a pittance compared to what you're worth," Byron returned.

The marshal stepped forward, blocking her view of Byron. Constance's mind swirled again. Worth? Her gaze went to the papers. Royalton was still there?

"You got a place we can lock him up until I'm ready to leave, Ellis?" the marshal asked. "I've got all the proof I need."

"I'll take him to the bunkhouse, boss." It was Hank that answered.

The papers on her lap grew blurry as tears welled in her eyes.

"You don't have proof of anything," Byron shouted.

"Miss Jennings positively identified you as the man who shot her," Marshal Adams said. "Between that and all I read, you could swing from a rope."

"It was her! She's the one that brewed the tea for her aunts," Byron yelled.

Constance couldn't hold in the gasp that split her lips. Ellis tugged her against his side, growling, "Get him out of here, Hank."

Byron's bellows continued to echo through the

house. "Miss Jennings," the marshal said above the noise. "I'd like you to read those papers before I leave. Just in case you need to add or change something."

"I'll wait, too, until you've read them, Miss Jennings, if you don't mind," John Hempel said. "I'd be happy to serve as your lawyer."

Constance frowned, glancing at the thick packet Ellis was lifting off her lap. An eerie sensation overtook her as he helped her stand. "Come on, you can read these in the office."

Ellis led her to the office and set her behind the desk. His insides were a jumbled mess of frustration and fear, yet the love they shared gave him hope she'd understand, even after reading the packet of papers.

Constance grasped his hand as it slipped off her shoulder. "Will you read them with me?"

The trepidation in her blue eyes had him leaning down and kissing her forehead. "If you want me to."

She nodded. "I want you to."

He cleared the corner of the desk and sat. "Go ahead," he said. "You can hand me the pages as you finish them."

An array of emotions threatened to rip him apart as he read. The urge to throttle Byron Carmichael for all the man had put her through ate at him more strongly as he moved from one page to the next.

Then, as the report of Mr. Parsons's findings ended and the legal paperwork of updating the property deeds for Royalton floated before his eyes, fear settled in his chest. Constance owned thousands of acres of land in Virginia. She had no need to stay in Wyoming.

As she handed him the last piece of paper, she stood and moved to the window. The profound emotions he felt for this woman left his eyes misty, and the thought she might no longer want to marry him made something akin to panic cloud his ability to read any more. It didn't matter. The last sheet was a legal documentation of her worth. But she was priceless to him.

He moved to stand behind her, wanting badly to touch her, but at the same time afraid to. Constance pressed a hand to the glass, and his gaze went past it, to the headstone sitting amongst the glittering white snow.

It had only been by the grace of God that Constance hadn't perished in that alley in England. Intense gratefulness had him grasping her upper arms and turning her about. The tears streaming down her cheeks made his throat thicken.

"He killed them," she whimpered. "He killed those two sweet little old ladies."

He tried to speak, but anything he could have thought to say would have gotten trapped in his throat.

"He poisoned them, and I—I let him."

"No," he said, gripping her arms firmer. "No you didn't. You—"

"Yes, I did," she insisted as she pressed the back of a hand to her lips. "I helped him brew the tea he brought for them."

"Oh, sweetheart." He pulled her to his chest, folding both arms around her shuddering shoulders. "You didn't know. You were trying to help."

She nodded, but her arms wrapped around his waist tightly as her sobs increased. He wished there was something more he could say, more he could do than simply hold her, but his mind couldn't conjure up anything. Other than how much he loved her. He rocked her slowly, softly, and kissed the top of her head. And when she slumped against him, as if completely worn out, he tightened his hold.

It was a few moments, before he felt her spine stiffen and she lifted her face. Still holding her tightly with one arm, he used the other to wipe the last bits of moisture from her cheeks.

A shaky smile pulled at her lips, but quickly disappeared as she whispered, "Those papers didn't mention the authorities in New York."

"What authorities?"

"Byron's wife said they were looking for me. That's part of the reason I wrote to Ashton, I was afraid they would put me in jail."

Hoping to ease her mind completely, he said,

"I'm sure Parsons spoke to the authorities. If it'll make you feel better, we'll have Hempel contact them."

"I was such a fool. I should have known Byron was up to no good. I should have questioned the tea. I should have read the papers I signed. I should—"

Ellis held her head still, and lowered his face to hers. "Shh," he whispered against her lips. "Shh."

Her hands spread across his back, kneading at the muscles that had been strained tight since Link had leaped into the wagon. Her lips moved beneath his then, sweetly, impishly.

He cupped the back of her neck and deepened the kiss. Her mouth opened for him, igniting the desire that hovered right beneath his skin, waiting for the simplest signal from her. He didn't calm the stirring kisses until her hips were grinding harmoniously against his.

She shook her head as she pulled away. Breathing heavily, her breasts heaved against his chest. "You make me forget everything else."

The shimmer in her eyes fertilized a full smile to form on his lips. "I'm glad."

She grinned, and then with a deep sigh, leaned her head on his shoulder. "Byron's an evil man, but I feel guilty he'll die."

His smile disappeared. Not able to fully agree with her guilt, he held his silence. He ran his hand down the length of her hair.

"All because he wanted a few acres of land," she whispered.

He stepped back. "It's more than a few acres, Constance."

"I read that." She shook her head. "I don't understand why my aunts never told me they were paying taxes on Royalton all those years."

"I can't say for sure," he said, "but maybe they didn't want you to leave." His mind caught, fearful she might think he had tried to dupe her. "I didn't read Eli's letter until after the holiday party, and once I got to Ashton's, well, other things held my mind." He knew that was only part of it. "Actually, I was afraid to tell you, just like with Ashton's will. There's this deep part of me that fears you leaving beyond everything else. I've never done anything like that before, purposely withheld information, yet I did it twice to you."

She tilted her head, as if contemplating his words. Her lips parted as if she was about to say something, but closed again.

Afraid anything he might say would be wrong, he pulled his eyes away from the ones searching his face. His gaze landed on the window for a moment. "We can move to Virginia," he said, bringing his gaze back to meet hers. "We can sell out, and move anytime you want. Anywhere you want."

"Leave Heaven on Earth?" She shook her head

sternly. "Not on your life, Ellis Clayton. This is where I want to live."

"What about Royalton?"

She shrugged. "Maybe your brother can help us figure out what to do with it." Her gaze caught and captured his. "Us," she repeated. "Everything I have today, tomorrow or a hundred years from now, I want to share with you." Running a finger over the center button of his shirt, she continued, "I don't just want to be your wife, Ellis, I want to be your partner. I want us to be a couple that shares everything, including our love." She waved a hand. "I don't have a clue what to do with an acre of land, let alone thousands. I need you, Ellis. I need you."

Relief left his body so swiftly he trembled. "I need you, too," he whispered, filled with appreciation for the trust she had in him. "In every breath I take."

"Every breath," she whispered, brushing her lips against his. "That's how I feel about you." She kissed him sweetly as her fingers undid the top button of his shirt. "You told me last night never to doubt your love for me." She undid another button. "And I won't. Not ever. But only if you never doubt mine for you."

Her fingers unfastening buttons had his blood heating up and her words had his heart overflowing. "Never," he said. Yet needing to know, he asked, "So you forgive me?"

The grin on her face was endearing. "Yes, I forgive you. I was never angry over you not telling me. I understand the fear of being separated from you." A tender blush rose on her cheeks. "I like knowing you don't want me to leave."

"Never." He tugged her hips forward, pressing their bodies close. "Ever. Don't doubt that, either." Though he was extremely serious, he couldn't help but teasingly run a hand over the peak of her left breast. Payback for the havoc her fingertips massaging his chest caused.

"Never," she said, running her tongue along his collarbone.

A groan rumbled up his throat as his swollen shaft jolted inside his britches. "Damn, you are a minx." He cupped her behind, pressing his erection against her.

She giggled, swaying her hips invitingly. "And you love me."

"Yes, I do." Knowing he couldn't keep this up much longer, he nibbled on her earlobe for a moment before saying, "Want to know something?"

"Yes," she mumbled against the skin.

He suckled on the lobe one last time before saying, "Link is able to perform marriage ceremonies."

She snapped her head up. An excited glow covered her face. "He is?"

"Yep. Reverend Stillman doesn't make it around

in the winter months, and ordained Link to perform the necessities in his absence." Her gaze went to the desk, and he read her mind. "Whether Carmichael was married or not won't matter once you sign that piece of paper John Hempel drew up. It makes your marriage to him null and void, and Newton's here to notarize it." If she needed more incentive, he gestured toward the fading light outside the window. "It looks like we're in for plenty of overnight guests." Grinding their still-merged hips, he finished by saying, "I really don't want to be sneaking around my own house come midnight."

"You don't? I recall doing that once, and it was very fun."

"Minx," he growled. Her sweet laugh tickled his lips. Pulling back he teased, "But if that's the way you want it."

She grabbed the back of his head and kissed him until he thought he might burst. Only then did she release him to whisper, "Let's go find Link."

Epilogue

With shaky fingers, Constance fastened the top button of her dress and pulled at the material to make it lie flat.

"It's fine." Ellis brushed her hands aside and kissed the bare skin the low neckline of the summertime gown revealed.

"Stop." She pushed his head aside and attempted to scoot off his lap as the front door slammed shut, but he held her tight. The heated, playful kissing they'd engaged in moments before still had her blood racing, and she tried to calm it by leaning her head against his.

"I knew we should have gone upstairs. We could have locked the door," he said.

"Shush," she insisted, placing a swift kiss upon his lips.

"Sheesh!" Angel exclaimed, bounding through

the office door. "You two are gonna wear the lips right off your faces."

Even though her heart sang with happiness, Constance conjured up a stern look. "Angel Clayton," she said warningly.

The chuckle Ellis let out didn't help the situation. Giving him a steady glare, Constance clambered off his lap.

Angel swiped the back of her hand across her mouth. "There, washed out."

The happy glint in Angel's brown eyes made Constance shake her head. "Some days I do believe you're hopeless."

Angel laughed. "Yeah, but you love me."

Ellis hooked Constance's hip, pulling her back to his side. "Yes, we do, scamp. How was your trip to town?"

"Good. I saw Jeb." Angel laid a stack of mail on the desk. "His mail-order bride will be arriving within the week. He told me to tell you thank you, Constance. Said he'd never have been able to order one if you hadn't given him and Miles Ashton's place. He was picking up a new icebox. Said his bride was gonna need one in this heat."

"I suspect she will," Ellis commented.

"I gotta go unsaddle my horse," Angel said, spinning about. "I got the stuff I need for that little fawn I found. I'm sure it'll take to the bottle Link found for me." She paused in the doorway. "I may be a while, holler when supper's ready."

"We will," Ellis assured. He stood and as soon as Angel had disappeared, he pulled Constance into an embrace. "Can you imagine if we had more like her running around?" He kissed her nose. "We'd never have any privacy."

Ellis's love had healed her in so many ways, yet a thought that caught Constance off guard every once in a while sliced her from head to toe.

"Hey." Ellis lifted her chin. "What is it?"

She shook her head and attempted to smile, but it didn't fool him. "It's silly," she whispered, "I know, but sometimes I…" The lump in her throat grew too large to talk around.

"I've told you before," he said softly, "this country is full of orphanages. We can start sending out letters today if you want."

"But would that be the same?" She'd never voiced the one fear she still harbored, and flinched at the way his face grew somber.

The knuckle beneath her chin moved to slide up the side of her face. His eyes examined her face for several silent moments before he said, "I watched one wife die bringing a baby into this world, and I'll be the first to admit it almost brought me to my knees." His fingers spread out, combed through her hair, until his palm held the back of her head. "But,

Constance, the thought of losing you outdoes that. I don't think I could live through watching you die."

Her heart lurched, aching at the thought of him in pain. Of him perishing. She'd never live through losing him. "I never thought of it that way. I'm sorry."

He shook his head. "Don't apologize. You haven't done anything wrong." His arms folded around her then, sheltering her, loving her. He kissed her temple. "You have no idea how wonderful it is to know I don't have to worry about that."

She leaned back, and though she saw truth in his eyes, still asked, "Really?"

"Yes, really," he said, dipping one finger beneath the neckline of her dress and instantly finding her still-hardened nipple. "I find it freeing to know I can sample this delightful body as often as I choose without having to worry you'll become pregnant."

"I like having you sample it," she admitted, leaning back to give him more access.

"My greatest wish is to make you happy, and what else I said is also true." His other hand unfastened the top three buttons. "We can send out letters or have Hempel do some checking."

"Maybe someday," she said. The delightful rush heating up her system was hard to think beyond. "But right now, I like devoting all my time to you and Angel."

He folded the edges of her dress open, exposing her breasts completely. "I like having your devoted time." In a quick swift moment, he'd swept her off her feet, cradling her in his arms. "Like right now." He kissed the center of her breastbone. "Angel will be busy for hours trying to get that baby deer to eat."

She wrapped an arm around his neck. "I suspect she will be."

"We've been married six months, and still all I can think of is getting you into my bed, how there's no place I'd rather be."

"I know," she whispered. "It's Heaven on Earth."

"Yes, yes, it is."

She nuzzled the side of his face and nibbled on his earlobe. Her love for this man continued to grow each passing day, and showed no sign of slowing down. "Ellis?"

"Hmm?" he mumbled, carrying her out of his office.

"If you put me down, I'll race you up the stairs."

He chuckled. "I don't want you worn out before we get to our room."

"Trust me," she said, unbuttoning his shirt. "I won't be worn out." The glimmer in his eyes had little sparks igniting inside her. "But I might be naked by the time I get there."

"Minx," Ellis said. "No wonder I love you more

every day." He lowered her to the floor as she wriggled against his hold.

She took off for the wide staircase, letting her dress slip off her shoulders as she ran. By the time she got to their bedroom door, she wasn't completely undressed—still had to step out of her pantaloons. And Ellis, bless his heart, had paused along the way to grab her dress, slip and the camisole top she'd left in her trail. She'd always need his help, and he'd always need her. She had no doubts.

* * * * *

A sneaky peek at next month...

HISTORICAL

IGNITE YOUR IMAGINATION, STEP INTO THE PAST...

My wish list for next month's titles...

In stores from 7th December 2012:

❏ Some Like It Wicked – Carole Mortimer

❏ Born to Scandal – Diane Gaston

❏ Beneath the Major's Scars – Sarah Mallory

❏ Warriors in Winter – Michelle Willingham

❏ A Stranger's Touch – Anne Herries

❏ Oklahoma Wedding Bells – Carol Finch

Available at WHSmith, Tesco, Asda, Eason, Amazon and Apple

Just can't wait?

Visit us Online

You can buy our books online a month before they hit the shops! **www.millsandboon.co.uk**

1112/

Book of the Month

MILLS & BOON

MICHELE HAUF
FOREVER WEREWOLF

nocturne

We love this book because...

Werewolves Trystan and Lexi's relationship comes under threat when he discovers a deadly secret about his heritage that could force him to choose between love and destiny in this thrilling paranormal romance.

On sale 16th November

Visit us Online

Find out more at
www.millsandboon.co.uk/BOTM

1112/BOTM

MILLS & BOON® Book Club *2 Free Books!*

Join the Mills & Boon Book Club

Want to read more **Historical** stories?
We're offering you **2 more**
absolutely **FREE!**

We'll also treat you to these fabulous extras:

- 🌹 **Books up to 2 months ahead of shops**
- 🌹 **FREE home delivery**
- 🌹 **Bonus books with our special rewards scheme**
- 🌹 **Exclusive offers… and much more!**

Treat yourself now!

Visit us Online Get your FREE books now at
www.millsandboon.co.uk/freebookoffer

0712/H2Y

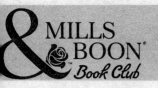

MILLS & BOON® Book Club

2 Free Books!

Get your free books now at
www.millsandboon.co.uk/freebookoffer

---

r fill in the form below and post it back to us

HE MILLS & BOON® BOOK CLUB™—HERE'S HOW IT WORKS: Accepting your
e books places you under no obligation to buy anything. You may keep the books
d return the despatch note marked 'Cancel'. If we do not hear from you, about a
nth later we'll send you 4 brand-new stories from the Historical series priced at
.50* each. There is no extra charge for post and packaging. You may cancel at any
e, otherwise we will send you 4 stories a month which you may purchase or return
us—the choice is yours. *Terms and prices subject to change without notice. Offer
lid in UK only. Applicants must be 18 or over. Offer expires 31st January 2013. **For
l terms and conditions, please go to www.millsandboon.co.uk/freebookoffer**

rs/Miss/Ms/Mr (please circle)

rst Name

urname

ddress

Postcode

-mail

end this completed page to: Mills & Boon Book Club, Free Book
ffer, FREEPOST NAT 10298, Richmond, Surrey, TW9 1BR

Find out more at
www.millsandboon.co.uk/freebookoffer

Visit us Online

0712/H2YEA

Special Offers

Every month we put together collections and longer reads written by your favourite authors.

Here are some of next month's highlights— and don't miss our fabulous discount online!

On sale 16th November   On sale 16th November   On sale 7th December

Save 20% on all Special Releases

Find out more at
www.millsandboon.co.uk/specialreleases

Visit us
Online

1212/ST/MB3